Beyond Illusion:
Leading from Reality

CARL TOWNSEND

iUniverse, Inc.
New York   Bloomington

Beyond Illusion: Leading from Reality

Copyright © 2009 Carl Townsend

Scripture not marked or marked as NKJV taken from New King James Version
Copyright 1979, 1980, 1982 by Thomas Nelson, Inc.
Used by Permission. All rights reserved.

Scripture marked as *The Message* taken from THE MESSAGE
Copyright 1993, 1994, 1995 used by permission of NavPress Publishing Group

"Divine Servant" is the copyrighted and trademarked creation of Christian artist, Max Greiner, Jr. Used with permission. For further information on Greiner drawings, paintings, and sculpture, contact the artist at: Max Greiner Jr. Designs, P.O. Box 552, Kerrville, TX 78029 (830) 896-7919. The picture shows the stature as it is displayed in Houston, TX.

iUniverse books may be ordered through booksellers or by contacting:

iUniverse
1663 Liberty Drive
Bloomington, IN 47403
www.iuniverse.com
1-800-Authors (1-800-288-4677)

ISBN: 978-1-4401-9110-7 (pbk)
ISBN: 978-1-4401-9111-4 (cloth)
ISBN: 978-1-4401-9112-1 (ebk)

Printed in the United States of America

iUniverse rev. date: 12/04/2009

Contents

Acknowledgements

Wayne McCroskey
Toni Anderson
Donna Johnson
Norma Sullivan
And many, many others who have helped me walk in faith beyond my wildest dreams.

Dedication

This book is dedicated to Tim Anderson who taught me so much about leadership. For me to be able to walk with Tim for even a few years was a rich, rich blessing. You'll get to meet him a bit when we get to Chapter 6. Come to think of it, he also shows up in quite a few other places here. Thank you Tim!

Introduction

There is no doubt that we see a failure of leadership today. My bookshelves are loaded with books on leadership. Unfortunately, the information in these books doesn't seem to be helping much. Most of the leadership that is out there seems to fail. We need something else. Why is it that the leadership in our political systems, our businesses, and often even in our churches seems to fail? What is missing?

+   +   +   +

This book is not organized as any type of 1-2-3 process to helping you lead. God doesn't work that way. Instead, I'm taking you on a journey. I'll tell you lots of stories. We'll meet some very interesting characters along the way. Take Nehemiah, for example. What was he really asking God for in that first chapter of his book? It will surprise you—it wasn't a wall. The wall was a vehicle. A means to an end. And what was the end?

This book is not meant as an extensive course in leadership. There are plenty of books on types of leadership, how to be a leader, and even the meaning of the word. OK, the meaning of the word is easy. A leader is someone who has followers. The primary purpose in this book is to shed some light on some of the characteristics that, to a very large extent, are missing with our leaders today.

I like the sign I saw on a former pastor's desk.

"There they go. I must go after them, for I am their leader."

The job of the leader is to lead the followers to Place. Something that is already real to the leader. The leader is already living and breathing the reality which others only see dimly, if at all.

Part I: Failed Leadership

As we start the journey I want to spend a short two chapters on something you already know. Things aren't right. People we think are leaders or people we have elected to leadership aren't leading. Many of the so-called leaders have been taking us for a ride. We've been promised change, but there is no change. No justice has been brought to those who have been unjust. Two wars with no end in sight, An infrastructure in decay. A government that is unable to stand up to Wall Street, the health care industry, and major corporations. Paralysis. No stallions leading—just a bunch of geldings. Too much of what we call leadership in Washington, many communities, sometimes in churches, and in other organizations has become nothing more than power struggle to get power and keep it. That isn't leadership.

This first part of our journey is hard to look at, but keep your eyes open. There are clues here. There is hope.

Chapter 1: We are not in Kansas Anymore

Toto, I've a feeling we're not in Kansas Anymore.

Dorothy, in *The Wizard of Oz*

There is no doubt that we see a failure of leadership today. As I write this, political leaders are unable to forge a path out of two wars we were led into by lies and greed. Today we see the economic system that has fueled capitalism for years is collapsing from greed and mismanagement; and much of the existing leadership has been unwilling to change, passing the costs of their selfishness and mismanagement to the next generations and the generations after them. When Katrina struck, the existing organizations that we had formed to meet such needs were bound by hierarchies of command, ineffective leadership, regulations, and poor policies. The people who got things done when Katrina struck emerged as active groups from churches and organizations that had a common passion and vision to change things. Also these groups had leaders with vision. Political leaders at all levels of the government have become geldings lusting for more money and power rather than the stallion servant leaders we need. The public educational system teaches humanism with little ethical or moral absolutes. The people responsible have yet to be held accountable.

The leadership in many churches doesn't seem much better. Today many leaders who are studying church growth have reached a common conclusion. They see many churches failing from outdated structures and unable to build the type of Church that Christ was really talking about.

Mike Regele (co-founder and president of Percept Group, Inc.), and Mark Schulz, writing in *Death of the Church*, state:[1]

> *In the face of these waves of change, the institutional church in America has two options. Either it will go about its business as usual—and be swallowed up by obsolescence and die by default. Or the church will choose to die—and thus find life.*

And from George Barna, founder and president of Barna Research Group writing in 2001:[2]

> *I've concluded that within the next few years America will experience one of two outcomes: either massive spiritual revival or total moral anarchy.*

And that revival hasn't come yet.

Don't get me wrong here. The Church will be here until the Lord comes. I am an incurable romantic when it comes to the Church. I'm talking about a radical change here that is needed in how the Church does missions.

Take a look at the North American institutional church. This is what we are generally talking about when we talk about our spiritual community. Anyone doing Church Growth studies on the church in North America will tell you we have a problem. The young people are abandoning the institutional church in massive numbers.[3] Some 80% of the church funding is from the Builder generation. As that generation dies off, so does the funding base.[4] (My church does not have this problem. We have a large number of young people and we are aggressively training them for servant leadership.)

Don't read this wrong. This does NOT mean the younger generations are without faith. Many of these young people have a strong faith. It is just that their faith is often no longer institutionally driven. Those Millennials will no longer choose to join any institution. The church, as an institution, has failed them. What they want to join is a vision, a passion. Something that will change the world. They work from small groups; but the groups are highly relational and unlike those of even the Boomers. Often they live in their small groups.

I have a friend who is a nurse at a local Christian college. She has college kids coming into her office who are sick, sometimes emotionally broken, and even an occasional student trying to commit suicide. She tries to get them to come to her church. They won't go. Her church along with others like hers is dying, unable to attract the younger generations. The kids do, however, have a strong faith. Some of them go to a new form of community that is quite different from what is known as the institutional church. Others see the campus, their campus friends, and the chapel service as their church community. The institutional church as we know it isn't relevant to them.

I had breakfast with an elderly lady a few days ago. She loves her church and shared with me some of what she liked about it. I asked about the youth there. There were none.

A few days later I was on Facebook with a young friend in another city. She and her husband were heavily involved in missions and using their gifts to do some wonderful and creative mission work. But, she said, we don't do church any more. They have their own network of people on Facebook and in their personal network. That is their "church". A few days later they left to work for a few weeks at a Christian orphanage in Uganda.

I really don't blame the Millennials. If I were their age I would have no reason to seek my spiritual directions from most of the institutional churches that I see. George Barna and other Church Growth leaders all say the institutional church, as we know it, is dying. The institutional church they see doesn't look anything like the church in Acts. So what is a Christian supposed to do today? If the church is supposed to be the miracle and primary influence in a culture, it is certainly a miracle that the North American church has so little influence in today's culture.

> *In this historic moment, we live caught in a worldview that no longer works and a new one that seems too bizarre to contemplate.*

Margaret J. Wheatley, *Leadership and the New Science: Discovering Order in a Chaotic World*

In the old worldview, or Western thought, people, organizations, and the world functioned much as a machine, with systems organized to work like clocks in a deterministic world. Left-brain thinking dominated. Churches were structured institutions with a hierarchical structure much like the businesses in which we spend the rest of the week. Prophets were dangerous—they upset the status quo.

The Conference

I sat at a conference room at a seminary as part of a very small group. A leading teacher at the seminary who did international church planting was sitting at the table along with a visiting pastor. This pastor had worked with a major church research organization to survey his city (paying the organization $15,000) and then planted a church based on the survey results. The first Sunday the doors were open the pastor drew a remarkable 600 people. Now he was drawing about 300 a Sunday—still a good attendance. The pastor wanted to know what he should do next.

I watched this leading church planter who taught at the seminary as he meditated a bit and then turned to the pastor.

"Nothing we have here at the seminary can help you on that," this church planter replied.

After a short pause he continued quietly with an interesting statement.

"What you need to do is to go through your Bible and write down every command that Christ left His followers. Our churches have violated every single one of them. You should lead from each of those commands as Christ meant the Church to do."

He then gave a few examples. That was it—that's about all he told the pastor. We've built our churches and have trained our leaders on worldly paradigms that are no longer relevant. The world doesn't run as an ordered clock anymore. To put it bluntly, God is still creating. God is big on surprises that involve the hearts of men and women, not programs or buildings.

For most Americans, the media sends images to us as consumers to buy whatever product they think will meet our needs. The attractive girl stands next to an automobile tire and tries to convince us that if we purchase the tire the pretty girl will want to ride in our car. Ridiculous, but we buy the tire. Or if the girl buys a certain expensive makeup product she will look beautiful to the guy. Or if the guy buys a certain sport car he will be manly. Preposterous; but it works. The pastor tries to sell Christianity the same way, telling us that if we buy his or her brand we will have success and happiness.

So what happens? It's a type of do-it-yourself religion that makes us happy, meets our immediate needs, and is fun. We pick from this program, that program, or whatever in terms of what we want. There is no threat and we don't have to change. Take what we need from whatever "store" is there. Churches copy this with their shopping mall mentality and build close to the freeway so people don't have any trouble getting there when they need to buy something spiritual. As long as we stay busy, the noise drives out our deeper needs.

It is like the patient who goes to the doctor and discovers he has early-stage cancer. The doctor wants to do chemotherapy and radiation. The patient doesn't like this answer, so he or she is going to shop for a doctor who will give them the desired answer. Spiritually, we often do the same thing. We look for the church that fits *our* definition of what Christ is all about and doesn't threaten our own paradigm of living, our illusion. That way, we don't have to change. A recent ARIS survey of

54,000 Americans indicated 76% of American adults identified themselves as Christians.[5] Really?

Spiritual leaders come into this much as the doctor to that sick patient. The pastor tells us what we want to hear and we might stay around and enjoy the ride and finance the church. But what we hold onto is an illusion. The Enemy has deceived us. If the pastor tells it like it is—the reality—we might bail out and choose to protect our illusion. Or we might kill the leaders. That's what they did to Martin Luther King, Dietrich Bonheoffer, and Jesus. And this is what is being done and what was done to thousands of others—even as you read this.

The New Leader

The new leader must lead from a vision of reality that those around him often see only as illusion. When Jesus came into our world, he entered a world in which the spiritual environment was much as it is today. The institutional religion had collapsed. Judaism had become no more than routine observances of rules and liturgies. The Sadducees were in charge of the Temple, but had sold out to materialism. The Temple had become a marketplace. The Pharisees owned the religious agenda; but that was an empty religion. Jesus constantly chided both groups, seeing them empty of any spiritual reality. The people were spiritually searching and came to John the Baptist, then Jesus. That was threatening to the Jewish leaders. Look what happened to John the Baptist and Jesus. Can you see the parallel to the world today?

Jesus led from a vision of reality that even the disciples could not understand or see until after his death and the coming of the Holy Spirit. *Their* view was a coming "king" who would throw off their yoke of slavery to the occupying Romans and set the nation up again as a chosen kingdom. Even after the resurrection of Jesus and he was spending the last few moments with his disciples they asked him:

"Lord, will You at this time restore the kingdom to Israel?"

Acts 1:6

They still didn't understand, still in their illusion. Still in their small story. And Jesus was leaving them, saying soon they would have the Holy Spirit helping them to start His Church. The whole thing did not look well at all to them now. The reality of what would happen within just a few weeks was an illusion to them now. They could not believe or see it.

Unfortunately for most of us, we build an illusion around our story that somehow, in some way, things will keep on going. And we keep on going like we have always gone. We stay in our illusion and try to muddle on. Like the old cliché, however, if you keep on doing what you've always done, you will keep on getting what you've always got. Unless there is a sense of desperateness (dissatisfaction), it is difficult to initiate change. This sense of desperateness is already sweeping our nation.

I like the story in the Bible of blind Bartimaeus. Jesus is leaving Jericho on his way to Jerusalem for the last week of His life. This man is screaming to Jesus for mercy, and those around the man tell the man to shut up. Jesus asks those around Him to bring the blind Bartimaeus to Him. Then Jesus asks what seems like a really stupid question.

"What do you want Me to do for you?"

Mark 10:51

The reply of the man is the heart cry of each of us.

"Rabboni, that I may receive my sight."

Mark 10:51b

Each of us is trapped in our illusions and we can't see what God is really doing and what our part might be in the Kingdom Enterprise. Until we can see that and claim authority in our lives in terms of this, nothing changes and we remain trapped in our illusions. Jesus will give us that vision if we ask, just like He did with Bartimaeus.

The Enemy is constantly distorting reality. God is continually working in our lives; but we are often so blind-sided that we miss the clues from God.

Moses kills an Egyptian and gets tossed to the desert. He's had no experience for surviving in the desert, so Pharaoh expects him to die there. God then gives Moses a forty year survival course on how to survive in the desert. Then Moses sees the real shocker—God is also preparing him for leading the Israelites through the desert. What we would look at and call a death sentence was in reality an illusion. The reality was an agenda that was far beyond anything Moses could image.

I love the story of Joshua as he embraces the leadership task of taking this ragtag generation of Israelites raised in the desert into a fortified "Promised Land" after this same nation had failed on their first call. Again, this nation faced a window of opportunity through which they had to go with all the risks that went with it. The Land was no longer an illusion. This new generation saw the reality and began moving to take it. Which generation of these Israelites do you identify with?

Looking at Nehemiah you see another interesting illusion. Nehemiah is a man with incredible management and leadership gifting. As the story opens, he is working as an underemployed cupbearer for a heathen king in a remote country. The reality is that it is all a big setup by God to restore the Israelite nation and prepare it for the coming Messiah. Against all odds, the king not only allows Nehemiah to go to Jerusalem to build a wall, but also provides him with materials and security for his journey.

What about Esther? Abraham? Noah? And a long string of others? Where are you in this?

Notes:

1. Regele, Mike. *The Death of the Church*. (Grand Rapids, Michigan: Zondervan, 1995)
2. Barna, George. *The Second Coming of the Church*. (Ventura:

Regal Books, 2001). The actual quote came from Bara at a conference in Portland.

3. For more information see Reggie McNeal's *The Present Tense: Six Tough Questions for the Church.* (Hoboken, NJ: Josey-Bass, 2003). Reggie currently serves as the Missional Leadership Specialist for Leadership Network. His statistics when I heard Reggie (2005) showed a North American church attendance from about 60% in the Builder generation in North America to 10% in the Millennials. Most of these numbers are in his *The Present Future* book and from multiple sources. Current surveys often show a higher percentage for the Millennials today, but remember that the Millennials reject institutionalism. Their definition of "church" is quite different from that of a Builder, making the measuring of the generational breakdown difficult. Reggie McNeal has written several books, with my favorite *A Work of Heart: Understanding How God Shapes Spiritual Leaders.*

4. My own church does not have this problem. We have a very large base of young people. We intentionally train these for servant leadership. This past summer we had a group of these travel to South Korea with our senior pastor and they lived for a time with some North Korean Christians who had escaped the persecution and life in North Korea. Our kids went up with them on fishing boats off the east coast of North Korea and launched weather balloons into North Korea with tracts. Our kids came home. The North Korean Christians planned to go back into North Korea where they will be persecuted or perhaps die for their faith.

5. American Religious Identification Survey (ARIS) from Trinity College in Hartford Connecticut, 2009. The survey was made between February and November of 2008. The summary is at:

6. http://www.americanreligionsurvey-aris.org/reports/ ARIS_Report_2008.pdf.

Dialog

With which character in the Bible do you most closely associate? Why?

1. How would you describe the larger Church today?

2. Do you have a church? Why or why not? If you have a church, how would you describe it?

3. What is God telling you about your response to the failure you see?

4. How do you feel about the lack of leadership today? Are you discouraged or fearful as you look at you own life and what is going on in the world? Why?

Chapter 2: Living in the Illusion

*When one realizes
one is asleep,
at that moment
one is already half-awake.*

P.D, Ouspensk, Russian journalist

One of the most recent movies that had a very deep impact on my life was the movie *The Illusionist*. After watching this movie, I was sharing with a small group how much the movie had affected my life. The effect of the movie really shocked me. I could not move from my chair for the hour and 45 minutes of the movie. The group challenged me as to why it had affected me so. I said I didn't know why. I needed to watch the movie again to see why.

This wonderful movie is based on a short story by Steven Millhauser, "Eisenheim the Illusionist". The short story, in turn, was loosely based on a real incident that happened in Vienna around 1914. The name of the real prince was Archduke Franz Ferdinand. The Emperor at that time was Franz Joseph I of Austria. You see the actual portrait of this Emperor in an illusion by Eisenheim in the movie. Ferdinand's wife was Sophie, the same name as the tragic heroine in the film. Historically, the Duchess and the Crown Prince were together assassinated on 28 June 1914, an event that some believe triggered World War I.

The scenery in the movie is beautiful. The filming of the movie was done in the Czech Republic. A real castle in Czechoslovakia was used for some of the filming. The costumes were all exquisite. You feel as if you are there—you are immersed and mesmerized by the story, participating with the other characters. The music for the movie has won awards. The entire ensemble of the primary actors and actresses are all outstanding. The Eisenheim character is loosely based on a real magician at the time, Erik Jan Hanussen, who was murdered by Nazi soldiers in 1933. For the movie, two professional magicians were hired to help with the illusions and train the actors on how to do the illusions.

Near the beginning of the movie there is a flashback to Eduard (the illusionist) as a young boy playing with a girl (Sophia). The young girl is fascinated by his illusions. This girl, however, is of noble birth and destined to be a princess or queen. Eduard is a commoner. That would be like trying to mix oil and water. The girl's father comes with his solders and drags the daughter away as she screams, with the father forbidding the young man to play with his daughter again. If this young man does, the father warns that he and his family will be put in jail. In his despondency, you see Eduard pack his suitcase and leave town that night. At the moment you don't know where he is going and what he plans to do. You find out later.

With the flashback over, the movie actually begins fifteen years later as Eduard—now a handsome young man—returns to Vienna as a famous illusionist, Eisenheim. He is performing at the theater in Vienna. The reviews of his performances describe Eisenheim's shows as riveting. One night the crown prince and his intended show up for a performance. The young girl he once played with is now a beautiful young lady and you are only days away from the crown prince announcing his engagement to this young lady. She is being forced into the marriage as part of a political game. It looks completely hopeless for Eisenheim. He loves her deeply but is told by the police inspector and another friend that his love being fulfilled is impossible and can only lead to his death or jail if he continues in his quest. Eisenheim doesn't stand a chance. You can guess how the story will go—but wait….

After some distance through the story, a startling and very incredibly tragic event happened. I was shocked as I watched it. I was screaming. It's as if I was hit in the stomach by a ten-ton truck. This is not the way the script was supposed to go. They've got the wrong script. I don't like this movie. I'm quitting. But you can't move from your chair.

Ever been there in your life? I was there when my wife died.

"God, this isn't the right script. I don't like the script. Give me another script." All God would say to me is that I hadn't seen the last act.

As the movie nears its inevitable ending, you see the police inspector walking down a lonely road. Everything this police inspector had dreamed of is gone. His vision is shot. Nothing left. Not even Eisenheim is there—at least in the inspector's illusion. No purpose in life. It is then you see a small boy come up and he gives the inspector the first clue to the reality. How so much like Jesus who tried to tell us that the first clues of the Kingdom will come from the child. As the eyes of the inspector follow the small child, the final scenes of the movie begin to pass before your eyes. The darkness is pulled back and you see clearly the reality of what actually happened. The inspector screams as he realizes what really happened. You scream and fall out of your chair. You realize the Illusionist and the movie director have been playing with your mind. At the same time, some type of spiritual awakening has begun in Austria.

Isn't that ending like the Emmaus road story in Luke? Remember those two depressed followers walking down that lonely road after the crucifixion? They are talking about the events of the past weekend and the crucifixion. Everything they had dreamed about, their visions, everything they had believed in was shot to pieces. They were expecting a king who would overthrow the Romans and restore the Israelite nation to its former glory again. Now they believed their hero to be dead, their visions shattered. As they shared their lost dreams, a stranger comes up to join them. The stranger joins the conversation with them and they are surprised that this stranger doesn't seem to know what happened the last weekend. Trapped in their illusions, they did not recognize the stranger as the risen Christ. Not until they broke bread with Him that evening. Then, the Bible says, their eyes were opened and they saw the reality.

Now move back in time just a short time before that Emmaus road story. We see a group of women who are grieving as they walk through the early morning darkness to the tomb of a man they had loved. The man they expected to be the Messiah. He had been cruelly crucified on a cross earlier and now He was gone. The women had spent the previous evening (after sundown) preparing spices to anoint the body as was their custom. The mother of Jesus was not with them as they arrived at the tomb. Apparently the mother was too grief stricken to visit the tomb at the time. The group included Mary Magdalene, Joanna, the wife of Herod's steward, Mary, the mother of James (a follower and possible financial supporter), and Salome, who was possibly the mother of the sons of Zebedee. Their vision had been shattered. They had expected Jesus to be the "Messiah" who would lift their nation from the bondage of their life of poverty under their Roman rulers and free them. Now He was gone. Dead. But they were holding an illusion.

Their concern as they traveled to the tomb was how to move the massive stone that would block them from reaching the body. They found the stone already moved and an angel at the tomb. The angel tries to tell them Jesus had risen from the dead; but that doesn't match with their illusion. They leave to tell the others of their strange experience. The reality of the risen Lord was too difficult for them to believe. They were living in their illusion and small story.

Peter and John, on hearing this report from the women, rush to the tomb. John stops without going into the tomb and looks into the tomb in astonishment. He sees the grave clothes; but their neat folding is not what one would have expected if the body had been stolen. Impetuous Peter rushes into the tomb and saw the linen clothes as well. Then Peter and John apparently left.

Then we see Mary Magdalene arriving at the tomb for the second time and struggling to find clues as to what has happened. Of all the women and men, she is the *only* one who returned to the tomb and stays there, weeping as she struggles to find what she has lost. She, too, carries the illusion but is *desperate* for what she has lost. Mary Magdalene was the woman from whom Jesus had cast out seven demons (Luke 8:2).

Mary stands sobbing uncontrollably. She is gutted by what has happened. Through her tear-streaked eyes, she struggles to see the man who comes behind her, believing Him to be the gardener. From within her illusion, she asks if He knows where the body is and if so to please tell her. She stands alone—just like you and me—before we see the reality.

"Mary…"

Mary's illusion is suddenly shattered. She recognizes the voice and realizes that she is no longer alone. Her wilderness has become Place. She sees the reality for the first time. The woman who had the most to be forgiven of and the woman who was the most desperate was the first person to see the risen Lord.

It is to this woman, Mary, to whom the risen Lord gives the first "Go tell…". She was the first evangelist. She was the first to obey and went to tell others about the reality. She is the leader. Jesus had risen from the dead.

Isn't that like our life? The Enemy is constantly distorting reality. Deceiving us. God is continually working in our lives, trying to help us see the reality. But we are often so blind-sided that we miss the clues from God.

What illusions are you trapped in? You can't really lead until you see the reality.

The Cell Phone Story

Sometimes God enters our life in such a quiet way we can miss seeing Him. Just a week ago I pulled my cell phone from my pocket to check for calls and found the front face of the phone had shattered. There was nothing else in that pocket but the phone. The face looked as if it had been hit hard by an ice pick. In the face of the phone was a tiny hole and I could see cracks radiating out from the tiny hole. This round hole looked like it had been drilled into the screen. The screen was unreadable. I stared in disbelief. There was no physical reason for the screen to break like this. The warranty would not cover this. I had no service contract. The phone contract had over a year to go and the price for a replacement phone would be about $360.

I left immediately for the store where I purchased the phone, taking my receipts with me. I did not take my credit card or any of those little coupons they are constantly mailing me. I don't know whether it was faith or not; but I did know I didn't have the money to buy another phone.

When I got to the store and went to the cell phone department, I saw the salesperson there was not the right salesperson which I needed to help me. I had bought a memory card there some months ago, only to discover when I got home that the memory card didn't work right. When I returned to the store with it, this same salesperson wouldn't replace it, saying it was new and not defective. Another salesperson, overhearing the discussion, grabbed the card and checked it in the repair department. It was defective and he replaced it and checked the replacement to be sure it worked.

So there I was again. A defective phone, no service contract, and the wrong salesperson.

It was then a salesman came over from another department (television department) to greet me. He wanted to know how I was doing. I told him I was fine, but the phone they sold me was not. This was not the salesman's department; but when he saw the problem, he immediately told me I was going to need a high-level person to help me. He took charge of helping me with my problem, got me connected to the right person, and in a few minutes I walked out of the store with a replacement phone—absolutely free.[1]

My guess is most people would walk away and not think much about the incident, maybe praising the store. That's an illusion. Sure, they did a great job but think a minute. The reality was that God was giving me an incredible message. The phone could not break that way on its own. There was warfare. This salesperson interceded for me. In the same way, I stood before God as a sinner and did not deserve any mercy, particularly with this phone. Jesus interceded for me, just as this salesperson did with the phone, and rescued me and paid the price to do that. Wow! What a message when you see the reality!

Jesus and the Illusions

Jesus made at least two trips to Nazareth where He grew up as a child. The Bible tells us, however, He was not able to do much there *"because of their unbelief"* (Mark 6:1). The problem in Nazareth was that they saw a carpenter's son, an illusion. They never saw who Jesus really was. Like the people of Nazareth, we become trapped in our illusions and cannot pray in faith beyond this. The Enemy deceives us. We have an academic faith, but not a faith that enables us to act.

Just days before His crucifixion, Jesus was throwing the money-changers out of the temple so the sick could get to Him for healing. Quite a shock to the status quo. Notice it was the children in the story who saw the reality. Not the priests, scribes, and other so-called "spiritual leaders". The children were the leaders in this story.

Then Jesus went into the temple of God and drove out all those who bought and sold in the temple, and overturned the tables of the money changers and the seats of those who sold doves. And He said to them, "It is written, 'My house shall be called a house of prayer,' but you have made it a 'den of thieves.'"

Then the blind and the lame came to Him in the temple, and He healed them. But when the chief priests and scribes saw the wonderful things that He did, and the children crying out in the temple and saying, "Hosanna to the Son of David!" they were indignant and said to Him, "Do You hear what these are saying?"

And Jesus said to them, "Yes. Have you never read,

'Out of the mouth of babes and nursing infants

You have perfected praise'?"

Then He left them and went out of the city to Bethany, and He lodged there.

Matthew 21:12-17

The adult religious leaders were trapped in their illusions—the laws and making sure everything was done properly to their covenant of law. Jesus, operating under a covenant of grace, was trying to reach those who needed healing. The kids saw the reality and were praising God.

I remember when my wife Sandy was doing summer missions in St Louis and teaching inner city kids how to read in an old church the mission group was using. The older people who came to church there (and didn't even live in the neighborhood) were upset that the kids were messing up the hymnals and otherwise not treating things properly. Sandy was more interested in reaching the kids. The other church leaders were trapped in their illusions.

The Tournier Story

In 1984 my wife and I took a tour with a group through Germany, Austria, Jordan, Israel, and Italy. When we got to Rome, the group part was over and most of the group planned to fly back home through Copenhagen. My wife and I broke with the group at Rome and planned to travel up to Florence, then Geneva (and other locations in Switzerland) and then on to England before heading home. Sixteen years earlier (1968) I had managed to hear the renowned author and doctor, Paul Tournier, speak in Berne. This time, before my trip, I wrote a letter to Paul Tournier, thanking him for what his books meant to me. Outside of the Bible, no writer has influenced me more than Tournier. At the time Tournier was considered by many to be the leading doctor in the world. He was based in Geneva. Doctors who had patients for whom they had given up would send them to Tournier, and they would get well. Later (Chapter 7) we will look at what Tournier did; but what happened on this particular trip was most astonishing. I did not have his address; I just sent the letter to him with Geneva, Switzerland as the only address I knew. In the letter, I asked permission take him to lunch as my wife and I passed through Geneva. I gave him the date and hotel where we would be staying.

Tournier got the letter and wrote back, saying he would be delighted to join us for lunch. As we traveled with the tour, we constantly shared with our group about the wonderful opportunity we would have to lunch with this great doctor when we got to Geneva. We were really excited about him accepting our invitation.

As we waited at our hotel lobby for someone to meet us, a gentleman came in and asked for us. He wasn't Tournier. As he came over to us, he shared with us that Tournier was very sick and could not join us. This gentleman whom Tournier had sent was Tournier's own doctor. Would we like to join him and his wife for lunch?

Sandy and I had a wonderful lunch with this doctor. Whereas Tournier would have spoken French, this doctor was originally from America and spoke English. I was lunching with the doctor for perhaps what was the greatest doctor in the world. I was completely unaware that in five years (1989) I would be in

Switzerland again—this time in a Swiss hospital, fighting for my life with an illness that is often misdiagnosed in the States. At that time my life would be totally dependent upon the Swiss medical system.

The illusion here was that I had lost an opportunity to meet an incredible doctor. The reality was that I did meet an incredible doctor who could provide me with critical information I would need in only five years.

Not long after arriving back home, I got a letter from Tournier's wife. Tournier's first wife had died, and Tournier had married again. Tournier's current wife was a concert pianist. She wanted to tour the United States and asked if I could help her set up a concert schedule. I had no skills or knowledge on this, and wrote her that the person she should contact was Ken Medema. Ken is a brilliant, but physically blind, Christian concert pianist who really prefers smaller groups where he can interact with his audience. Ken may be physically blind, but he sees better than almost anyone I have ever met. Ken does many concerts and has a great deal of knowledge on this. Moreover, Ken was someone she should definitely meet at a personal level when traveling here if she had a strong interest in music ministry. Ken is extremely gifted in using music to heal and initiate personal transformation. In addition, I had Ken's address and sent it to her. If my reports are correct, they did meet and she greatly enjoyed the experience. God writes very interesting scripts for our lives.

Paul Tournier died only two years after my lunch in Geneva with his doctor. The world lost a great man. *The healing begins, Tournier taught me, when we see the reality.* We will come back to see what he taught in Chapter 7.

In the next chapter you will see what happened five years later on my return to Switzerland.

Notes:

1. No—I will not share with you the name of the store where I purchased the cell phone. If you went to a store

of the same chain in your area you would probably not see what happened here. The salesperson in the store who became my intercessor seems to have disappeared from the local store. I haven't been able to find him in the store again.

Dialog

1. In your morning devotional, pray for God to astonish you that day. Keep your eyes open, then journal what happens.

2. Did what happened fit your agenda?

Part II: The Illusion – The Perceived Wilderness

Ever felt like those Israelites on the edge of that Promised Land? These jokers had been released from their bondage in Egypt by a series of miracles. When the Egyptian army tried to follow them, the army drowned in that river. God provided food and water as they crossed the desert. He gave them some rules to live by now known as the Ten Commandments (which have been thrown away in our public buildings because we insist on living by our own rules). There they stood. On the edge of that Promised Land (or Promised Time). They did this spy job on the land. Two of them—Joshua and Caleb—said we can do it. The others said it was impossible. The purpose of that mission was not to see if they could do it. It was theirs already. The purpose was to get a vision of what God was about to give them.

They blew it. With the exception of Joshua and Caleb, they spent the rest of their lives in the wilderness. They were in an illusion. They could not see the reality and take the risk of stepping out on that reality as their own.

How about you? Feel like you are in a wilderness? Lost hope? It's only an illusion. God is out to do a number on you. You will find, however, life is serious business and does have risk.

Chapter 3: Facing the Leadership Illusion

My body was shutting down. Hiking high in the Alps on a beautiful day, a paralysis was starting to sweep through my body starting from my feet and hands and moving to the lungs and heart...

Unknown to me, this attack on my body had actually started two weeks earlier. Back then (May, 1989) I had just finished speaking at a Christian technical conference near London. At the last day of that conference, something much like a traveler's "stomach flu" had struck me. In addition, something had also altered my immune system so that my body's immune system began attacking my own cells of the neural system, physically destroying my neural system.

Now, ten days later in Zermatt, my wife and I were enjoying a ride on a tram and then shopping in the tiny remote village. The Matterhorn played hide and seek with the tourists as we jostled about the village streets. After shopping, we started hiking at the foot of the Matterhorn. As the hike began, I noticed a strange tingling in my feet. My wife noticed my feet weren't behaving right and commented, asking if I was tired.

"Sure," I said, "but this doesn't seem like tiredness. It is like I am sending commands to my feet and the feet aren't responding too well."

The next morning as we prepared to leave Zermatt, we realized the problem was even more acute. After breakfast I had difficulty climbing the stairs back to our room. It was as if I was carrying my suitcase up the stairs; only I wasn't carrying anything. As we prepared to checkout, I realized I couldn't lift my suitcase. My wife joked I had bought too much. Then she lifted my suitcase with no problem.

"Let's get out of here—quickly."

Zermatt is high in the mountains and could provide little medical help. An express train was leaving Zermatt in a few minutes. We got an electric taxi to get to the train station while Sandy checked us out of our hotel. We left Zermatt on the express train to Interlaken. With a single train transfer, we would to be at Interlaken by lunch.

The symptoms, more commonly called Gullain-Barré Syndrome (GBS), were already being experienced by my body and something had actually begun destroying the neural system in my feet and then the legs. Although the GBS initially targeted the myelin sheath surrounding the nerves, in my case the GBS continued into the axons of my nerve cells to destroy them as well. And the nerve cells, a doctor told me later, have very little restoration capability. We believe today that Franklin D. Roosevelt never had polio—it was this same Gullain-Barré Syndrome, and he never walked again.[1]

On the train, I sat quietly as this famous express dropped through some of the most scenic mountains in the world at more than 100 miles an hour. A paralysis was slowly moving up my legs. I tried to unzip my backpack, suddenly realizing my fingers would not work right and whatever this was had paralyzed my fingers and started to move up my arms. The paralysis was moving toward my lungs and heart moment by moment. I was in a foreign country with no clue as to what had happened or how to get the medical attention I would need to save my life. I was already in shock, one of the symptoms a doctor would look for later.

We arrived in the small resort town of Interlaken by lunch. As we headed to our hotel where we had reservations, Sandy would move the suitcases and then me. I already needed support for walking. The hotel found us an English-speaking doctor who came into his office that Saturday afternoon. Sandy helped me get to his office. By now I could hardly walk, even with support. A quick check by the doctor and he picked up the phone to call the hospital, giving directions to the person on the other end in German. Then he turned to me.

"This is serious, but not life-threatening. You are headed to the hospital. It is very good you got me in."

The first statement was true. It was serious. The second was not. GBS is life-threatening in its acute stage. I was in a tiny resort town in a remote area of Switzerland with a life-threatening issue shutting down my body. Today I believe this doctor was able to diagnose the GBS in his office, something my own doctor later said is quite unusual.

At the hospital in Interlaken, three people met me as I staggered though the door with my wife's support. One, a doctor, started getting my oral history in English. Another was a nurse who started taking blood samples for laboratory work. A third person started the administration work. All working simultaneously. Then I was taken to a hospital room. A team of doctors were quickly assembled (on Saturday afternoon) and I was under intensive observation. My wife told me later the doctors were checking in on me all through the night, as the lungs had a 50% risk of shutting down.

The next morning I awoke with a gray-haired gentleman leaning over and examining me. Then he went back to some other doctors and they started talking in German. One of them came over shortly and spoke to me in English.

"The doctor who was just here? He is one of the top neurologists in the world. He just happened to be in this small resort area. Without him, we would have flown you by helicopter to Bern. This doctor knows what this is. He is just back from an international conference on what you have. The doctor has a treatment that is not experimental. We will start it after a few more tests to confirm his diagnosis. To use the treatment, we must be 120% sure of the diagnosis."

Within only a few hours, they started their treatment, which was certainly bold. Massive doses of steroids went into my body intravenously. They knew exactly every side effect I would experience and started counter medication for the side effects before I experienced them. In addition, they had me in intensive care and were watching for any additional side effects (such as double-vision) that I might experience. By the second day the GBS was no longer advancing in my body and they started slowly decreasing the steroids. But by then, I was paralyzed from the shoulders down and the neural system was physically gone. State-side doctors later told me that the neural system, unlike other cells, has very little, if any, restoration capability. For 48 hours the doctors had wrestled with trying to stop the relentless destructive progress of the GBS and had finally won. But the neural system had already experienced major destruction.

I lived in the hospital intensive care unit for two weeks. From my window at the hospital I could look out at the Swiss mountains. I could see the north face of the Eiger mountain where Clint Eastwood filmed *The Eiger Sanction*. I could see the restaurant where they filmed the James Bond *On Her Majesty's Secret Service*. Hang gliders gently floated in the thermal currents over the other mountains. And I hung for days between life and death.

After three weeks (two in intensive care) my steroid dose was down to a few pills a day and I was told I could go home. I was still totally paralyzed from the shoulders down. They gave me enough medication for 24 hours, telling me after that I would need to be under a state-side doctor within the 24 hours for more medication. Miss a dose getting home and I would have major withdrawal symptoms and could die. Sandy also was trained to give me shots with a blood thinner to prevent clotting. Without the shots, a clot in the legs could move to the lungs and kill me. An ambulance and nurse shuttled me to the Zurich airport.

On the plane I sat paralyzed with my wife. I was like a heavy sack of potatoes in the airplane seat. At the Interlaken hospital they had trained her with three different ways to move me without injuring her back. As we waited in the plane for takeoff, the captain came on the speaker.

"Folks, sorry to inform you but our alternate generator is out and we can't fix it here. We will need to fly back on a course that will keep us almost constantly over land. It will be three hours before they can clear this course for us and we can take off."

Sandy and I stared at each other. I had medicine for only 24 hours. That would give me less than 21 hours to get to Portland and under a doctor's care. And this clock had started ticking when I left Interlaken—several hours ago.

"What do we do?" she said.

"We pray."

After arriving at O'Hare, there was a transfer to my Portland flight. The attendants there did not believe I could not move and actually dropped me as they moved me to the gurney for loading. Sandy was on the phone at the time calling relatives. There was no paramedic at the airport to check me out after the attendees dropped me. At O'Hare, no one can hear you scream.

I arrived in Portland for the ambulance that was waiting for me about two in the morning local time. A friend from our church met us and took care of my wife (now exhausted) as the medical team took over.

At the hospital in Portland, the steroids that now saturated my body had increased my appetite so that people came to visit me just to watch me put down a meal. This little guy (5' 2", 130 lbs.) could wolf down a breakfast that included a stack of toast, several eggs, a stack of bacon, and multiple glasses of orange juice in a little over 15 minutes. Where was it going? No muscles were burning it, and the elimination system was shut down. I soon found the answer. My body could warm a small room with the heat it was generating.

I was laying there paralyzed from the shoulders. My lungs were still functioned, but were very weak. As I lay there, my own doctor came in.

"Carl, it's a miracle."

A miracle?

"Carl, if this had happened stateside, it would probably have been misdiagnosed. Two, we have nothing to treat it. Three, even if we knew what the Swiss doctors did, we would not have been able to do it here. You were at the one place in the world we could have gotten you back alive."

Then he walked out of the room. So this is miracle. I found out later all three of the things he told me were correct.

Slowly they continued to reduce the steroids, continuing the blood thinner. Within only a few weeks they started my rehab. I wanted them to start on the legs and arms. They started their therapy with silly exercises having me move my arms against their resistance. The exercises had a fancy name; but I was frustrated. I wanted them working on the legs and arms. Finally they told me why they were doing what they did.

"Carl, your lungs are weak. You can't move enough oxygen through your lungs for anything more than this now. We need to build the lungs up first."

Now a message came as prophecy. Like me wanting those arms and legs, we flail about trying to accomplish things in this world. To lead, we have to *wait* until we can move enough oxygen from the Holy Spirit. In the Bible, *pneuma*, which is used for the Holy Spirit at times, is the Greek word for the wind (see John 3:8, Hebrews 1:7). It is the word from which we get pneumonia, a disease of the lungs. At Pentecost, the stronger Greek word *pnoe* is used, which refers to a blast, explosion, or rushing wind. Pentecost and the coming of the Holy Spirit had to come before Peter could do what he did with the lame man at the temple gate. They had to wait. I had to wait.

During the next few months at the hospital I constantly wrestled with trying to get my body back. In working with the therapy, I was able for the first time to come to grips with the real damage, my own feelings, and the process of recovery. It was frustrating to wake up in the morning and find yourself trapped in a body that could not respond to commands. I found myself praising God each time I gained a little strength. When my fingers finally got strong enough to work the simple light switch on the bed, I would sit there throwing it back and forth for hours just celebrating my new discovery. I could not even sit up in bed for almost four months. At home on the weekends, Sandy had to take care of me: dressing, undressing, showers, and the toilet. I was trapped in a body that had no strength.

They took measurements of the neural system. The neural system was gone.

Some time later as I walked again my wife asked me a very interesting question.

"What did you think when the doctor told you that you would never walk again?"

"When did he say that?"

"He was right by your bed. I saw and heard him tell you this."

"I never heard it."

The doctor's words that had been so devastating to her, driven her to a prayer meeting where she poured out her heart with tears in prayer with others, were never heard by me.

"Don't you realize," I told her, "that that statement is theologically incorrect? If he had said a 5% or 10% chance of walking, I might have heard. But not 0%. That leaves out God and what He can do." My mind was filtering out any negative messages. I could not take a risk of taking ownership on any of that.

The doctor brought in some catalogs and asked me to pick out two wheelchairs. I would need them, he said, for the rest of my life. The neural damage was major, as many axons were destroyed. I threw the catalogs away, asking only for a temporary wheelchair. Maybe rent one. This upset the doctor, so he sent a psychologist in to help me deal with the reality of the situation. I tried to help the psychologist see the reality of the situation.

One time as the doctor was leaving the room I asked him what the neural system was doing. Do the neurons grow back, or are the messages to the muscles being re-routed to the muscles through other neural pathways?

"You don't understand, Carl." he said, "The neurons grow back very little, if any. And it takes a long time. The damage here is major."

My doctor would check on me each day, asking me to grip his hand in a handshake. There was nothing there. He would smile, as if acknowledging his prognosis was correct. I would try to work the light switch by my bed. I couldn't at that time.

Soon they had me in the swimming pool; the goal was to teach me how to walk again with the water taking some of my weight off the legs. I was walking all over the pool the first day. The next day my therapist told me the doctor's report.

"The doctor said you shouldn't have been able to walk in the pool."

"That's his problem," I told her. "It isn't mine."

After about a month back in the states they did an extensive analysis on my neural system. After the tests, the head neurologist at the hospital came into my room. He had a puzzled look on his face.

"We have done in the States what the Swiss doctors did there. It doesn't work. The tests even now show you still have the GBS. Yet all of the therapy indicates you are getting better. We can't explain it. So we'll keep going the direction we are going now."

In another experiment they put sensors on my ankle and connected them to a scope. The doctor asked me to think about moving my foot. I could think the image; but the foot did not move. On the scope, however, the electrical signal from the ankle probe went off the screen. The doctor was more than surprised.

"What? How did you do that?" she asked.

"Want to see it again?" I asked and repeated the spike on the scope.

"Wow! If you could get out of here on that, you would be out of here today."

I turned to my wife.

"She says there is a way to get out of here today."

And then there was the eye doctor. As they worked with me

in rehab, I noticed my eyes did not work right. I had massive headaches after reading only for twenty minutes and the eyes didn't focus right. I eventually got to the eye doctor, who took some tests and then peered into my eyes with his microscope. He refused to make any changes at that time, telling me to wait until the drugs and GBS were out of my system. Some months later I returned and he repeated his testing and examined the eyes again. Then I watched as he fell back in his chair in shock.

"What did you see?" I asked.

"When you were here before, I saw nothing in the eyes but gray garbage. The neural system in the eyes was damaged along with the rest of your neural system. The muscles of the eyes could not focus the eyes as the nerves there were destroyed. None of that is there now. The eyes are clear, the nerves are fine. I will write you a new prescription for your glasses, but your eyes are *five prescription levels better* than before you had the GBS. Somebody upstairs likes you."

Every day as I continued on this journey, I was reading the story of the lame man in Acts 3. What really happened back there? The man was forty years old and suddenly walking and running. Look at the miracles:

1. There were no muscles. If you haven't used those leg muscles a few days, they become very weak and useless. He had not used his muscles in over forty years and they knew it.
2. Unused muscles, when stretched, will cause incredible pain. You have to slowly work them and massage them gently. There was no pain here with this man.
3. Walking and running are *learned* experiences. This guy had never been taught to walk, much less run.

As I poured over the scripture story, I asked myself many questions I had never asked before. The man who was healed appeared to have no faith. What did Peter do? John was with Peter. What was John doing? What did the religious authorities see? What did the religious authorities do in response? Why was he healed? Where was the faith, or vision, of healing? *Who is the leader in this story?*

And one of the most important questions of all: *Where am I in the crowd that day? What do I see? Do I see the reality or an illusion?*

Even more important, as I read this story over and over again, *I began to live in a spirit of expectation.* Who is Peter today? I treated each person who visited me as a Divine Encounter. Could someone really visit my room and speak the word for me to walk again and I would walk? Any one (or more) of these visitors could be Peter. What was God's agenda here?

I did notice something, however, about the Bible story. We don't know the man's name. What happened violated all known laws of science—and the religious leaders knew it. The healing was not given to him primarily for his sake, but for the birthing of the Church. In other words, the giftings had little to do with Peter or the lame man. The gifts were given for the coming of the Church and the Kingdom. The Bible says the Church grew by about 5,000 men that day (see Acts 4:4).

Within a few months I was walking again, and in slightly over a year I was no longer even using a cane.

The doctors propagated an illusion to me. The illusion was bounded by a mindset in our Western civilization. It was based on a closed Newtonian physics system that says God created the world and it is a closed system. Now the world is running down to the chaos from which it was created. Everything is deterministic.

> *Three centuries ago, when the world was imagined as an exquisite machine set in motion by God—a closed system with a watchmaker father who then left the shop—the concept of entropy entered our collective consciousness. ... then why does life flourish? Why does life result in newness..., not deterioration and disintegration?*[2]

Margaret Wheatley, *Leadership and the New Science: Discovering Order in a Chaotic World*

From the day we are born those of us in the Western World still live and act into the illusion of the Newtonian physics. Unless we can break free of this Newtonian physics illusion we can never experience healing and lead in the necessary transformation.

Follow the story in the next chapter and see the illusion that every one of us experiences.

Notes:

1. Goldman, AS *et al. "What was the cause of Franklin Delano Roosevelt's paralytic illness?"* J. Med. Biogr. 11:232-240, 2003).
2. Wheatley, Margaret. *Leadership and the New Science: Discovering Order in a Chaotic World.* (San Francisco, CA: Berrett-Koehler Publishers, 3rd Edition, 2006)

Dialog

1. Read the story of the lame man in Acts 3 and 4. Where are you in the crowd that day?

2. Do you believe a lame man who had never walked for forty years walked that day?

3. Do you believe this story can happen today? Does it?

4. If you believe it could happen today, why do you think we don't see more of it?

5. Two smelly and uneducated fishermen become leaders in this story. What does that story of Acts 3 tell you about leadership?

Chapter 4: The Illusion We Each Face

There is nothing lost that may be found if sought.

Shakespeare

In 1991, just two years after my GBS, I was beginning to walk without a cane. We then discovered my wife (Sandy) was diagnosed with an acute form of leukemia. The diagnosis was late and the leukemia was moving so fast in her body that they were not sure they could even get the catheter for the chemotherapy into her body quickly enough to start the chemotherapy. They succeeded. Miracle 1. They did get the chemotherapy completed; but as the cells returned after the chemotherapy the leukemia cells were still there. The fact she was still alive after the first chemotherapy was the second miracle.

The next chemotherapy was stronger; but her white cells did not return after the chemotherapy. As pneumonia moved in, we prayed for a third miracle. I would make daily trips to the hospital with my weak legs, occasionally falling in the hospital corridors as I continued to recover from my own GBS. We got the miracle again. A new genetic drug that had been on the market for only a month kicked her white cells back to normal in 24 hours, and there were no leukemia cells or side effects. Miracle 3. She was jumping up and down on the hospital bed and they sent her home.

After her remission, the doctors now told us that there was

a 90% chance the leukemia would return within a year without a bone marrow transplant. The cells that would return would be those resistant to the chemotherapy and the doctors would have nothing to fight them. Her younger sister had died at the age of two from leukemia. Her marrow had a good match for a transplant with both her brother and her sister. Moreover, her white count had always been defective since I had known her. The marrow transplant had a 50% chance of success. We didn't like either odds, but the transplant option was the best alternative and could be done in three months. For the transplant they required the leukemia to be in remission (which it now was) and Sandy would need to be "well"; that is, in good physical condition. She was. We elected to have the transplant done at the Seattle Fred Hutchinson Cancer Research Center, about 3 ½ hours away from Portland where we lived.

The transplant went well and for a time after the transplant she was an outpatient at the Center. One day during that time as outpatient she went catatonic during a lunch at our apartment. An ambulance rushed her back to the hospital where she remained for three weeks as they tried to find out what had happened. During that time she had no short-term memory, seemed oblivious of her surroundings, and was trying to jump out of windows. She had to be restrained to her bed and watched 24 hours a day. After three weeks the MRI showed brain lesions, most probably (they said) from the whole body radiation used to destroy the defective blood cells and marrow before the transplant.

I called Peter Batchelder in Portland, my pastor at the time and who had a rich gifting in intercessory prayer. He said they would start fasting and praying. Soon Carol called from Portland, a friend who is also a mighty prayer warrior. She said she was driving up from Portland the next morning. I told Carol it didn't make much sense, as Sandy would not recognize her. Carol said I didn't understand and would see me the next morning.

As Carol and I walked into Sandy's room the next morning, Sandy was sitting up eating breakfast and completely normal after three weeks of being lost to any reality. A neurologist was called in, even though it was Saturday. He did some behavorial tests and then announced she was perfectly normal except for no memory of the past three weeks. They would do another MRI but the lesions, he said, would not be there. They did another MRI. The lesions were no longer there. I requested a copy of the medical report. The report called it "spontaneous remission", which is how the doctors spell "miracle". Another miracle.

Sandy made it through the bone marrow transplant and was back home in Portland a month later by Christmas; but she was weak and still had recovery ahead at home. By April she was off the medication to prevent rejection. Within another month, however, a rejection process had set in. Unlike with a kidney transplant or that of any other organ, with a bone marrow transplant the entire body is foreign to the new bone marrow and immune system. The new immune system sees the entire body as foreign cells. The marrow is matched very carefully before the transplant to insure rejection doesn't happen, but the doctors told us there is still a mystery and most of the decisions are made by the computers based on probability studies. They have the drugs to stop the rejection process; but in Sandy's case the diagnosis was made too late and the anti-rejection drugs were started too late to help.

The Emasculation

As I stood at the bed of my dying wife, the nurse took me aside and told me what I would see during those last thirty minutes of her life. As I stood there holding Sandy's hand, the minutes ticked by exactly as the nurse had told me. Thirty minutes later she went home to be with Jesus.

As I stood there in my loneliness, something happened to me. There are basically three needs, John Eldredge says, of any man: an adventure to embrace, a battle to fight, and a woman to pursue.1 The man has to hear from his father that he has the strength for the adventure, the strength for the battle, and the strength for the pursuit of the woman. Without that message the man is severely damaged. As I stood alone, I did not have the strength for the adventure for the healing of Sandy. I did not have the strength for the battle to pull her back from death, and I did not have the strength for the pursuit. I had no authority, no power. I was emasculated. Everything connected with my manhood was gone.

And Satan said, "Gottcha!"

But Satan is the Great Deceiver. I actually stood in Christ with more authority and power than I had ever had before in my life. I was, like every man and woman, trapped in an illusion. Satan was holding me captive. I was in a massive illusion.

The Pain

With the loss of my wife, a flood of emotions poured over me again and again like the pounding surf when a storm hits the beach near me. Some of the emotions had names, like Grief. Others were just there with no particular name.

There was a feeling of Guilt. I should have stood between her and the Enemy. I should have told the Enemy to buzz off. He had no right to even touch her, much less take her life. That was an illusion. I had been standing between her and the Enemy, I had been telling the Enemy to buzz off. I almost lost my own life doing that.

I had Guilt because I didn't have enough faith. After all, Jesus said if I had faith as a grain of a mustard seed and believed; it would be done. It wasn't done. I didn't have enough faith. I'm guilty. Yet I know if I could go back in time I would make the same decisions. We had faith that the decisions we made would lead to victory.

I was Angry. In many ways it was the major emotion I had to deal with. I was well aware the doctors made multiple mistakes. I knew where those mistakes were. Sandy didn't have to die. I'm going to sue the doctors. I started the research for that. Nothing, however, could bring Sandy back to me. She was gone. If I tried to sue, the process would take years and the anger would destroy me. God said I had to forgive. Ouch. I was angry at God. Most of all, I was angry at myself.

And then there was Abandonment. Sandy had abandoned me in dying. God had abandoned me. God had no right to take her back. If He was all-powerful, it was His fault. This time it was Jesus speaking to me.

"The toughest battle I had to fight," Jesus said, "was dying for you on that cross. Every man has to have a battle to fight. There on that cross was the biggie of a battle for Me. I had to hear from My Father at that time that I had strength for the battle. Instead My Father turned His back on Me at the time I needed Him the most. God could not look at the sins of the world on Me at the time. Look at My own words from that cross—'Daddy, why have You abandoned Me?' I know more than anyone else what abandonment is like. I have not and will not abandon you."

So abandonment was another illusion from the Enemy. Sandy was still alive with Jesus—and well. I would see her again.

Sometimes God seemed far away and I could not even hear Him. Sometimes God was in my face and we would wrestle and argue.

The Horse Story

Two years after my wife's death, God spoke to me with a strange message.

"Carl, I want you to race a horse on the beach."

"What was that again?"

"I want you to race a horse on the beach."

"Lord, what is Plan B?"

"There is no Plan B."

A few days later I was traveling back from the airport with my niece, who was visiting from Illinois.

"What do you guys do for fun here?" she asked.

"We go to the beach, rent a horse, and race it on the beach." I replied.

Dumb answer. I had never raced a horse on the beach. Something had tripped. An agenda had begun. A few days later my brother-in-law called me.

"Carl, she wants to do that horse thing. Wanna go with us?"

"Sure."

A few days later he called again.

"We found where to rent the horses. What kind of horse you want."

"Fast."

Boy, was I stupid.

A few days later I'm at this beach on a beautiful day with the mountains on my left and the Pacific Ocean on my right. An infinite beach was before me. I'm sitting on this huge stallion that wants to race. I was afraid.

I kicked the horse and the horse immediately shot off like a bullet from a gun. I had asked for a fast horse and this dude was fast. I'm holding on for dear life to whatever I can hold on to, trying to stay on this thing. The reins lay limp somewhere on the saddle. My teeth were chattering as the horse threw me up and then down as he raced full speed down the beach. There was a look of panic on my face. My hands were turning blue because I'm holding on to that saddle horn so hard. My seat was getting sore fast. The horse was totally out of control and tearing down the beach at as fast as he could go. I wasn't steering him—he was going where he wanted to go. I was just trying to survive. I had no authority. I had no power. God had taken me back to the exact same place He had me when I stood before my dying Sandy.

And God said, "Gottcha."

As I raced down the beach on this out-of-control horse, God continued talking. God definitely had my attention.

"Let go, Carl."

"God—are you crazy? It takes both hands holding on to the saddle horn just to stay on this thing."

"Let go, Carl. Take the reins."

"No, NO—The reins won't keep me on this thing and I can't hold on with one hand."

"Remember Moses?" God continued.

"What about Moses?"

"He had everything in Egypt. Money, education, women—whatever he wanted. Then he killed an Egyptian and was thrown into the desert to die. He lived there for forty years with nothing. It was an illusion. I was training him for a job during those forty years. After those forty years he's standing barefoot before this strange burning bush with nothing, absolutely nothing, but this stupid stick in his hand. What did I tell him to do?"

"Throw down the stick. That was the only possession he had left."

"OK. That saddle horn is your stick. Let go. LET GO, Carl. NOW! Take the reins!"

What a risk! God wants me to risk! Slowly I balanced myself and took the reins. As I pulled back on the reins, the horse came to a gentle stop. I did have authority, I did have power. The horse was giving me authority. I had been under an illusion.

I knew I had to win here a different way. Slowly I walked the horse and got in touch with his power under me. I felt his muscles, his rhythm, passion, and his heart. I went down when the horse went down, up when the horse went up. I could make him go left or make him go right. I was building a heroic intimacy with the horse as we walked. Then I brought the horse up to a trot, still maintaining the rhythm and heroic intimacy. Finally, we were back to racing again, but this time together. As the horse and I tore down the beach, I was singing that majestic song Shine, Jesus, Shine at the top of my lungs whizzing by others staring at me as if I was some kind of crazy guy. I had the reins in one hand, and the other hand was high in the air in praise. With the gorgeous ocean to my right, the beautiful beach before me, and majestic mountains at my left—I was at a place I had never been before. I was touching the adventure again.

Sometime later I stepped down from the horse; I had a wild look in my eyes. My hair was swept back, my face looked windblown, and my adrenaline was rushing. I was no longer emasculated. I had authority.

God continued to speak.

"Carl, I am wild like that horse. If you don't believe it, read your Bible. Look at Abraham, called to sacrifice his only son who had been promised to him by Me to build a chosen nation. Look at Noah building a boat on a sunny day on dry land without a cloud in sight. Look at Moses, waving that tiny stick over the water and watching the water separate. And it wasn't a shallow stream—the Egyptian army drowned in it a few minutes later. Look at Shadrack, Meshach, and Abednego in the fiery furnace. Look at Esther, who was called to save her nation by marrying a heathen Gentile king. And—top this—look at this virgin woman who has never known a man conceive and bear a son. And then this guy grows up, they crucify Him on a cross, and then He rises from the dead. Top that! I am wild."

"Carl, you were created in My image. You were in My mind's eye before you were born. You are created wild, like that stallion. Like Adam, you weren't created in the Garden. You were created in the wildness outside the Garden just like Adam. You were born to be wild. You have more power now than you have ever had. But you must run under My authority. Like the horse, you must run under My authority with the power that I give you. You were created for that purpose. I want you to lead from that authority."

What does that mean? What is this journey God is taking me on? As I would soon find out, God was breaking me from an illusion that each of us faces. Nothing is what it seems.

The Task

As I walked away from the horse, I was praising God.
"Two thumbs up, God. Great message."

"Wait up, Carl. I will go with you."

"What?"

"I got a job for you."

"Going to India again? That last mission trip was strange and I was scared, but we did it fine. I'll go again if You want me to go to India."

"Nope."

"What about London again? That it? I came back paralyzed from the shoulders down and it took me over a year to walk again, but if that is what You want I will go."

"Kindergarten stuff, Carl."

"What? I almost died on that. What is this job You want me to do this time?"

"Carl, I want you to rescue a human heart."

Silence.

"God, the rescue of a human heart is the hardest mission on the face of the earth."

"I know, Carl. I've been doing it a few years."

"Maybe we could go to London again. How about that?"

"Carl?"

"OK, You're on; but I know nothing about this."

"Yes you do. Listen up, Carl. Here's your first course. Begin by letting Me hold the reins. Don't even try to be the hero on this."

"Ok. You got the reins. What next?"

"You cannot rescue a human heart unless your own heart has been rescued. You have to get rid of all that anger, guilt, feelings of abandonment, grief from losing Sandy—all of that."

"God?"

"Yes?"

"Did you set Sandy's death up so I would change for what you want me to do now?"

"Carl, I am omnipotent, so in a very real sense her death was a part of My plan. Look at the story of Job in your Bible. Satan wanted to test Job, but Satan had to ask and get My permission.

I had an agenda and Job had to trust Me in that agenda. Just so, your task is to find My agenda and trust Me in it.

"But the pain was so much in losing Sandy. If I let the heart go, it will be vulnerable again. I can't handle that much pain again."

"The pain will heal if you give Me your heart and let your heart be vulnerable again. Trust in My love for you. The whole purpose of Creation is for intimacy with Me, to feel My love in an incredible relationship. Release your heart to Me and My grace. That is the only path you have for healing."

"God, take the reins. Take my heart. Let's go for it. I am ready to rescue that heart.

"One other thing, Carl. It's hearts, not heart."

"Oh, God."

Not long after that I got this email. It was from a lady who had been reading one of my books and could not put it down. She had lost her husband some eight months ago and was still hurting.

"How long," she wrote, "after the loss of a spouse does it take for the healing to take place?"

"The correct answer," I replied, "is the rest of your life. But you are asking the wrong question."

"What is the correct question?"

"The correct question is this: What is God trying to do with the loss of your spouse? The guilt, the sense of abandonment, the anger—it is all an illusion. The reality is that God is trying to do something with you. Find out what that is."

This question can easily shift to whatever that event is in your life—the loss of a job, loss of the house, bankruptcy—the question is really the same because God is trying to get your attention. What is God trying to do with you?

"Think of a stream or river that is flowing peacefully and has for years. A storm comes. A hurricane or maybe a tornado. After the storm has passed the river is still there, but it has a new course. Nothing you can do will return the river to the course it once had. In spiritual mapping, the storm is called a confluent event. The death of that spouse is a confluent event in your journey. Nothing you can do will return you to the previous course. You must embrace the new course God is giving you."

The Message of David and Those Smooth Stones

Want another example? Look at David facing Goliath. Goliath was nine feet nine inches tall. That would be measured to his forehead. With the helmet, you are looking at over ten feet. He's with the Philistines on one mountain range and the Israelites on the other with a valley between them. Each morning and evening this big Goliath dude is out there roaring up and down the valley. His challenge echoes up and down the valley and strikes fear through the entire Israelite camp.

"Send me your best man. If I can crush him, you are mine."

David has come out from taking care of the sheep at home to bring some food to his three brothers fighting there. He's a teenager. Nothing is impossible. Let me at 'em. The brothers should have been happy. He had some news and food from home. In this case those brothers, instead of being happy to see David, rip the kid up. Who is taking care of the sheep back home? Why isn't David back there with them? Why is he even here in this dangerous place?

Soon the other soldiers pick up the chant and are harassing David. David went to Saul; but he got the same message from Saul. Goliath is out there roaring and carrying on. Saul eventually let David use his armor; but the armor was too heavy and David becomes the entertainment for the evening for the soldiers as David staggers around with the heavy armor. The soldiers are loving it and laughing.

The soldiers were in an illusion. Only David saw the reality— God's chosen nation against one heathen man. The Bible tells us that David took the armor off and then picked up five smooth stones from the brook.

> *Then he took his staff in his hand; and he chose for himself five*
> *smooth stones from the brook, and put them in a shepherd's*
> *bag, in a pouch which he had, and his sling was in his hand.*
> *And he drew near to the Philistine.*

1 Samuel 17:40

Why smooth stones? David had used stones before in his slingshot. David knew that if the stones had any sharp edge they would not go true to their mark. David had one chance to slay Goliath by hitting the one spot Goliath was vulnerable, and the stone would have to go true to its mark.

Now how did stones get smooth? From getting beaten over and over again through the years in that brook. Sometimes the stones would shatter and the process would have to start over again. Eventually one of them became the smooth stone that David used to slay Goliath.

Where is the Goliath in your life? Is he the messed up supervisor you have at work? Is he the missing father that you never had growing up that didn't tell you the messages you needed to hear? Nope, he is none of those. That Goliath is the anger, the guilt, the bitterness, the loneliness that is lodged in your own heart over these circumstances. Give it to Jesus, and He will make those smooth stones you need for those Goliaths. Once your own heart is open, you can then launch out to help God slay the Goliaths in the hearts of others. Like David, you become the leader when you see the reality and step in faith beyond your illusions.

Facing Your Own Illusion

Every person reading this is faced with the same devastating illusion that I faced as I mounted that horse. We don't see the authority God has already promised us. Because of what happened back there in the Garden, we are born captive to an illusion and deceived by the Enemy. We have the challenge of seeing what God is really doing and hearing what God is saying. God wants to give you the authority for what He is asking you to do. You are invited to the battle and you are called to the adventure. What is your response?

Notes

1. Eldredge, John. Wild at Heart: Discovering the Secret of a Man's Soul. (Nashville: Thomas Nelson Publishers, 2001)

Dialog

1. In 1 Chronicles 12:32 it says the sons of Issachar had "an understanding of the times, to know what Israel ought to do...". These men could see what God was doing and advise the Israelites what they should do in a given situation. What do you think is the relationship of suffering to seeing what God is doing; i.e., seeing the reality as opposed to the illusion?

2. How does this seeing what God is doing relate to leadership in terms of God's purpose for your life?

3. Identify three periods of suffering in your own life and write about them in your journal. Share with a friend what these stories mean to you in your spiritual journey.

4. What is the relationship between the leadership that emerges from our suffering and the servant leadership that Jesus taught about and lived?

5. Who are "the sons of Issachar" in your own life?

6. Do you have any sense of God asking you to do something? Is there any fear in this?

Chapter 5: The Illusion of the Lost Place

He who has once had the experience of belonging in a place, always finds a place for himself afterwards; whereas he who has been deprived of it, searches everywhere in vain.

Paul Tournier, *A Place for You*

With the loss of Sandy, I was without Place. There is no darker night than a night without Place. When Adam and Eve sinned and were cast out of the Garden of Eden, they lost Place. When Cain killed his brother the curse God placed on him was that he would be a wanderer for the rest of his life. Cain would never have Place again. The Tower of Babel was an attempt by Man to build a Place and reach God on his own. The early settlers in America were looking for Place. The early pioneers to my own city of Portland were looking for Place. Our missions to space, again, are another attempt to find Place that was lost back there in the Garden. For many, we seem to be living in exile, lost to Place.

This desperate need on the part of Man to find Place again, to the extent of risking everything, is only found in Man. No animal shares this. The world was created as perfect for man, with the animals named by Man and servant to Man. Man had Place through his intimate relationship with God. With the Fall this Place was lost. Man is searching for Place again with whatever risk it takes.

The Exile

- Mary once had Place when she was a child. Now she had just left an abusive and alcoholic husband. As a child Mary had found Place in the home where she grew up. Now, divorced and alone, she was without Place and had no use for the ex-husband and her church—both of which had failed her. She told me she had lost her faith. Yet she had been healed of an aggressive cancer with a very high death rate. She felt she was in exile and couldn't see what God was doing in her life. She was trapped in an illusion.
- I shared a meal with Arlene a short time ago whose husband had just died. She had also lost Place. After decades of her own personal exile without Place she had found Place with that husband. Now he was gone and she was an exile again. Or was she? Was her lost place an illusion? As I ate the meal with her, I felt I was in a *very* sacred Place—*I* had found Place again as I talked with her.

The story repeats itself with the orphan, the war refugee, the soldier in a foreign land, the man who has just lost his job that he loved, the woman who watches the church she loved and where she had accepted Christ dissolve and she grieves this loss, the mother who has just lost a child, or a family who moves from a place they loved to a new home in a strange land.

God always rewards the person who is desperate enough in his search for Place—Place will eventually be found. The Prodigal Son in the Bible story found Place once he was desperate enough. The older brother never found it.

When Sandy and I married in 1970, we married at Thanksgiving and then headed out from her home in Illinois to my new job in Portland, Oregon. Our objective was to beat the winter snows. The moving truck made it to Portland within a few days. We hit a blinding snowstorm in the Midwest; but we continued on through it and arrived in Portland and quickly rented a house. We were moved into our rented house by Christmas.

So there we were, exiles in a new land with no family and trying to build new traditions and see what we could salvage from the traditions of the past. The house had a ten-foot ceiling; so to start we got a monster tree for the living room. As a kid we use to flock our family tree using some kind of Lux soap mixture. Somehow we flocked the dude that we bought, hauled it in, and had that first Christmas together. We decorated the tree with strings and strings of new lights all hooked to an electronic box I built that flickered the tree lights to three channels of Christmas music. Then on Christmas day we took off up Mt. Hood where I skied and she played in the snow. Then we came back, lit a fire in the fireplace and had beef fondue by the fireplace. Not a bad set of traditions from which to start. The point of this story is that when one Place was lost, God was leading us to another Place that was richer and deeper. This was our first Christmas together.

At Sandy's death I sold the house (which I then owned) and bought another house near my church. It became Place for almost another 15 years. I helped launch over six ministries from that house. It, too, became Place along with my church.

The church I then knew at Sandy's death eventually dissolved and on a recent Sunday afternoon a group of pilgrims from that church who had scattered to other churches met in a home and wept together. Place was lost again. Or was this lost place an illusion?

A few days later my computer stumbled into a video concert on YouTube in which thousands of young people were praising God. I joined with them in praise. The site had already experienced over a million hits.[1] I had found Place again.

Change is a part of life. It's how we deal with the change that is important. I like the story Tournier would tell of the trapeze artists. It reminded me of my own life growing up in New Orleans. Our family would often go to the Pontchartrain Beach in the evening and watch the free trapeze artist show. We didn't go to watch the artists swing from the bars. Instead, we went to watch them as they let go of one bar and swing to the next, suspended in space for the moment.

Life, Tournier said, is like that. We are constantly moving from one place to the next place. Each movement is a risk of faith. The last bar is death itself. If you've done the others right, that leap to the last bar isn't hard at all.

Looking at Biblical Exiles

A look in the Bible shows the importance of Place to men and women through thousands of years. The word "land" is used some 1717 times in the Bible (KJV). The word "place" is used 715 times. As a comparison, the word "mission" isn't used at all, the word "repentance" is used 26 times, "pray" is used 313 times, and "prayer" 114 times. Place was very important in the biblical stories. Let's look at a few of these stories and their relationship to our own journey to Place.

Abraham's Journey to Place

Terah and his family were called from Ur of the Chaldeans to move to the land of Canaan. Abram was one of Terah's sons, and Abram means "high father".

> *Terah took his son Abram, his grandson Lot son of Haran, and his daughter-in-law Sarai, the wife of his son Abram, and together they set out from Ur of the Chaldeans to go to Canaan. But when they came to Haran, they settled there. Terah lived 205 years, and he died in Haran.*

Genesis 11:31-32

Terah never got to where God called him. He stopped with his family at Haran, a center of moon worship at the time. Terah was an idol-worshiper.

And Joshua said to all the people, "Thus says the LORD God of Israel: Your fathers, including Terah, the father of Abraham and the father of Nahor, dwelt on the other side of the River in old times; and they served other gods. Then I took your father Abraham from the other side of the River, led him throughout all the land of Canaan, and multiplied his descendants and gave him Isaac. To Isaac I gave Jacob and Esau."

Joshua 24:2-4

After Terah's death in Haran it was Abram who was called by God to Canaan and took the risk of leaving Haran and moving to Canaan when he was 75 years old. What was Abram looking for? Place is shaped first in vision and faith, and then becomes reality as the risk is taken. Hebrews 11:10 tells us of Abraham's vision.

*By faith Abraham obeyed when he was called to go out to the **place** which he would receive as an inheritance. And he went out, not knowing where he was going. By faith he dwelt in the land of promise as in a foreign country, dwelling in tents with Isaac and Jacob, the heirs with him of the same promise; for he waited for the city which has foundations, whose builder and maker is God.*

Hebrews 11:8-10 (emphasis added)

It was in Canaan that God made the covenant with Abram when he was 99 years old and changed his name to Abraham, which means "father of a multitude". Abraham was waiting for a city whose foundations and builder was God. Some translations say that he was *looking* for this city. The more correct translation is *waiting*, in a proactive sense, expecting to find the city. He was *expecting* to find Place. God was leading him to a Place he did not know; but he traveled in expectation with all the related risks. He took action in his search for Place. He wasn't hoping to find Place. He had faith that this city existed, that it was real. And it was.

Canaan was a temporary Place for Abraham until his descendants, the Israelites, came there many, many years later. These descendants then claimed it as their own. Abraham never owned any land in Canaan.

Jacob's Journey to Place

Isaac was Abraham's son of promise, and Isaac eventually became the father of Jacob and Esau. The relatives of Terah had continued to live in Haran. Later, as Abraham was old, he sent a servant back to the Paddan-Aram area to bring back a wife for Isaac, his son. Haran was a city in the the Paddan-Aram area. The servant returned with Rebekah who became Isaac's bride. Rebekah was the daughter of Bethuel, and Laban was Rebekah's brother.

Later, Isaac sent his own son Jacob back on a similar journey to Paddan-Aram to get a wife there from the daughters of Laban, Isaac's own father-in-law. Jacob (which means trickster) had stolen his father's birthright which should have gone to Esau. Esau was out to kill him. Jacob was sent as an Exile to a land he had never known. Jacob was in a wilderness, a desert, and lonely beyond description.

Now Jacob went out from Beersheba and went toward Haran. **So he came to a certain place** *and stayed there all night, because the sun had set. And he took one of the stones of that* **place** *and put it at his head, and he lay down in that* **place** *to sleep. Then he dreamed, and behold, a ladder was set up on the earth, and its top reached to heaven; and there the angels of God were ascending and descending on it.*

> *And behold, the LORD stood above it and said: "I am the LORD God of Abraham your father and the God of Isaac; the land on which you lie I will give to you and your descendants. Also your descendants shall be as the dust of the earth; you shall spread abroad to the west and the east, to the north and the south; and in you and in your seed all the*

*families of the earth shall be blessed. Behold, I am with you
and will keep you wherever you go, and will bring you back
to this land; for I will not leave you until I have done what
I have spoken to you."*

*Then Jacob awoke from his sleep and said, "Surely the LORD
is in this **place**, and I did not know it." And he was afraid
and said, "How awesome is this **place**! This is none other
than the house of God, and this is the gate of heaven!"*

*Then Jacob rose early in the morning, and took the stone that
he had put at his head, set it up as a pillar, and poured oil
on top of it. And he called the name of that **place** Bethel; but
the name of that city had been Luz previously."*

Genesis 28:10-19 (emphasis added)

What had been wilderness was an illusion. It was now Place.
Bethel means "House of God".

Jacob lived in the Paddan-Aram area working for Laban for
seven years to marry Rachel. Then Laben tricked the trickster at
the marriage and Jacob found he had married Leah instead. Jacob
then worked another seven years to marry Rachel. Tradition has
it that all of his children except Benjamin were born there. Now
he wishes to return home, to Place.

*"And it came to pass, when Rachel had borne Joseph, that
Jacob said to Laban, "Send me away, that I may go to my
own **place** and to my country.*

Genesis 30:25-26 (emphasis added)

The problem is that Jacob is deadly afraid of Esau. He thinks
that Esau will kill him on his return. Jacob is there again in the
wilderness of his life in which he has an encounter with an Entity
who he felt was God Himself.

> *Then Jacob was left alone; and a Man wrestled with him until the breaking of day. Now when He saw that He did not prevail against him, He touched the socket of his hip; and the socket of Jacob's hip was out of joint as He wrestled with him. And He said, "Let Me go, for the day breaks."*
>
> *But he said, "I will not let You go unless You bless me!"*
>
> *So He said to him, "What is your name?"*
>
> *He said, "Jacob."*
>
> *And He said, "Your name shall no longer be called Jacob, but Israel; for you have struggled with God and with men, and have prevailed."*
>
> *Then Jacob asked, saying, "Tell me Your name, I pray."*
>
> *And He said, "Why is it that you ask about My name?" And He blessed him there.*
>
> *So Jacob called the name of the **place** Peniel: "For I have seen God face to face, and my life is preserved." Just as he crossed over Penuel the sun rose on him, and he limped on his hip.[2]*
>
> Genesis 32:24-31

The name of the place, Peniel, literally means "Face of God." Jacob had found Place again. Jacob's name is now Israel. Jacob literally means supplanter, or trickster. Israel means Prince with God, or ruling with God. Jacob now has authority. The wilderness was an illusion.

Jacob left this Place with a limp. I could relate to this, as after the GBS I now have my own limp. Why didn't God finish the healing he started with me? Does that mean I should believe and pray more for the healing of the limp? Reggie McNeal answers that in one of his incredible books.

> *All leaders limp. Leaders become leaders, in part, because they are willing to wrestle with who they are, who they want*

to become, how they can overcome some deficit in their own lives. They often need to be admired, even loved, need to bring order to some chaos that is within them. And almost always, these vulnerabilities are established in the leader's family of origin, the early community that begins to shape the leader's heart before the young child can even speak.

Reggie McNeal, *Work of Heart: Understanding How God Shapes Spiritual Leaders*

Moses had a speech impediment and Aaron had to speak for him. The Apostle Paul had a thorn in the flesh.

The story continues as Joseph, the son of Jacob, was carried away in slavery from Place to Egypt. Joseph was even in a prison for several years. God had a plan, however, and it was Joseph's trip to Egypt that later saved the Israelite nation during a time of famine.

A Nation's Journey to Place

Years later we see a nation's journey from captivity in Egypt to a promised Place. How like our own journey as we travel from the captivity of sin to the freedom in Christ. On reaching Place, however, they could not go in. Captive to an illusion, they remained in the desert for the rest of their lives, never taking ownership on a Place already bequeathed to them. The window of opportunity was lost. It was the next generation (with the exception of Joshua and Caleb) who went in. How like with our own lives, as we often stand on the edge of our own Place but stay in the desert, afraid to take the risk, until we die. We live the illusion on the edge of the reality, never embracing the reality *that is already ours*. People very often stay in their small story and illusion, never seeing the reality.

Our Journey to Place

Like those early Israelites, many of us are trapped in a desert of our own making, afraid to take the risk.

- There is George, He's offered a wonderful job and ministry opportunity in another city, but is afraid to step out and take it. Maybe he thinks he doesn't have the skills to take it? Maybe he has too many friends here to move there? If he doesn't act at this window of opportunity, the window will close and the opportunity will be gone forever. George prays, talks with mentors, and eventually decides he must take the risk.

- There is Joan and Bill. They have been hurt by the church they are in. Some friends invite them to a new and spirit-filled church; but they are afraid of being hurt again in that church even though they believe the Holy Spirit is calling them there. Soon the Holy Spirit is no longer tugging at their hearts for the move. The friends invite Joan and Bill to a seminar the church is sponsoring at a retreat center. They find so much love and care poured on them that they decide to visit the church. They soon find Place at this church and become members.

- There is Amelia. She's been hurt by a husband who eventually abandoned her. She's hurt and decides she won't marry again. A wonderful man comes into her life and she marries him, finding Place and joy in the relationship. Then he goes home to be with Jesus. There you go—she's been abandoned again. Again she decides she won't marry again. No man can fill God's spot. George loves her and realizes the door to a woman's heart has no doorknob on the outside. The only way he can win her is to create Place outside of her heart and make it so incredible that she chooses to come in; i.e., she opens the door. And yes, she eventually chooses to come into that Place and let him into her heart.

How can we be released from our desert and capture our opportunity? Notice some things here in the Israelite story. When they went into the Promised Land some observations are common to answering that question today as we go into our "Land" even at the personal level. Read it in Joshua.

- They did not go into Place in their own strength. They had only the Presence of God before them.
- They went in faith, taking all the risks that were a part of taking hold of the opportunity. They were willing to be vulnerable.
- They went into Place on the Lord's timing and strategy— not their own. They had to wait in the desert until the window of opportunity was theirs.
- They *expected* a miracle as the Jordan River dried up before them.
- Praise and music was an integral part of the taking of Place.

Where do you see Place in your own life that you cannot go into yet? Is it God's vision? How is He telling you it can be done?

Released from Captivity

And then there is the story of this same nation of Israel in captivity some years later and the promise of their release. In the next chapter we will see what Jeremiah says about the *heart* in this. This was part of a letter the prophet Jeremiah sent to the captives in Jerusalem. Look in this passage and see what Jeremiah says about *Place*.

> *For I know the thoughts that I think toward you, says the LORD, thoughts of peace and not of evil, to give you a future and a hope. Then you will call upon Me and go and pray to*

*Me, and I will listen to you. And you will seek Me and find Me, when you search for Me with all your heart. I will be found by you, says the LORD, and I will bring you back from your captivity; I will gather you from all the nations and from all the places where I have driven you, says the LORD, and I will bring you to the **place** from which I cause you to be carried away captive.*

Jeremiah 29:11-14 (emphasis added)

This prophecy was given to a nation; but it also refers to you. Notice the promises here in this passage. There is a long list, but notice these two:

- God *will* release you from captivity.
- God *will* restore Place in your life—a place of intimacy with Him.

That's a promise, not a possibility. It is the covenant word of God. Its completion is based on a single command:

"…when you search for Me with all your heart."

How about your own life? Where is the captivity in your life? What Place has God called you to go into and risk? Where is the wilderness in your life? Where do you see Place?

The Reality of Place

Quite often we may think we are in a dark place, lonely, and depressed. We don't realize we are called to this Place, God is here, and we are really surrounded by an army we can't even see. I like the story in 2 Kings 6 in which the servant sees them going into a situation where winning seems hopeless. Elisha prays to open the servant's eyes, and he saw a whole mountainside full of horses and chariots of fire surrounding Elisha!

Therefore he sent horses and chariots and a great army there, and they came by night and surrounded the city. And when the servant of the man of God arose early and went out, there was an army, surrounding the city with horses and chariots. And his servant said to him, "Alas, my master! What shall we do?"

So he answered, "Do not fear, for those who are with us are more than those who are with them." And Elisha prayed, and said, "LORD, I pray, open his eyes that he may see." Then the LORD opened the eyes of the young man, and he saw. And behold, the mountain was full of horses and chariots of fire all around Elisha.

2 Kings 6:14-17

That was true also of Jacob as he anticipated his fate with Esau as he returned home. Our vision is limited by our belief. So often we stand and think we are alone. We do not see God's army with us.

Are you Elisha or the servant? Can you pray for God to open your eyes?

Spiritual Mapping of Places

When we think of our journey to Place, we realize that the search is a very dynamic process and won't be fully realized until we reach heaven with Jesus. It is for heaven that we were created in the first place. We were created, are being created, and will be created for eventual life with Him in heaven.

In the Old Testament we see the tent sanctuary was a simple structure that could easily be set up and dismantled as the Israelites followed the cloud of the Presence of God. Later the nation built a more permanent structure of the temple as Place to enable the people to grapple with the true concepts of worship and experience the Presence of God. People waited in awe for the reemergence of the High Priest on the Day of Atonement. The smells, the sights, and drama of the worship experience were rich with pageantry, signs, and wonders as they were caught up in the Presence of God among them. The Temple became Place.

When Jesus came, He spoke of the completion of the Old Covenant—if they destroyed this temple (Place) God would raise it up in three days, referring to His own body. Something had happened by then to the people since those early days when that first temple was built. A creeping institutionalism had led them to a form without power, a performance mentality that elevated humanism and legalism. Rituals became meaningless behavior patterns. They missed the Messiah when He did arrive. Even with the signs and wonders Jesus did, they could not break loose of their institutional mindset. They had lost Place. They thought Place was a piece of real estate.

In a very real sense, we look for places where God has broken through to us in our physical world. These become confluent events in our lives and even in history. A *confluent event* is an event in time that changes the course of history (or even our personal life) forever from that point. The death and resurrection of Christ was a confluent event.

Jacob found special places both going to and from Paddan-Aram. Although the sites were physical places, they were important because God broke through there.

Abraham found one near what is now Jerusalem where he met Melchizedek (Genesis 14:18). Where are these sites in your own life? Where are the places where bindings need to be broken? Where are the places where you meet God and they become Place?

When we realize that the warfare is really for the hearts of men and women, you learn to see that there can be bindings in the heart that can prevent one from seeing and acting on the reality. Confluent events from the past have bound the heart. As with a region, the spoken word of God can reveal and break the bindings and release the heart.

I like the story of Daniel's vision of the Glorious Man in Daniel 10. Daniel fell on his face and those with him fled. Only Daniel saw the visitor, who appeared like Christ Himself.

Then he said to me, "Do not fear, Daniel, for from the first day that you set your heart to understand, and to humble

*yourself before your God, your words were heard; and I have
come because of your words."*

Daniel 10:12

The visitor gave only two reasons why Daniel could experience
the vision and Place:

- Daniel had humbled himself before God.
- Daniel was desperate to understand.

How desperate are you? How humble before God?

The Final Destination and Place

As Jesus stood before his followers, He made an astonishing
statement about Place.

> *"In My Father's house are many mansions; if it were not so, I
> would have told you. I go to prepare a **place** for you. And if I
> go and prepare a **place** for you, I will come again and receive
> you to Myself; that where I am, there you may be also."*

John 14:2-4 (emphasis added)

At the time this was spoken, the custom of a Jewish marriage
was quite different than our contemporary marriages. There was
no engagement. On the agreement of the families involved, the
woman became betrothed to the man. At that point they were
considered married; but the marriage was not consummated. The
man would then go away and build a house for his beloved. When
the house was completed he returned, took his bride, and carried
her to their house. They would then have the wedding ceremony
and the marriage would be consummated.

As Jesus spoke these words, we can imagine Him looking
away to a marriage ceremony nearby. Jesus is saying the marriage
with those who follow Him has already taken place. Now Jesus is
going away to prepare a Place. Then He will come again for His

bride (The Church) and take her to His Place and the marriage will be consummated.

In Chapter 12 we will look again at Place and the leader's relationship to this.

Notes:

1. The URL I watched is http://www.youtube.com/ watch?v=M7SMUf6QcyQ. The song here is sung by the song's author, then Brooke Fraser. Since I initially watched it she is now Brooke Ligertwood and the web site has over four million hits and is rated 5-star. Notice the generational age group of her audience. Compare this with what was said in Chapter 1.
2. It is difficult, at times, to track who is speaking or acting in this passage. In my Bible when the Entity is speaking or acting, the pronoun is capitalized. When it is Jacob, there is no capitalization. And yes, the place name is spelled differently in the two references. The reasons are uncertain.

Dialog

1. Did you have Place as a child? How does that affect you now?

2. Where do you find Place now in your own life?

3. Can you identify some Bethel Points in your own life where God has broken through?

Part III: From the Wilderness to Vision

So often we fail to recognize that the very wilderness we are struggling to survive in is there to prepare us for God's Plan for our life. Before we can lead others, we must see the vision God has for our personal life. In these next sections we will follow the life of Nehemiah and how as a leader he received his personal vision and how he responded. I often like to call the book of Nehemiah in the Bible *Leadership Management 101*. Unfortunately, we can't use this textbook in the public schools today. What this means is that if you understand what Nehemiah did from these next two sections, you will know some leadership secrets that most of our leaders today (including many pastors and spiritual "leaders") have never learned. Join me for the journey and some incredible stories and insights.

Chapter 6: The Path from the Wilderness: Seeing from the Heart

It is with the heart that one sees rightly; what is essential is invisible to the eye.

Antoine De Saint-Exupery, *The Little Prince*

A spiritual awakening which does not awaken the sleeper to love has roused him (or her) in vain.

Jessamyn West

To reveal one's heart and to lead from this in love is the highest form of leadership.

Carl Townsend

Every way of a man is right in his own eyes,
But the LORD weighs the hearts.

Proverbs 21:2

Whatever that vision is for your life, it involves the heart.

And when Jesus went out He saw a great multitude; and He was moved with compassion for them, and healed their sick.

Matthew 14:14

"The first of all the commandments is: 'Hear, O Israel, the

71

> *LORD our God, the LORD is one. And you shall love the LORD your God with all your heart, with all your soul, with all your mind, and with all your strength.' This is the first commandment. And the second, like it, is this: 'You shall love your neighbor as yourself.' There is no other commandment greater than these."*

Mark 12:29-31

The Journey of Nehemiah's Heart

Look at the story of Nehemiah. Nehemiah was an underemployed guy working for a heathen king, Artaxerxes I, in Shushan (or modern Shush) in what is now southwest Iran (see Appendix A). The year was 444 BC. These friends of Nehemiah were reporting to him about the early waves of Jews returning to the area of Jerusalem. These friends had been spiritually mapping the Jerusalem area and came to give Nehemiah a report. It wasn't good. The people there in Jerusalem had no vision, no passion, no security. Nothing. The city walls were in shambles, the gates were burned with fire, rubbish and ruins all about, and the Jews who had returned were in disgrace.

At this point both Nehemiah and his friends held the same information. Nehemiah's response to the information, however, is quite different from that of his friends. His heart is with his people. He is broken with compassion, he weeps. He can't eat, can't sleep for four months. There was a burden, a concern. He is consumed by his burden.

Notice that this first prayer of Nehemiah (in Nehemiah 1) is driven from Nehemiah's concern and heart. A burden.

> *And I said: "I pray, LORD God of heaven, O great and awesome God, You who keep Your covenant and mercy with those who love You and observe Your commandments..."*

Nehemiah 1:5

Nehemiah uses the personal name of God (*Yahweh*) in his prayer. To understand this, look at the very accounts of creation in Genesis 1-2. Genesis 1:1 — 2:3 describes a creation referring to God as *Elohiym*, or a depersonalized being or deity who rules.

Starting in Genesis 2:4 the story of the creation begins again. This time, however, you see a shocker. It's a different author for this version. The word LORD (*Yahweh*) used for God for the first time, referring to a very personal and intimate God. A God who makes covenants with His people and keeps them. Nehemiah begins by referring to God as *Yahweh*, this personal and covenant-keeping God. Shortly Nehemiah will play one of these covenants back to God and claim authority on it being completed.

> *...please let Your ear be attentive and Your eyes open, that You may hear the prayer of Your servant which I pray before You now, day and night, for the children of Israel Your servants, and confess the sins of the children of Israel which we have sinned against You. Both my father's house and I have sinned. We have acted very corruptly against You, and have not kept the commandments, the statutes, nor the ordinances which You commanded Your servant Moses.*

Nehemiah 1:6-7

Now we see that Nehemiah confesses to God the sins of both the nation and himself and his own house. This "confess" means "to be sorry for" and, more than that, to turn away from.

Then we see something extremely interesting,

> *Remember, I pray, the word that You commanded Your servant Moses, saying, "If you are unfaithful, I will scatter you among the nations; but if you return to Me, and keep My commandments and do them, though some of you were cast out to the farthest part of the heavens, yet I will gather them from there, and bring them to the **place** which I have chosen as a dwelling for My name."*

Nehemiah 1:8-9 (emphasis added)

Notice that the prayer at this time is not for the construction of the wall, but rather *for the nation to return to Place.* Nehemiah takes authority for this vision from the covenant God had made with Moses. That covenant, in turn, was based on the Plan of the Israelite nation being the channel through which Christ would eventually come. This return involved both a physical and spiritual return to Place. Nehemiah stands on the authority of that covenant.

As Nehemiah concludes his prayer, he asks for two things:

> *O Lord, I pray, please let Your ear be attentive to the prayer of Your servant, and to the prayer of Your servants who desire to fear Your name; and let Your servant prosper this day, I pray, and grant him mercy in the sight of this man."*

Nehemiah 1:11

- He asks for the opportunity to present his vision to the king.
- He asks for the success of the vision.

Nehemiah does not ask for God to step up and do the vision he holds. Rather, he asks for the *opportunity for himself* to do his part of the vision and for success. The wall Nehemiah will lead in building is not even mentioned at this point.

There is now a four month delay between the time Nehemiah gets this report and when he can do anything about it. Nehemiah is sad as he stands before the king again after the four months. Being sad before the king then could cost Nehemiah his life. When the king asks why he is sad, we see a fearful and shaking Nehemiah praying again.

> *Then the king said to me, "What do you request?" So I prayed to the God of heaven.*

Nehemiah 2:4-5

As Nehemiah begins to speak, we see he was not idle during those four months he waited. Nehemiah already has the specifics of his vision (to build the wall), a plan and strategy, and a list of the resources he needs. The vision of Nehemiah is to restore Place. The vehicle that he will use is the wall.

How does this apply today? George Otis, Jr. has done a lot of research on stories of where cities and even regions have been totally transformed by the Holy Spirit. I don't mean just a sense of revival. I mean where the city or region is totally transformed economically, politically, spiritually, agriculturally—any way you could measure it. And it is a sustained transformation. In every single case this incredible transformation was driven by *only one or two people* who held a vision of the Holy Spirit sweeping their city or region and were willing to risk everything, even their life, to see that vision happen. And in some cases, the leader lost his life in the process.

How does that relate to my life? How does it relate to your life? God needs you for what He is trying to accomplish. He is waiting for you. Let me share the story from my own life.

The Journey of My Own Heart

Whatever this personal vision is that God has for your own life, it has something do to with your heart, a burden, a concern. One of the problems we have in moving and leading to the reality from the illusion is that we have been wounded too many times when we tried. When we gave our heart, we found nothing but pain and finally lose the ability to give from the heart again. We want to stay where we are, avoid the risk, and embrace our feeble and failing illusions as if they were reality. We have no stories that are strong enough to carry us out of the illusions, so we continue to embrace our myths. Every man and woman alive has felt these arrows. We are each wounded from what happened in a Garden a long time ago.

From my own arrows, I found it hard to give my heart to a woman. When I finally did, she took me to an incredible Place.

She showed me romance. Until then God seemed to be indifferent, an academic excursion. It wasn't so much that I lacked faith; it was just that I didn't have a big enough story to take my faith into until then.

To understand what my wife Sandy did in healing my heart, you must understand why God created woman in the first place. Adam named her "Woman", or "taken out of man" at first. Later Adam changed her name to "Eve", "mother of all living". What God named her, however, is what is important. It is what God named her that determines her purpose, authority, healing, and her role relative to Adam. When God decided to create woman, God named her *ezer kenegdo*.[1]

> *And the LORD God said, "It is not good that man should be alone; I will make him an* ezer kenegdo *comparable to him."*

Genesis 2:18-19

The word *kenegdo* is simple enough. It translates as "companion who comes along-side". But what of that word *ezer*? What does it mean? None of my English Bibles translate this accurately. The verse is often quoted in marriage ceremonies. But do you have *any* idea about what it really means?

The word *ezer* is used fourteen other times in the Old Testament; and in all other times it refers to a relationship between Man and God. In addition, almost all of the other times when the word is used it refers to a life and death struggle. It is a very strong word that means more literally *life-giver.*

> *I will lift up my eyes to the hills—*
> *From whence comes my life-giver[*ezer*]?*
> *My life-giving [*ezer*] comes from the LORD,*
> *Who made heaven and earth.*

Psalms 121:1-2

There is desperation here—the word implies the life of the Psalmist is at stake. It is literally a scream for help. In the Genesis verse, the woman is created as life-giver, *essential* for the Adventure to which the man is called.

Although the meaning of the *ezer kenego* phrase is very complex, we essentially see God is naming what He created as a life-giving companion for the man. In Genesis it means not just "mother". The meaning is far, far richer than that. She is the essence of life itself to the man. The man is called to the Adventure, but the woman is called along-side him in the Adventure.

During those years leading up to my paralysis from the GBS, Sandy and I had worked together with some 26 volunteers to build a database of churches for our city of Portland. At that time no directory of local churches existed. The pastors were like generals going into battle and not knowing where the soldiers were, how many they had, and how well the soldiers were trained. Many pastors did not seem to even know there was a war going on or what the enemy was doing. A general could be court-marshaled for that; yet that was exactly where the leaders were until that database was built. We identified over 1800 churches in the metropolitan area and their pastors with strategic information on each church. Only a year later in 1989 as I battled my GBS with Sandy along-side me, the city leaders were beginning to use that database to pull the pastors together for the first prayer summit. Major networking and praying began to take place. This led to a major Billy Graham Crusade in 1992, a month after Sandy's death. It was one of the most successful crusades the Billy Graham team had ever held. Later, in an interview with a PBS reporter, Graham said there were three reasons for the success—the first was prayer, the second was prayer, and the third was prayer. The database that was built enabled the leaders to begin pulling the pastors together to bring a massive prayer assault on the city.

This was one of the first crusades to collect extensive objective data on the Crusade results.[2] After the crusade we added a second database of the parachurch organizations who were meeting needs in the city. The resulting databases also included the names of and contact information for many, many Christian leaders in the metro area.

After the event, the primary visionary for the city and the man who started the prayer summits was struck with Parkinson's and could no longer serve the city pastors as he had been doing. His right-hand man died on a prayer summit in Japan. Another leader was battling chronic fatigue syndrome for years until he was suddenly miraculously healed in Doris Wagner's office in Pasadena. I tried to print the mailing list of prayer intercessors who had been a part of the Crusade. As the printer started, my computer suddenly burst into flames as I just stood frozen and stared in amazement.

With my GBS and Sandy's leukemia, I was very aware that Sandy and I were trapped in this same war. Both God and Satan were after the hearts of men and women in our city. I was going out to war and she would go out with me at my side, leading me on and carrying me off the field for healing and encouragement when I got hit. One of woman's deepest needs is to go out on the Adventure with the man. For both men and women this war and the battle are very real. It is not an illusion.

One day as Sandy battled the leukemia for her life, I came in the house and fell to the floor as if I was struck by some kind of Entity, although I could not see it. As this Entity struggled with me and we were wrestling and thrashing on the floor, I could not see who or what it was. I was fighting for my life, and sweat was pouring off of me. Finally, whatever it was left and I was left alone with my adrenaline still rushing and soaked with sweat. I got up, washed myself, and sank in prayer. Who or what was that? What did it mean? I felt like Jacob who had wrestled with an angel and then walked away with a limp for the rest of his life. I already had the limp. What was going on?

With the final loss of Sandy, my heart was shattered. Millions of tiny pieces. What was the meaning of life? Could my heart be put back together again?

That was 1992. During the time since then I often felt like I was in a wilderness or desert. Where was God in all this? Actually, however, this was an illusion. I was really in a lush rain forest with a reality that was yet to be seen.

The story repeats itself with any woman or man who is willing to take the risk. Just a short time ago a very dear friend, Tim Anderson, went home to be with the Lord. He was only 49, and he had married an incredible woman, Toni, only four years earlier. Although about the same age, Toni had previously married men who had failed her and had given up on marrying again for the previous 19 years.

Shortly before the marriage, four cars rear-ended Tim in one accident and then after that Tim was falling multiple times a day from the first injury which left him, as she married him, mostly wheelchair bound. Friends gave this marriage a year to last, as everyone thought Tim would not live that long. He lived four years in the wheelchair. He was in constant pain with diabetes, spinal nerve damage, damaged lungs, damaged heart, failing eyes, and damaged kidneys that would shut down at times. One doctor told me in his 25 years in the medical profession, he had never met anyone with as many physical problems as Tim had.

Tim ministered in a wonderful way to me and many others during this time, with Toni. During those four years they were married, he led over fifty people to the Lord. Toni kept up communication with hundreds, who prayed for Tim at her request, but who were also encouraged themselves through seeing Tim and Toni's faith through these struggles. Many, many others were touched with his deeply spiritual wisdom and discernment. Tim was discipling a small group of men weekly at their house when he wasn't in the hospital. They often came to visit him during his hundreds of hospitalizations. If he was out of the hospital for as long as two weeks, he considered that a major success.

Tim shared with me that he was falling two or three times a day during transfers from bed to wheelchair to car or from the shower. Often the falls would leave him unconscious. He had to choose each day, he said, whether to live or die. What a message!

"That's true of each of us," I told Tim. "We each make that choice to live (in Christ) or die every day."

"The difference, Carl," Tim told me, "Is that I would not have been able to choose to live without Toni."

Toni became his *ezer kenegdo*, going out on the battlefield with him and pouring constant love and encouragement on him. During the last few years of Tim's life Toni got little sleep. She was working an eight hour day and then coming home to be his nurse through the night. The transformation in her during those four years was miraculous. Their home became a very sacred Place where the two ministered to many people and others ministered and prayed for them.

With the loss of Tim, I felt a deep pain. Again, I had a damaged heart. Then I read the words of the Lord to Ezekiel.

> *I will give you a new **heart** and put a new spirit within you;*
> *I will take the heart of stone out of your flesh and give you*
> *a **heart** of flesh. I will put My Spirit within you and cause*
> *you to walk in My statutes, and you will keep My judgments*
> *and do them.*

Ezekiel 36:26-28 (emphasis added)

Huh? What does this mean? Am I in an illusion? If so, where is the reality? One thing is clear from this verse. It is God who has to give me the heart. Not the woman. In fact, a man cannot win the woman whom God gives him until he has already found his heart.

Let's look for a moment at another verse about the heart. This one has a promise and a condition that must be met before the promise can be fulfilled. It is in Jeremiah and we looked at it first in the last chapter. Now look at the same promise again and notice the condition:

> *For I know the thoughts that I think toward you says the*
> *LORD, thoughts of peace [Shalom] and not of evil, to give*

you a future and a hope. Then you will call upon Me and go and pray to Me, and I will listen to you. And you will seek Me and find Me, when you search for Me with all your **heart***. I will be found by you, says the LORD, and I will bring you back from your captivity; I will gather you from all the nations and from all the places where I have driven you, says the LORD, and I will bring you to the* **place** *from which I cause you to be carried away captive.*

Jeremiah 29:11-14 (emphasis added)

The word "peace" near the beginning of this verse is translated from the Hebrew *Shalom*, which is a strong word meaning health, wellness, prosperity, security, and peace.

Now notice the condition under which God will honor all of these promises:

"when you search for Me with **ALL** *your heart."*

With time, the arrow that pierces your heart becomes a sword God wants to place in your hand. God tells you to take the sword. First you believe; then you see.

The Story of the Heart

To get answers about the heart we must see how God has worked in history. God created everything. He was there before time. Christ was in God before time.

In the beginning was the Word, and the Word was with God, and the Word was God. He was in the beginning with God. All things were made through Him, and without Him nothing was made that was made. In Him was life, and the life was the light of men. And the light shines in the darkness, and the darkness did not comprehend [seize, possess] it.

John 1:1-5

The word used here for "Word" is *logos*, which means truth, reality. What is *real* existed from the very beginning. We create the illusions. Jesus was with God and is that which was, is, and will be real from the very beginning.

Love cannot exist without an agent. If God wanted to create Love, there had to be something to love—something in His own image. And this was all part of the plan before creation. Love is the most powerful force in the world. And this agent God creates in His image to Love must be free to choose to love Him. Love cannot exist without this freedom to choose. God created Man to love Him; but unless Man was created free to make the choice to return this love, love can not exist. For this reason God had to release Man as a free agent to choose. What a risk He took!

God created the world for Man; then God created Man. The idea of Man and of you was in the mind of God before the creation of the world. *God created Man for the sole purpose of loving, worshiping, praising, and serving Him.* Man was given authority in the world God had created for him. There is your purpose statement!

> *It's in Christ that we find out who we are and what we are living for. Long before we first heard of Christ, …he had his eye on us, had designs on us for glorious living, part of the overall purpose he is working out in everything and everyone.*

Ephesians 1:11 THE MESSAGE

> *For everything, absolutely everything, above and below, visible and invisible,… everything got started in him and finds purpose in him.*

Colossians 1:16 THE MESSAGE

As mentioned earlier, the word LORD (*Yahweh*) is used for God starting in the creation story and refers to a very personal and intimate God. When Adam and Eve were in the Garden, the Bible tells us they walked with God in the cool of the evening and had this intimate and sacred conversation with God. There was no death, no pain, and only the purest form of Romance.

Then Satan entered and stole the hearts of Adam and Eve. Their intimacy with God was shattered. When Adam and Eve sinned in the Garden, they released to Satan their authority they had on earth. Satan now had authority on earth. Still, as Adam and Eve were cast out of the Garden, God promised a Deliverer who would restore what had been broken and that He would restore the broken authority on earth (Genesis 3:15).

(Yahweh to the serpent about Christ)
And I will put enmity
Between you and the woman,
And between your seed and her Seed;
He shall bruise your head,
And you shall bruise His heel.

As time passed and other men and women walked the earth, there were those who looked in Faith to this coming Deliverer and in so doing rested again in the intimacy that had been lost. In Hebrews 11 you see this Hall of Faith, but even this short chapter leaves out so many names. The important thing here is that none of these of the Old Testament—Abraham, Moses, Isaiah, Nehemiah, Esther, Rahab—saw the historical completion of their vision; but they lived into this vision given to them by God as if it were *already completed* and so gained Eternal Life. They found this intimacy again with God (see Exodus 33-34). Today, God calls each of us to look back in faith to the Christ Event in history, and then live into the vision to which He is calling you today. That is the only way to find this intimacy and healing and find our heart again. It is the only way to see the reality. All of reality is only seen through the lens of that Christ Event.

When Christ was tempted at the beginning of His ministry Satan told Christ that all kingdoms of this world were his. That was a true statement. At the Cross, Christ took back this authority and then commissioned His followers to go in His authority.

God pursued me—and you—through time to win us back with the death and resurrection of his own Son. In return for embracing and returning this love, God will give you the richness of that intimacy that was lost in the Garden. You can read this story in the Bible—the greatest romance story of all time.

Eventually, if we have chosen this relationship here with Him, we will be with Him after we have conquered death. Then we are fully healed with Him. We have found our heart again, and the reality finally embraces us with its full power.

What Next?

Looking again at Nehemiah, we see he had to wait. Four months. We see him praying and fasting during that time, but that wasn't all. When the king asks Nehemiah why he was so sad, it is obvious that Nehemiah had a plan, strategy, and a shopping list of what he needed. Sometimes God tells us to wait, but it is not an idle time. Moses had to wait 40 years in that wilderness as God took him through a preparation. Gideon had to wait until God had pruned his army. Abraham had to wait until his father died. Sometimes it will be the next generation before the vision is completed, as with Joshua and Caleb. The vision, however, will *always* be completed.

Notes:

1. Read *Captivating: Unveiling the Mystery of a Woman's Soul* by John and Stasi Eldredge for a more complete discussion of this phrase.
2. Results of the church growth data during the time of the 1992 Graham Crusade is available at: http://www.netadventures.biz/portchu.htm.

Dialog

1. What is the purpose of your life?

2. Do you live that purpose?

3. Is it the purpose God wants you to live?

4. Rewrite the prayer of Nehemiah in your journal. What do you claim? Under what authority?

5. What is God promising to you?

6. In what specific ways have you seen God acting in your life recently?

Chapter 7: Praying the Reality into Existence

We are working with God to determine the future. Certain things will happen in history if we pray rightly.

Richard Foster

Prayer is the great mystery. If God is all powerful, why did He let my wife die? Why weren't my prayers answered? Why have I lost some of my best friends and mentors to cancer and other horrible diseases?

Here is a God who can do anything. He is all-powerful and now has ultimate authority on earth. He can speak the word and the universe is created. He can raise Lazarus from the dead. Why does God need our help? Why, in fact, did He even need to create me? Or you? Of what use are our prayers to a self-sufficient God? And if God really loves us, why do some prayers seem to go unanswered? Or if the unanswered prayer is an illusion, what is the reality of prayer?

In Ezekiel 22:30-31 we find an amazing verse:

"So I sought for a man among them who would make a wall, and stand in the gap before Me on behalf of the land, that I should not destroy it; but I found no one. Therefore I have poured out My indignation on them; I have consumed them with the fire of My wrath; and I have recompensed their deeds on their own heads," says the Lord GOD.

In this verse we see that an all-powerful self-sufficient God is saying He will destroy a nation and execute judgment unless *one* man stands in the gap between the nation and God and prays, petitioning for the saving of the land. God wants to save the nation but will execute the judgment unless one intercessor stands and prays for the land. God leaves Himself totally dependent on the prayers of one man.

Here is another example of one man saving a nation:

Fed up, God decided to get rid of them—
and except for Moses, his chosen, he would have.
But Moses stood in the gap and deflected God's anger,
prevented it from destroying them utterly.

Psalms 106:23 THE MESSAGE

Why did an omnipotent God set up a system that depends on us?

God's problem is not that God is unable to do certain things.
God's problem is that God loves. Love complicates the life of
God as it complicates every life.

John Douglas Hall

What is Prayer?

You would think that for most folks prayer is defined like this:

Prayer is asking God to give us the resources we need to play our
roles for the day.

We smile at this definition and often deny that's how we pray, but isn't that more often the reality as we define it? We are so sure that our agenda is God's agenda that we pause in our schedule for a quick break and ask Him for what we need to get over the next hurdle in our agenda. Then we wonder why our prayers seem to fall on deaf ears.

This is really a poor definition, and the reason is in understanding the key word in this definition: *roles*.

Dr. Paul Tournier had great success in healing people where other doctors had failed. When others asked him what he was doing different, he explained that healing was a whole-person experience. You could not separate the person into physical, emotional, and spiritual parts. The word for salvation in the New Testament, *soteria*, refers to total healing.

Tournier said that we spend much of our lives playing roles. The person playing the roles is wearing a mask. Tournier called this the *personage*. Sometimes when going to the doctor the doctor will ask me questions such as "How is your job going?" or "How's your love life?" He knows that my physical condition is directly connected with the answers to those questions. Unfortunately, however, he is still asking from within the personage and roles, such as web developer (on the job question) or lover on the second question. Most doctors don't go to the deeper level.

The real person underneath those roles and free of the roles and masks Tournier called the *person*. Tournier began the healing process inviting the patient to coffee or tea by the fireside. Then he would draw the patient out of the roles they were playing, seeing them as a unique *person* before God—free of any roles, masks, and games. [1]

For many this risk of moving outside of the personage was too much to take. Tournier helped initiate this, he said, by being open and free of roles and masks himself. He would take the risk first and share from outside his roles. Of course, at the moment you choose to step outside of your own roles you are vulnerable. That's why you had the roles in the first place. Yet for the healing, you have to take the risk.

If you are the counselor and trying to initiate healing, you must remember that if you wish to succeed as Tournier did you must step outside of your counselor role. [2] The healing won't take place until you are both outside of any roles. If you are in a small group at your church and sharing, don't expect real healing until someone leads and speaks from the *person* and outside of any roles. If you are a lover trying to win your beloved, you both must step outside of roles to see each other's heart. It is not so much an issue of going through a series of steps (taking a role yourself). That's personage. It's rather a surrendering of the heart to Jesus to discover Place.

The same is true in our relationship with God. For prayer to be real, we must free ourselves of the mask and roles before God. We must choose to be on His agenda—not our agenda. Once you step outside of your roles in relating to God, however, there is the risk and vulnerability. Can we dare to do this?

When we are praying from within our roles, we can't expect God to answer. To see God's answer we must step outside of the personage and pray from our heart, our burden. We saw in the last chapter how Nehemiah did it.

Here is a second definition of prayer that is often used:

Prayer is communication with God.

This involves both speaking and listening. If you are communicating with your spouse and you interrupt when he/she starts to speak, the communication rapidly fails because you aren't listening to your spouse. Prayer also, like communicating with your spouse, involves action. What are you specifically called to do in response to what your spouse says? What are you specifically called by God to do in response to God? How does this relate to what your spouse is saying?

> *We must no longer see prayer as preparation for action. Prayer must be understood as action itself, a way of responding, a potent spiritual weapon to be used in spiritual warfare against the most powerful forces in the world. Prayer is not undertaken instead of other actions, but as a foundation for all the rest of the actions we take.*

Jim Wallis

We see Samuel as an example of how to listen and respond to God. At the beginning of Samuel's life, we are told there is no vision in the land.

Now the boy Samuel ministered to the LORD before Eli. And the word of the LORD was rare in those days; there was no widespread revelation.

1 Samuel 3:1

Samuel, though, was able to hear the prophetic words that the Lord spoke to him and act on his calling. The Hebrew word for LORD here is *Yahweh*, referring to a personal God. By the end of the chapter Samuel is a man, and now there is vision and prophecy in the land.

So Samuel grew, and the LORD was with him and let none of his words fall to the ground. And all Israel from Dan to Beersheba knew that Samuel had been established as a prophet of the LORD. Then the LORD appeared again in Shiloh. For the LORD revealed Himself to Samuel in Shiloh by the word of the LORD.

1 Samuel 3:19-21

Notice this passage also identifies Shiloh as *Place*. It was a place where Samuel could hear, where the vision was birthed. Samuel listened, God spoke, and Samuel acted.

Prayer involves listening, as we can expect no answered prayer unless we know God's agenda, and the only way we can discern that is by listening to Him. Without that, you can only expect unanswered prayer.

Some people think Christian prayer is an illusion. They don't hear God speak and there is no listening, so there is really no prayer. Maybe they should find out why they can't hear God as a clue to their illusion of unanswered prayer.

My friend Toni told me that during their church building

they were asked to pray about an amount to give for their building project. No numbers were discussed at church and none were to be discussed between families. She heard many stories of couples who prayed separately as she and her husband did. Toni says she challenged this with Tim, "I have a number, but I'm not sure it's right." When they told each other the number to be given that God had given to each of them for a 3 year period (quite a lot), they had the exact same amounts. Some grumbled about the building money and some even left the church. Apparently they either wouldn't test God or didn't listen when he told them what to do (even if the answer was "nothing").[3] They lost the blessing.

Let me take you now to what is my favorite definition of prayer.

Prayer is an intimate lover's conversation with God, the lover's Creator.

Prayer is, as John Eldredge says,[4] an integral part of a Sacred Romance that is richer and deeper than any words can describe. In this Romance with my Lover (God), we have special places, special songs, special stories, and secret names He has for me that cannot be expressed to anyone else. Ah, there you go. In this type of prayer you are stepping outside of your personage and crying (*ezer*) from your heart. What might surprise you is that if you have trouble letting go of those roles in your prayer, you will find (as I mentioned earlier) that God steps out of that personage image you have of Him and reveals himself to you as Person. In the Old Testament translations, as I mentioned, you will often see the word LORD used for the Hebrew *Yahweh* when this happens. See Exodus 32:31-33:23 for an example of this type of praying between Moses and God.

From this perspective, the reality of prayer is not that of a prosperity gospel where God shoves blessings on us because He loves us and wants to bless us. It's more like a check system set up by most organizations. In this system, to cash a check from the organization it takes at least two signatures. In this analogy God has blessings for us; that is, the participation in the Kingdom Enterprise—seeing his Kingdom come on earth. With the death and Resurrection of Christ, God has already signed the check. Now He's waiting for your signature. Until we have signed the check and taken ownership on the Calling, the check is no good. It's not a matter of overcoming God's resistance, it is rather taking ownership of what God wants you to do to accomplish what God is doing, a partner in making what has already been accomplished in heaven accomplished here.

There are many different types of prayer. There is the prayer of thanksgiving. There is a prayer of forgiveness—either from our own sins or interceding for the sins of another or a nation. There is the prayer of intercession, praying for the healing or deliverance of another person or nation. The prayer of protection. A prayer of praise. All of these you can see in the Model Prayer that Christ taught His followers.

Another thing to remember. The reality of prayer is not a nice chit-chat with our lover. God has a job for you. The pain and suffering you have experienced is used by God to prepare you for warfare. Prayer is an action step. It is not a preparation for action, but is an action step in itself. Often this is experienced as intercessory praying, and it is some of the most powerful praying we can do.

Notes:

1. Tournier, Paul. *The Meaning of Persons.* (New York: Harper and Row, 1957) This classic book goes out of print, is reprinted, and appears again. Look for reprints on Amazon.com or find a used copy.
2. Biblical counseling involves using the Bible to provide answers to a problem. If this is a logical (or Newtonian) or academic exercise, you are on a failing paradigm. What we are talking about here is using the Bible for insights

on resolving an issue by faith. Want an example? A lady near me had fibromyalgia. She stepped out in faith and experienced healing through the help of a prayer leader with experience in intergenerational intercessory prayer. The binding was identified, prayed into strategically for release, and she was totally healed.

3. It was stated that if the answer to their prayer was to give zero, that was acceptable; but a prayerful response was requested of all members. Some of the couples exchanged pieces of paper with the amount they felt God was asking them to give and they would have the same amounts. Toni and Tim knew the amount the Lord gave them was not in their budget. At that point, after months of trying to sell the truck Tim could no longer use, it sold and was the breakthrough of their commitment.

4. Eldridge, John. *The Sacred Romance*, (Nashville, TN: Thomas Nelson Publishers, 1977)

Dialog

1. How would you define prayer?

2. If prayer involves a conversation with God, why do you think we don't pray more than we do?

Chapter 8: Guidelines for Strategic Vision Praying

It's the praying Christian who **looses** *heaven's expression here.*

Bill Johnson

Before looking at some basic guidelines for prayer, let's look at a few reasons why our prayers often seem unanswered. Remember that God loves us and everything that happens is inside of that context of His love for us. The battles we face here prepare us for the eternity we have with Him.

The Illusion of Unanswered Prayer

Here are some basic reasons a prayer may seem unanswered. Sometimes a prayer is answered, but in a different way than we expect. Sometimes the prayer is really unanswered, but it's our own fault.

Lack of Faith

Jesus made at least two trips to Nazareth where He grew up as a child. The Bible tells us, however, He was not able to do much there "*because of their unbelief*" (Mark 6:1). The problem in Nazareth was that they saw a carpenter's son, an illusion. They never saw who Jesus really was. Like the people of Nazareth, we become trapped in our illusions and cannot pray in faith beyond this. The Enemy deceives us. We have an academic faith, but not a faith that enables us to act.

Too often we pray on logic or reasoning and not by faith. Jesus said:

Why are you reasoning in your hearts?

Luke 5:22

We feel as if we don't have enough faith. Faith is not a feeling thing. Faith is given to us by the Holy Spirit. If you don't have enough faith for the vision God is giving you, confess this to God and ask God for the faith. Since God wants this vision done and you need the faith for yourself and for those who follow, God will give you the faith for it if you ask.

Lack of Understanding

Many times we pray a certain agenda, but at the same time we are unable to see God's agenda—our own agenda has blinded us.

I think of the time I came home from work one night very tired, as it was almost midnight. I reached in my pocket for my apartment keys, only to find there were no keys there. I faced a night with no bed, as it would be morning before the office opened for the apartments. It was too late to call any friends. I started praying to find the keys and searched first around the car. I went back to the mailbox to see if they had dropped there and maybe someone had found them and left the keys on top of the box. No luck. I drove back to work, continuing to pray to find the keys, and searched the parking lot where I had parked. No keys. I drove back home, pondering the expense of motel lodging as I searched once more for the keys there. I was on *my* agenda (finding the keys) and praying that way.

As I searched and was giving up hope, a neighbor came out of the apartment above me and went to the laundry room in the complex. I was curious why he was doing his laundry that late, and he was curious why I was coming in so late and why I couldn't get into my apartment. We shared our stories. I soon discovered he was a locksmith. Although my door had a bolt lock, he had me in my apartment within two minutes without damaging the door. The next morning at the apartment office their maintenance people made me new keys; but they also told me it was really quite impossible to open the bolt lock in two minutes.

I had been praying to find my keys. God had a relational agenda that involved me with my neighbor. Almost always the answer to prayer is some type of relational agenda.

Another example is the prayer of Moses after he came down from Mt. Sinai with the Ten Commandments, only to discover the orgy in the camp. In the prayer Moses acts as a true intercessor, *demanding* God to reveal His agenda. Moses places himself between the Israelites and God, asking God to kill him if God can't forgive the nation.

Later, we see the Israelites failed to see the agenda as they stood on the edge of the Promised Land. As we will see later in Chapter 17, this was their window of opportunity, the *kairos* moment, their Promised Time. Moses again intercedes but this time Moses knows the agenda and he prays into it (Numbers 14). His prayer moves the hand of God and the nation is spared. It is amazing to realize that we can move the hand of an omnipotent God if we set our heart to understand, know God's agenda, and humble ourselves before God.

In praying for a nation, city, area of a city, or even a relationship it is important to understand how God has worked in the area or person before—God's agenda. You can ask God to reveal this agenda and where the bindings still exists. Only then can you take authority to break the bindings and restore the coming of the Spirit. God will remove the binding, as the vision will be completed.

I like the way James explains this:

You ask and do not receive, because you ask amiss, that you may spend it on your pleasures.

James 4:3

Unforgiveness

There are times when a prayer is unanswered because of anger and unforgiveness. The relationship with someone is broken or perhaps we are angry at God about something and we need to forgive and release before God can act.

Betty Mitchell is a lady who has led a world-wide ministry and touches many, many people. One Sunday she spoke and started with asking each of us to write down the names of ten people we need to forgive on a piece of paper. I wrote my list and she started her message. At the end as we left the auditorium, I realized the person who should be on the top of my list was not even on the list. Satan blinds us to where the true brokenness is, preventing the healing from even being initiated. If any relationship with another person is broken, it is hard to hear God speak. This forgiveness is critical in seeing our prayers answered. If we ask God to reveal where things are broken He will answer that prayer.

Unconfessed Sins

God cannot look on sin and even turned his back on His own Son as He was dying on that cross as God's only Son took on the sins of the world—yes, yours and mine. And the Bible says that we are all sinners, and only can be saved by the grace (unmerited favor) of God.

…for all have sinned and fall short of the glory of God.

Romans 3:23

For God to hear our prayer, we must first confess where we have failed Him.

Lack of Desperation

When we are praying, how desperate are we for God to answer? Assume you no longer have bindings from unforgiveness, you have confessed to Him your own sins, you want that intimate chat with *Yahweh*, you have asked God for faith and for forgiveness for any lack of faith, and you even have an understanding of what He is doing in your circumstances. Are you desperate enough to do anything—including giving up your life—to see it happen? How desperate are you?

Look at the desperation in this story:

> *A woman who had suffered a condition of hemorrhaging for twelve years—a long succession of physicians had treated her, and treated her badly, taking all her money and leaving her worse off than before—had heard about Jesus. She slipped in from behind and touched his robe. She was thinking to herself, "If I can put a finger on his robe, I can get well." The moment she did it, the flow of blood dried up. She could feel the change and knew her plague was over and done with.*

Mark 5:25-29, THE MESSAGE

I love to listen to George Otis, Jr. as he tells hundreds of stories about God doing miraculous things in various countries about the world. The inevitable question comes back at him—Why isn't God doing it here? George's answer is very simple. We aren't desperate enough for the coming of the Holy Spirit. Once God sees us desperate enough we will see Him act. All of the stories from Otis are about desperate people. In city after city, region after region, it was always the same. Men and women desperate for the coming of the Holy Spirit.

Compassion in Prayer

When I was involved in doing city-reaching ministry, I was involved in very high-level strategic research with a team of wonderful leaders to define the harvest force and harvest field of the city. The database of about 1800 churches and over 600 parachurch organizations became a critical component of the results. This database became the nucleus for mobilizing for strategic prayer. None of this, however, would have had any value unless we had compassion for the hearts of the men and women in our city who had yet to meet the Lord. The battle was between the Lord and the Enemy for the *hearts* of the men and women in our city. It wasn't a data or information issue, it was a *heart* issue. Without compassion, nothing happens.

Sometimes God wants to teach us a lesson about prayer and compassion. A friend of mine—a single mom—had been sick for weeks. I had been praying over her, anointing her with oil in prayer, and doing all the stuff I thought I was supposed to do. Trying to be the hero, you know. Dragonslayer. Rescue the fair damsel.

But she wasn't getting better. Just worse. I couldn't figure it out. She wanted to be well. I wanted her well. God wanted her well. So what was going on? God is omnipotent, right? He should be able to get this job done.

Remember that story at the beginning of the last chapter? God is waiting for the prayers of *one* man (or woman). He needs one person to stand in the gap. And I better figure it out here. God's already signed the check. Now He is waiting for that second signature.

After several weeks she was getting really sick and in bed. She was having great difficulty breathing and sleeping. She wanted me to take her boys out for the night so she could get some rest. I brought them back late that night. Walking them to their door I really wanted them to go in quietly so as not to wake their mother if she was asleep. No chance. They barged to their mother's bedroom and soon charged back out as I was turning to leave.

"She wants to see you."

I followed them back and looked into the eyes of a very sick lady. Then the kids left the room.

"My mother dropped off my daughter and left," she rasped. "She said she didn't want to get what I have. You'd better leave, too!"

"I'm not leaving."

"You might get what I've got."

"I will not get what you've got."

I quickly realized something was happening and this had absolutely nothing to do with me or being a hero. It had everything to do with compassion. Her pain was my pain.

I took her hand and started praying. Something like 10,000 volts swept through my body and I started shaking. My legs gave out and I fell to the floor on the edge of the bed. I knew I had to hold onto the hand; but other than that I just tried to hang in there and pray until whatever it was stopped. Then I slowly stumbled back to my feet.

As I turned to look into her face, she was smiling. She was well.

"I'm leaving." I said. "You will be asleep in twenty minutes."

"Make it ten."

"You got it in ten."

I left.

The next morning I was still trying to process what had happened. I called her to check. She was already up.

"How you doing?" I asked.

"Fine. I'm fixing breakfast. I slept like a baby."

That next night after midnight I received a call from the church secretary.

"She just went to the hospital, Carl. The daughter is very sick and can't breathe. What do I do?"

The daughter had caught whatever it was from the mother.

"I'm on the way to the hospital to see them." I said. "Call Peter (the pastor) and just give him the information."

I knew the Holy Spirit would tell Peter what to do.

Peter was already at the hospital when I got there. We went in and started praying with the mother and daughter. This time I was like the student watching my pastor; but the compassion and "the taking on of the pain" was still there, just as Peter was doing now. The daughter was out later that day.

The lesson here is very profound. We need to let go of trying to be the hero. I like the way Graham Cooke explains it. He says he is at a lot of conferences where these other leaders give him their "business cards" that refer to themselves as bishops, prophets, and other highfalutin titles. His card says simply "Graham Cooke, servant of the Lord Jesus Christ". That's what it's all about. The only authority we really have is what He gives us, and we should exercise that with grace and compassion—neither virtues of which we choose. This authority is always a gift and, when given, is given to us in our desperation for our intimacy with Him—the One who does the healing and restores. It's fine to be the Dragonslayer; but you better know the true source of the authority and power and the agenda for which God is leading you.

Guidelines for Strategic Prayer

Now that you have some insights, let's take a look at some basic principles of strategic prayer.

Release any Unforgiveness and Ask for Forgiveness for Your Own Sins

What is remarkable about these Biblical prayer warriors is that they not only ask forgiveness for their own sins, but they also offer to take on the sins of those for whom they are praying as if those sins were their own as well. After Moses meets with God after the national failure at Mt. Sinai, Moses asks God to forgive the nation. He asks God, if the nation cannot be forgiven, not only to kill him but to blot him out of "the book that you have written":

> *Then Moses returned to the LORD and said, "Oh, these people have committed a great sin, and have made for themselves a god of gold! Yet now, if You will forgive their sin—but if not, I pray, blot me out of Your book which You have written."*

Exodus 32:30-32

Again in Nehemiah, we see Nehemiah taking on the sins of the nation as if they were his own and praying God to forgive these sins. This is a necessary step before the vision and reality can be taken.

> *...please let Your ear be attentive and Your eyes open, that You may hear the prayer of Your servant which I pray before You now, day and night, for the children of Israel Your servants, and confess the sins of the children of Israel which we have sinned against You. Both my father's house and I have sinned. We have acted very corruptly against You, and have not kept the commandments, the statutes, nor the ordinances which You commanded Your servant Moses.*

Nehemiah 1:6-7

Now for an interesting study continue reading the book of Nehemiah and identify each prayer Nehemiah made and see the heart of Nehemiah in each.

Pray to Discern God's Vision

I like the story in 2 Samuel 18:24-26 about the watchman on the wall. From his place high on the wall and with the help of King David below him, the watchman discerned a lot of information from the runner approaching the city. He knew who the runner was, that the runner was bringing good news, and that the news would be that the Israelites had won the war. Suppose at that point he came down from the wall and spoke this information into the people of the city. He could tell them they had won the battle. Yet they had not seen or heard the runner, and the words from the watchman would be perceived as prophecy. The information was, however, *already* true and the battle *already* won.

The prayer warrior is much like that watchman. From his or her Place in their intimacy with God they have already seen what God is accomplishing and take hold of that vision to pray it into existence. Moses did this in Numbers 14. He saw the vision of the coming Christ through the Israelite nation. This "Promised Land" was the center of the world at that time. They would be at the center of many major trade routes. As travelers passed through this Israelite nation they would be hearing the story of the coming Christ. The world would soon know of the coming child. Wise men would come from the East to see him. Moses, Joshua, and Caleb could believe and see this.

Later we see Nehemiah praying God's vision (quoting Moses) into existence to begin to lead a nation without vision, security, or passion back to the Lord.

Remember, I pray, the word that You commanded Your servant Moses, saying, 'If you are unfaithful, I will scatter you among the nations; but if you return to Me, and keep My commandments and do them, though some of you were cast out to the farthest part of the heavens, yet I will gather them from there, and bring them to the place which I have chosen as a dwelling for My name.'

Nehemiah 1:8-10

Like these leaders, we must as watchmen (or watchwomen) discern the vision and reality, and then pray it into existence as it is already accomplished in the heavenlies.

Now read this:

*Thus says the LORD who made it, the LORD who formed it to establish it (the LORD is His name): "Call to Me, and I will answer you, and show you great and mighty things, which you do not **know**."*

Jeremiah 33:2-3 (emphasis added)

The Hebrew word for LORD here is *Yahweh*, the intimate name for God—only known by those who are His chosen. The tense is future perfect; i.e., God will show or you will see. The command for that astonishment to happen is to call on God. The promise is that God will answer.

The Hebrew word used for "know" here is very important. From our Newtonian logic, we translate this as intellectually knowing. That is a far, far cry from what the LORD (*Yahweh*) is saying. Let's look for a moment at a verse in Genesis that will shed some light here. In Genesis 4:1 we read:

> *Now Adam knew* [yada] *Eve his wife, and she conceived and bore Cain, and said, "I have acquired a man from the LORD."*

Genesis 4:1

The Hebrew word for "knew" here is *yada*, and obviously is referring to a sexual intimacy. Now move ahead to Jeremiah 24:7 and read:

> *Then I will give them a heart to know* [yada] *Me, that I am the LORD; and they shall be My people, and I will be their God, for they shall return to Me with their whole heart.*

Jeremiah 24:7

Wow! The same Hebrew word, *yada*, is used here. It refers to God giving a heart to His people (and that's *you*) that they may know Him (intimately), a deep knowledge and experience that is beyond any words to describe. God wants you to know (*yada*) that He is *Yahweh*, you will return to Him, and He wants you to give your heart to Him. This *Yahweh* name, or YHWH, is the personal name of God who He chooses to use only with His people. This name implies the intimate relationship. In other words, the speaking of the *rhema* word may initiate healing, may be prophecy, may be tongues, interpretation of tongues, or another gifting. The purpose, however, is really a Divine Encounter that takes us to the very presence of God. Now read the Jeremiah verse again and put your own name in it. Take the intimacy that He offers.

Then I will give Carl a heart to know [yada] Me, that I am Yahweh; and Carl shall be My man, and I will be his God, for he shall return to Me with his whole heart.

Jeremiah 24:7

Now look at Moses at Mt. Sinai. He had just been given the Ten Commandments and returned to a camp that was in rebellion. Moses had broken the stones, symbolic of the nation that had broken their relationship with God. Moses pitched his tent outside the camp and called it the tabernacle of meeting (Exodus 33:7). It was there that Moses began an intimate conversation with God. Look at two verses in that conversation:

*Now therefore, I pray, if I have found grace in Your sight, show me your way, that I may **know** You and that I may find grace in Your sight. And consider that this nation is Your people.*

Exodus 33:13 (emphasis added)

*So the LORD said to Moses, "I will also do this thing that you have spoken; for you have found grace in My sight, and I **know** you by name."*

Exodus 33:17 (emphasis added)

In both verses the *Yada* word is used for "know", and the LORD word is translated from the Hebrew *Yahweh*, to reference a personal God. *Yahweh* will reveal His vision.

Pray Strategically into the Vision

Since the prayer warrior has already seen the reality and vision, the strategic prayer is much like an arrow into the heart of the enemy. You must speak the Word out loud.

And He has made My mouth like a sharp sword;

Isaiah 49:2

The job is done. In the very speaking of God's word with *dunamis* out loud *(rhema)*, it begins to happen.

Believe in the Vision and Act on it as if it has already Happened

You are not so much praying "If it is your will", but rather discerning the will and praying it into existence. Look at the Model Prayer Jesus left us.

> *Your kingdom come.*
> *Your will be done*
> *On earth as it is* [already done] *in heaven.*

Matthew 6:10

It's not so much a petition as a command. In praying, you are taking authority in the name of Jesus and asking Heaven to invade earth. This Model Prayer really has only three parts: praise and worship, asking heaven to invade earth, and praise and worship. All of that middle part of the prayer has to do with the invasion.

Encourage Feedback

As prayers are answered, encourage those for whom you pray to tell you what happened. This becomes the testimony for others to move ahead in faith (Hebrews 11:2) and also helps you as a prayer warrior to discern more of the pattern of what God is doing in the circumstances.

Praise God

Share what God is doing with your prayers. Sing about it in song.

> *I'm whistling, laughing, and jumping for joy;*
> *I'm singing your song, High God.*

The day my enemies turned tail and ran,
they stumbled on you and fell on their faces.
You took over and set everything right;
when I needed you, you were there, taking charge.

Psalms 9:2-4 *THE MESSAGE*

Sing about it even before others can see it, as it is already done. The Enemy hates praise music.

Secure Your Information

What you see, hear, and pray for is often very strategic information. Treat it that way. Don't necessarily share it with others unless directed by the Holy Spirit. Do share what God is doing.

Have Intercessory Prayer Warriors Praying for You

Once you are praying for the vision and reality, you are on the front lines and in a very vulnerable position. Have others who share your vision praying with you. Pray for the warriors, as they have now moved to the front line and are vulnerable.

What If I Don't Know this Jesus?

He knows you. He loves you. He wants to be your best friend. What this means, simply, is that He is willing to step into your prayer request simply to show you that He does love you and wants that intimacy with you. Ask Him to forgive your sins. Tell Him you want to change. Are you willing to take that risk? Be careful and think about it first. It may cost you everything you've got.

Dialog

1. Can you think of a prayer you made that you think was unanswered? Why do you think it was unanswered?

2. Can you think of a prayer in the Bible that was not answered? Why was it not answered?

3. What are some guidelines to praying you think could be added here?

Chapter 9: The Call

Your heart is free...have the courage to follow it.

Malcolm Wallace to his son in *Braveheart*

Why was I able to walk again after the GBS? Can we really visualize ourselves well again and drive the healing from that? Does this mean we can initiate healing for Attention Deficit Disorder, bi-polar problems, and perhaps even Alzheimer from nothing more than challenging the brain? If so, how do we challenge the brain? How does faith relate to that? How does our purpose in life relate to that?

God is Acting in Your Life

God is acting in your life and has a very bold vision He wants you to accomplish. There is a very interesting word in the German language that refers to a time-phase: *zeitgestalt*. As used here, it refers to God's pattern in history. A seed has a *zeitgestalt* locked within itself. A cabbage seed and a broccoli seed look alike, but one becomes cabbage and the other becomes broccoli. You can't get broccoli from a cabbage seed. The seed does not choose what it wants to be. It has a destiny locked within its being.

You have a destiny, time-phase, or *zeitgestalt* in God's Plan. We do not choose our zeitgestalt. It is a free gift (*charisma* in the Greek) given by God to each of us. It is not that we are called to mission—we *are* mission. And, as Elizabeth O'Conner taught me years ago: *Our greatest source of anxiety in our lives is our resistance and struggle against this destiny that is already written within our lives.* We have great difficulty in accepting this gift, rejecting the very calling of God in our lives. We constantly choose to live in our small story.

The Old Testament definition of sin was that of an archer missing his or her target. We each fail in hearing our calling and responding to it. The Psalmist talks of our being chosen by God.

> *O LORD, You have searched me and known me.*
> *You know my sitting down and my rising up;*
> *You understand my thought afar off.*
> *You comprehend my path and my lying down,*
> *And are acquainted with all my ways.*
> *For there is not a word on my tongue,*
> *But behold, O LORD, You know it altogether.*
> *You have hedged me behind and before,*
> *And laid Your hand upon me.*

Psalms 139:1-5

The apostle Paul also referred to the fact that we are chosen:

> *...just as He chose us in Him before the foundation of the world, that we should be holy and without blame before Him in love, ...*

Ephesians 1:4-5

Paul was not speaking just to the Jews as the chosen nation. In this verse he is writing to a church of both Jews and Gentiles (Ephesians 1:11-13). Those in Christ are chosen.

God loves you in a very special way. This is easy to comprehend at the intellectual level, but very difficult to appropriate into our personal lives. We find difficulty in receiving this love. We are chosen by God; yet we have difficulty in receiving our being chosen.

In the Old Testament the Israelite nation becomes the parable of our own relationship to God. They were chosen by God to carry the message to the world of the coming of the Christ Child. Yet as the Israelites stood on the very edge of the Promised Land (or Promised Time, as it more accurately translates), they could not go in. Trapped by their illusions, they could not see the reality. With the exception of Joshua and Caleb who could see the reality, the entire nation over the age of 20 spent the rest of their life in the desert and never went into the land that was already theirs.

How, like Israel, we stand on the edge of our own calling and destiny. Like the Israelites, we see our political organizations and institutions as giants and ourselves as grasshoppers. Yet we are already chosen by Christ to go in and take the land. We are called to participate with God in the redemption of the world.

The Call

God is calling you to participate with Him in the redemption of the world. The Greek word used in the Bible for "call" is *kalein*. It is used as a verb. It could be used when calling someone to a banquet or feast (Matthew 22:3, Luke 7:39, Revelation 19:9). The word was also used in calling someone to a court of judgment (Acts 4:18, 24:2).

The word *kalein* in the New Testament is often associated with other words. We are called to grace (*charisma*, gifts) (Galatians 1:6). We are called to *koinonia* (fellowship) (1 Corinthians 1:9). We are called to freedom (Galatians 5:13), peace (1 Corinthians 7:15), hope (Ephesians 4:4), sanctification (1 Thessalonians 4:17). salvation (2 Timothy 1:9).

The call is unique to us. Remember, God called Jacob and changed his name to Israel. In so doing, God established a covenant relationship with Jacob and His authority over him.

And God said to him, "Your name is Jacob; your name shall not be called Jacob anymore, but Israel shall be your name." So He called his name Israel.

Genesis 35:10-11

111

A parent names a child, and in so doing establishes a vision of their expectations of the child and defines their covenant relationship with the child as parent. A doctor names a disease, and in doing that gains authority in the healing process. Christ named demons before casting them out, and in so doing established His authority over them. In hearing and appropriating God's call on us by name, we affirm His authority over us and His purpose for our life.

Jacob's dream with the ladder to heaven at a place which was called Luz, became Bethel, or "House of God". On his journey back home he wrestled with the entity and the place becomes Peniel, which means "Face of God". Jacob's name became Israel, which means "ruling with God". In the New Testament Simon becomes Peter (Rock). Saul becomes Paul, a Gentile name that signified God had called him as a missionary to the Gentiles.

The name cannot be given until the man or woman becomes the name. Although the identity and zeitgestalt was there from before creation, the man or woman has to take ownership on it, and then the name is given. They now live with the authority of God through their life. The new name signifies the calling to that relationship and intimacy. The person now has a new authority in terms of the calling and the name that relates to that calling. The name of any place related to the event then changes to signify where this took place and the authority of the experience that happened there.

Once we reach our final Place—heaven, God gives us a white stone with our name on it:

> *He who has an ear, let him hear what the Spirit says to the churches. To him who overcomes I will give some of the hidden manna to eat. And I will give him a white stone, and on the stone a new **name** written which no one knows except him who receives it.*

Revelation 2:17 (emphasis added)

Why is it so hard for us to see the reality? The Enemy deceives us. We observe through our senses, and then we create what we believe to be reality from what we observe. This perception of reality is then stored as dynamic patterns in the brain. It's not a bit storage as in a computer. Rather, the brain stores information as circulating and dynamic patterns. By the time we are three years old, there are already 100 trillion neural connections in place that play the patterns that define how we interpret reality. Our concept of what we believe is reality is shaped very early and we make decisions against what we think is reality. This perceived reality is a broken perception—an illusion created in a Garden long, long time ago.

My sister was teaching a writer's class and to illustrate this had two drama students do a classic drama trick for the class. She had one male drama student (an actor) barge into the class and get into a sudden loud, angry, and boisterous argument with a woman "student" in her class. (This was the first day of class and the "student" was really also an actor.) The basic script for the two drama students was very balanced; that is, the problem was just as much the man's as the woman's. She then had her students write what they observed. Only one student in the class caught the truth of the story and saw it as balanced.[1] Although each student observed the same information through their senses, each interpreted it differently based on their past perceptions of reality.

With my own GBS, I was asking the doctors about their prognosis for my own recovery. I wanted to know what was happening to the neural system with time. The GBS affects only the peripheral neural system and (unlike polio) does not even get in the spine. It is an auto-immune issue in which the immune system sees its own cells as foreign and begins destroying them. The GBS had destroyed the myelin sheath that surrounds the peripheral nerves and enables the signals to move from the brain to their destination (and vice versa) quickly. The sheath acts as an insulator for the electrical signal, much as insulation on a wire.

In many GBS cases this is repaired quickly. In my case the GBS also went into the peripheral neural cells and began destroying axons of the neurons. There was major, major neural damage. The myelin sheath can grow back quickly; but the neurons are the slowest growing cells in the body. The body replaces some 300 billion cells in the body every day. Neurons are replaced, but slowly. The longest axons in the human body, some of those now destroyed, were in the sciatic nerves. The sciatic nerves are the longest nerve in the body and run from the base of the spine to the lower limb. These single-cell fibers of the sciatic nerves may have a length of a meter or even longer. Those axons can take years for restoration, if ever. It is believed the angel who struck Jacob struck him on the sciatic nerve.

We are learning, however, that the neural system can be rewired. Both the peripheral and central nervous system. Doctors working with children who may have experienced childhood abuse often use hypnosis to pull up hidden memories in an attempt to prove the abuse. Unfortunately, the results will not be conclusive as the child does have the potential to rewrite the stored images circulating in the brain. How can the doctor separate the reality from the illusion?

The human mind can also travel forward in time, projecting a story based on past views of reality and play it as if it were a reality. A guy might project forward with a vision of a date with an attractive lady. Even more interesting, suppose this lady has been wounded over and over again from relationships in the past and has no vision of herself as well or that she can make a marriage work. The guy who loves her, however, visions her as well in his own mind and relates to her as a well woman. *His* reality is her as a well person. *Her* vision of the reality of herself is that she is broken. Through his love for her, she can eventually take ownership on his vision of her and with God's help and power she experiences her own healing. His reality becomes her reality. His love, God's love, and grace actually physically rewires her mind. I have seen this happen.

There are even more interesting aspects of healing. Can the mind project forward from an illness with a vision of healing (faith) and initiate physical healing? If so, what is the spiritual dimension of this? Where does illusion become reality in this?

In 1999 Dr. Paul Hegstrom, founder of Life Skills International as well as a professional counselor and author, had two heart surgeries in a single day and then a stroke. The doctors operating on his brain for the stroke told him later that 40% of his brain was destroyed. As he recovered and began his speaking engagements again, he had difficulty with them. He said the words would form visually in his brain, but he would occasionally have trouble speaking them and apologize to his audience. With time, however, all of this was healed and in the interview I heard you would never know he had experienced a stroke. As most people do not recover from this type of stroke or recover poorly, the interviewer was asking him about how he accomplished this.

To achieve this, Paul said, his brain had to rewire itself. There are far more neurons there than needed for practical purposes. The brain had to rewire itself so that some of the unused neurons took up the tasks lost to missing neurons. In addition, the neurons left can grow more dendrites and synapses. New neurons can grow. [2] Scientists have long known the brain can rewire itself, but they didn't know how to initiate this. Paul's progress was real and objectively measured with brain scans.[3]

Paul said that he had to first *will* the brain to rewire itself. The illusion of the healing had to become reality, with the unhealed brain as illusion. A key part of this strategy is that Paul had to speak the new reality out loud. The brain is trained from childhood to believe and trust your own voice. Speaking the vision out loud initiated the healing.

The Greeks had an interesting word for words spoken with authority—*rhema*. In fact, the familiar passage in Ephesians 6 indicates the spoken word of God (*rhema*) and prayer are the only offensive weapons the Christian has in spiritual warfare.

*And take the helmet of salvation, and the sword of the Spirit, which is the **word** [rhema] of God; praying always with all prayer and supplication in the Spirit, being watchful to this end with all perseverance and supplication for all the saints.*

Ephesians 6:17-18 (emphasis added)

The Bible was not written at this time. The words of the Bible, however, are truth, reality, or *logos*. When the right verse is spoken out loud at the right time in power and authority, it becomes *rhema*.

In Genesis, we see God spoke the created order into existence.

Then God said, "Let there be light"; and there was light.

Genesis 1:3

In the same way, if we speak God's agenda out loud with his authority we can initiate the healing and carry it to completion. This is what Dr. Paul Hegstrom was doing to initiate his healing and rewire his brain. He would speak the verses out loud.

Look again at the Model Prayer Christ taught us. It begins by establishing the authority of God (*Our daddy, which art in heaven…*), then goes on to claim, in authority, that what has already been done in heaven is to be done on earth. It is far more than a petition, but rather a *rhema* word, a word spoken in authority for the completion of God's agenda (already completed in the heavenlies) on earth through us taking God's authority on earth.

Your kingdom come.
Your will be done
On earth as it is [already done] in heaven.

Mathew. 6:10

Now let's put some concepts here together. Look at Isaiah's name. It means "God is Salvation". Every time God calls Isaiah by name the promise of the coming Christ is told. When God calls Isaiah by name, the *rhema* word is spoken again. Look at the Isaiah 49:1:

The LORD has called Me from the womb;
From the matrix of My mother He has made mention of
My name.
And He has made My mouth like a sharp sword;

Isaiah 49:1 -2

The Hebrew word used for LORD in this verse again is *Yahweh*, or YHWH, and refers to a personal and intimate God. Isaiah's mouth will speak the *rhema* word.

The Dichotomy

Can we really make something happen if we have enough faith? Look for our first clue in the very words of Christ.

So Jesus answered and said to them, "Have faith in God. For assuredly, I say to you, whoever says to this mountain, 'Be removed and be cast into the sea,' and does not doubt in his heart, but believes that those things he says will be done, he will have whatever he says. Therefore I say to you, whatever things you ask when you pray, believe that you receive them, and you will have them."

Mark 11:22-24

I had faith that my wife would be healed. Where did I go wrong? Or did I? I wrestled with the guilt that maybe I needed more faith. I was in an illusion.

I had a very dear friend who died last year after four years of struggling with multiple and major physical issues. A few months later another dear friend and major mentor of some 30 years died of cancer. Does this mean God has abandoned me? No, I firmly believe God loves me deeply. I believe God has final authority here, and His Kingdom has been, is being, and will be restored on earth.

This is not the world God created. The world we live in was severely broken at the Fall. Man demanded his independence, becoming angry at the One who gave him the world. The world that was created was perfect for Man. Adam and Eve gave the authority that God gave them to Satan, destroying the relationship and intimacy they had with God. God sent His Son to restore His authority here on earth and releases that authority to us to accomplish His Kingdom work. God loves you and His mercy wins over justice because He loves you. It is Man who has embraced evil and God has responded with goodness. What happened to Sandy was the work of the Enemy and no one in the world is immune from the Enemy's work. My job is to release my own independence, quit trying to judge God, and to know God for who He is and submit to God's agenda.

In addition, there is far more to this faith issue than that. Now look at the same statement from Christ recorded by a disciple with the condition stated:

And whatever you ask in My name, that I will do, that the Father may be glorified in the Son. If you ask anything in My name, I will do it.

John 14:13-14

Keep going. Here it is again by another disciple:

*If you have faith as a mustard seed, you will say to this mountain, 'Move from here to there,' and it will move; and **nothing** will be impossible for you. However, this kind does not go out except by prayer and fasting.*

Matthew 17:20-21 (emphasis added)

Don't stop.

If you abide in Me, and My words [rhema] abide in you, you will ask what you desire, and it shall be done for you. By this My Father is glorified, that you bear much fruit; so you will be My disciples.

John 15:7-8

If you want to be in the mountain moving business, the agenda must also glorify God and be a part of the Kingdom Enterprise. It should lead to fruit. The work also includes a lot of prayer and fasting. God wants to take the evil and use it for His purpose. That may or may not include what you *think* is your agenda.

There is even more to these words of Jesus if we take a hard look. *The actual meaning of these verses is exactly the opposite of what you would expect.* Jesus was not telling His disciples they needed more faith. What He was really saying is that if you have just a tiny bit of faith in God's agenda you can get into this mountain moving business.

Through the Eyes of the Child

It is very, very often that children can embrace this truth far easier than the adult. They have not been exposed as much to the cultural and logical boundaries that limit our vision and faith.

There are children playing in the streets who could solve some of my top problems in physics, because they have modes of sensory perception that I lost long ago.

J. Robert Oppenheimer

A denominational leader shared with me a story of some children from a church some sixty miles from Portland. It seems a businessman in Portland decided to build a pornographic store not too far from a major intersection where I lived. These kids (very young) came up with their leaders from their church and did a prayer march around the store. Then the group went on home to their city and church. That night the store burned to the ground and one man in the store died in the fire.

I asked the denominational leader if we could have them visit our church and share with us about the story.

"You want the kids up?" he asked.

"Nope—I want the teachers up to speak to our kids."

"The teachers teach a very simple faith. Nothing that you haven't heard before. The difference is that these kids are raised isolated from most of our culture. They don't really know reality as we perceive it. They don't know that what they did was not reasonable. They saw what they did as reality and went ahead and did it."

I love a story Graham Cooke tells about seeing through a child's eyes. The Lord told Graham he wanted him to plant a church. This was a pretty spiritually desolate area as far as any church plant went. Many others had tried to plant churches there and they had failed. Graham did not want to add himself to the list and he told God that. God told Graham the others hadn't been listening to Him, and that's why they failed. God told Graham to go ahead and plant a church there, but to plant a church for the children.

So Graham honored his call. They started with a handful of kids and soon had a large group of eager kids. Graham taught them how to love Jesus, discover their gifts, and take all the risks with that discovery. One kid told Graham her Grandma had arthritis in her leg and she wanted to learn how to pray for Grandma to be healed. He helped the kid pray for Grandma's healing. Grandma went to the doctor and they found the leg with the arthritis was suddenly healed. The doctors decided they better check the other leg. It was also healed. Pretty soon the adults started to show up to find out what was going on. Soon they had a multi-generational church, planted with the help of those kids. The kids became the leaders.

Now look at what Jesus said about the children and reality:

*Then Jesus called a little child to Him, set him in the midst
of them, and said, "Assuredly, I say to you, unless you are
converted and become as little children, you will by no means
enter the kingdom of heaven. Therefore whoever humbles
himself as this little child is the greatest in the kingdom of
heaven. Whoever receives one little child like this in My
name receives Me."*

Matthew 18:2-5

*Then little children were brought to Him that He might put
His hands on them and pray, but the disciples rebuked them.
But Jesus said, "Let the little children come to Me, and do not
forbid them; for of such is the kingdom of heaven."*

Matthew 19:13-15

The clues to finding our authority lie in first understanding
where God is working and then seeing what the children see.

Through the Eyes of the Heart

The calling and destiny will always have something to do with
the heart, a burden of the heart. On that old Emmaus road story
(Chapter 2), the first clue they had to the reality was a burning
of the heart.

*And they said to one another, "Did not our **heart** burn
within us while He talked with us on the road, and while
He opened the Scriptures to us?"*

Luke 24:32 (emphasis added)

The word used here for "heart" is from the Greek *kardia*.
It refers to the heart and feelings. I also like the Greek word
kardiognostes, which refers to a knower of the heart—a heart-
knower.

In Ephesians 6:6, the heart is mentioned again.

*...not with eyeservice, as men-pleasers, but as bondservants of Christ, doing the will of God from the **heart**, with goodwill doing service, as to the Lord, and not to men, knowing that whatever good anyone does, he will receive the same from the Lord, whether he is a slave or free.*

Ephesians 6:6-8 (emphasis added)

The burden, calling and gifting is always birthed from the heart.

Notes

1. One person in the class got it right. My sister asked him why, and his answer was that he was a fanatic at reading mystery books.
2. Fields, R, Douglas. "New Brain Cells Go to Work", *Scientific American Mind*, September, 2007, Volume 18, Number 4. Also see Begley, Sharon. "How the Brain Rewires Itself". *TIME* (January 29, 2007)
3. Hegstrom's book *Broken Children, Grown Up Pain: Understanding the Effects of Your Wounded Past* (Kansas City: Beacon Hill Press, 2006) is also available from Amazon.com and other sources. Paul Hegstrom's website is at http://www.lifeskillsintl.org/. You can find several interviews with Dr. Paul Hegstrom at: http://www. sidroth.org/site/News2?abbr=rad_&page=NewsArticle& id=6205&security=1042&news_iv_ctrl=1185.

Dialog

1. If you knew you could not fail and had unlimited resources, what would you do with your life?

2. How do you see yourself as chosen?

3. Where do you see yourself as chosen and by whom?

Chapter 10: The Audacity of Faith

Faith is to believe what you do not see;
the reward of this faith is to see what you believe.

St. Augustine

The leader is always stepping out in faith. What he or she sees is real in the heart of the leader, but has yet to appear to the rest of us. The leader is always moving on his or her faith.

Not long before Sandy and I became engaged she boarded a plane with me for an Easter holiday trip to meet my parents. This was also her first flight in an airplane so she had considerable anxiety. I had flown many times, and I sat relaxed waiting for the plane to begin its runway dash to skies as the engines began to roar. Sandy was obviously frightened, holding tightly to the armrest with a panicked look in her beautiful eyes. Soon this monster machine that weighed almost 500 tons when it was loaded roared down the long runway and into the air. A short time later we arrived at my parent's home and we had a wonderful time there.

Now if you are just looking at one of those airplanes on the ground it doesn't look very logical that the 500 ton monster could defy gravity and fly. You might say we had "faith" that the airplane would fly. But was that really faith?

From my perspective I knew the physics of why the airplane flew and also had taken many, many flights. Some four years earlier on a 707 flight out of New York to Paris my flight had almost crashed. The plane had tilted on takeoff. The incident report I got later indicated we lost 25% of our altitude as the plane slid sideways into the city. Then the plane oscillated the other direction and we lost 33% of our altitude as it again slid sideways into New York. Stuff was falling out of the overhead bays. People were screaming and crying. With the motors roaring, I saw nothing out of the windows but water as the plane started coming down. Eventually the runway appeared and I could see the fire trucks and other equipment. The report I got later indicated the plane had lost its hydraulic system and the pilots had to manually get the huge 707 plane, still on takeoff, turned around and back to the airport. As I sat in this plane with Sandy some four years later, I was sure praying the Good Lord would keep all the thousands of parts in this plane together for a safe flight.

Sandy's perspective was somewhat different. Without a knowledge of the physics of how the airplane flew and zero experience of flying any other plane, she was really stepping out believing that she could trust me on the flight, the airplane, and most of all—the Good Lord.

Where, then, is faith in all this?

The Reality of Faith

You don't really see any specific definition of faith in the Bible, but you do see stories that illustrate faith.

Now faith is the substance of things hoped for, the evidence of things not seen. For by it the elders obtained a good testimony. By faith we understand that the worlds were framed by the word [rhema] of God, so that the things which are seen were not made of things which are visible.

Hebrews 11:1-2

Or, in a more contemporary expression:

Faith is being sure of what we hope for and certain of what we do not see.

125

Faith is the *substance* of the things we cannot see. Hope does not imply action or demand that we do anything and provides no substance for action. Faith, in contrast, is proactive. It *demands* we do something. It demands we step out on something that is there that we cannot see physically—only spiritually. Yet it has already happened in the heavenlies. Faith has substance.

In reality, faith always springs from a relationship. Faith is the result of believing someone. It is an unconscious process of acting on something *because we believe someone*—not because we believe *something.* Faith is beyond reason. If we are acting on reason, it isn't faith.

> *Faith is not a conscious thing; it springs from a personal relationship and is the unconscious result of believing someone.*

Oswald Chambers, *Approved Under God*

During the first few months that I had the GBS, the doctors told me that it wasn't reasonable that I would walk again. I had to step out in faith beyond reason. It had to be a proactive step on my part. And there was a relationship, and it wasn't with the doctor. It was with God. If I had believed (or had faith in) the doctors I would never have walked again.

The loss of my wife, three years after the GBS, was another step of faith. A big one. In this case I was angry with the doctors, with my prayer partners, and with God. And that anger would not bring my wife back. The bottom line, I realized, was to find out where, if, and why my prayers failed me. Or maybe they didn't fail me? I had to begin a long journey involving the best of prayer warriors (both living and dead) to find my answer.

In this desperation, I also traveled internationally. I remember in 1995 in Seoul, Korea when I climbed the famous prayer mountain there. George Otis, Jr. was speaking that day up the mountain and he held us spellbound with stories of what God was doing around the world. When lunchtime arrived, the leaders realized they didn't have enough food for the crowd that had come that day, so we had to choose between listening to more Otis stories or lunch. Nobody left for lunch. Finally the Good Lord multiplied our loaves and fishes and we adjourned for lunch. During the break I hiked up the garden trail that led past stations in the life of Christ. Finally, on arriving at the cross, I fell prone with others from nations around the world in worship at the foot of the cross. After some time I had to return down the trail to get to the afternoon session on time. Seeing Tom White at the session, I asked a question that had been on my mind as I descended the garden trail.

"Tom, what is up there beyond the cross? I didn't have time to go further."

"Carl, there is nothing there beyond it but an empty tomb."

What do you see beyond that cross? Do you stop at the cross or do you see the empty tomb? Do you have any clue of what happened on Pentecost a few weeks later when they were hit with the Holy Spirit? What happened when Peter met the lame man at the temple gate not long after that? Peter had taken a proactive step of faith in *waiting* as God had commanded them. Peter took another proactive step of faith with the lame man when he told him to stand up.

This proactive step of faith in my personal travels led me to the discovery that the prayers and God had never failed me, but were leading me to a new Place. Both the death of Sandy and the GBS were necessary steps to that Place.

In the fictional story of the film *Indiana Jones and the Last Crusade* we see Indiana Jones (Harrison Ford) on a quest with his father (Sean Connery) for the Holy Grail, which is assumed to have healing powers. As they reach the end of the quest while pursued by the Nazis, Jones almost reaches the Grail but is separated from it by a large canyon. His father lies dying behind him, desperately needing a healing drink from the Grail. Jones sees no way to cross the massive canyon which seems infinitely deep and dark. You then watch as Jones takes one step into the canyon and shifts *all* his weight to that foot with nothing but empty space under the foot. Jones risked everything. Suddenly a stone appears below his foot. Another step forward and another stone appears. Taking one step at a time, he reaches the Grail (and another test) before he takes the contents of the Grail back to his dying father and brings the healing the father needs. But Indiana Jones needed to step out in faith for the stone or the Grail would never have been his and the healing would never have happened.

So often the healing we need is just as close as Indiana Jones was to that Holy Grail in this story. To get to it, however, we have to take a step and a risk that seems beyond any reason. We have to put everything in the hands of God and trust Him completely. The belief precedes the action. Without it, no healing will take place. This belief can only be achieved through intimacy with God.

On that plane trip with Sandy I already had plenty of testimony of what God was doing in my life and I had faith in God that He was taking me to another Place. And the person who would lead me to that Place was sitting right beside me. It was a relational thing with God. I could lean back and relax on this flight.

The Intimacy Issue

Since faith is built on a relationship, an intense and intimate relationship with God is essential to see the larger story and your role in this story. This intimacy with God is a critical aspect moving from the illusion to reality, particularly as it relates to our prayer life. If you want to see the reality of what's going on around you and understand your part in the larger story God is taking you on, you must have this intimacy with Him. This whole thing is not an academic excursion. It's a risk-taking trip that involves putting *all* your weight on something that isn't even appearing to be there to those around you.

Here's a classic example. God hardened Pharaoh's heart so that God could show His wonders to the Israelites and that would become a testimony through the ages of what God could do. Moses had to put all of his weight in his mission.

> *Now the LORD said to Moses, "Go in to Pharaoh; for I have hardened his heart and the hearts of his servants, that I may show these signs of Mine before him, and that you may tell in the hearing of your son and your son's son the mighty things I have done in Egypt, and My signs which I have done among them, that you may know that I am the LORD."*

Exodus 10:1-2

In Hebrews 11:1 the writer refers back to this as a *substance* from which we can build more faith. Look at that verse again.

> *For by it the elders obtained a good testimony.*

What God has done for us in the past becomes those stepping stones to get to the next step that we have yet to see but where we must risk. Look at the message that Moses gives the Israelites in Deuteronomy 11. In this passage Moses first claims authority on the testimony of what God has already done. Then he points them to the present with what they need to do now, and then finally he claims authority on their future as they move to the Promised Land. He builds their faith on what God has already done, and literally plays this message over and over again to them as they move forward.

Can you think of anything more stupid than what Moses did to rescue this nation? The Israelites were the economic engine for one of the most advanced civilizations of that time. Here's old Moses—80 years old—standing there with nothing but a silly stick going in to Pharaoh. Then, to top it off, God tells him to throw down the stick (Exodus 4:1-5). Moses had to throw away the only thing he was left holding. Moses took a faith step.

The same thing is true with us. God really wants to astonish us, just like He did with Moses. Do you have any idea about what God wants to do to rescue you? First, however, there must be this intimacy. Then He speaks. Then we must let go of what we are holding. Then God will astonish you.

The sole purpose for God creating you is for intimacy with Him. Can you hear that? See it? Taste it? Act on it?

Now let's take this to another level and look at the last moments of Elisha's life. Elisha is dying. Elisha had a deep intimacy with God. The King knew it, and comes to Elisha to get advice on a coming battle.

> *Elisha had become sick with the illness of which he would die. Then Joash the king of Israel came down to him, and wept over his face, and said, "O my father, my father, the chariots of Israel and their horsemen!"*

2 Kings 13:15

Notice that King Joash is grieving as he identifies where his own securities lie (Elisha, chariots, and horsemen) and the fact he was losing one of these. Joash does not mention the Lord as a security.

Now notice how the dying prophet replies.

> *And Elisha said to him, "Take a bow and some arrows." So he took himself a bow and some arrows. Then he said to the king of Israel, "Put your hand on the bow." So he put his hand on it, and Elisha put his hands on the king's hands. And he said, "Open the east window"; and he opened it. Then Elisha said, "Shoot"; and he shot. And he said, "The arrow of the LORD's deliverance and the arrow of deliverance from Syria; for you must strike the Syrians at Aphek till you have destroyed them." Then he said, "Take the arrows"; so he took them. And he said to the king of Israel, "Strike the ground"; so he struck three times, and stopped. And the man of God was angry with him, and said, "You should have struck five or six times; then you would have struck Syria till you had destroyed it! But now you will strike Syria only three times."*

2 Kings 13:16-17

The king did what Elisha asked. He opened the east window and shot the arrow through the window. The window is a symbol for the *kairos* moment, a window of opportunity through which the king must act (see Chapter 17 for more on this word). Elisha then asks the king to take the arrows and strike the ground. The king takes the arrows and strikes the ground three times. Whoops! What happens? Elisha becomes angry and tells the king he will only defeat the enemy three times. He should have struck six times. If so, he would destroy the enemy—as it is, he will only defeat the enemy three times. What do you think it was like when the king prepared for that fourth battle, only to realize the Lord's anointing was no longer on him and he could not win?

Many of us stand like Joash as we go into our battles. We don't have enough vision, faith, and boldness to strike the ground boldly. We are trapped in our illusions. We only strike three times. An illusion of faith. More like a lack of faith. I know people standing there now. I see them as healed. God sees them as healed. They are in an illusion. They see themselves as missing the healing they need. They need to take that faith step—in a relationship, in a ministry, or perhaps for a job. As a result, they never see the reality and the larger story of what God is doing. They aren't astonished. They don't lead. Unless we step out and risk with what God tells us to do, we won't have the incredible testimony about what God could have done.

God wants to do a number on us, but we don't have enough faith to step out of our illusion. God wants to astonish us, but often we don't have the bigger faith vision for accomplishing that. We stay in the comfort zone of our small story, just like Joash. How many times did you strike the ground today? God wants to astonish you. Can you pray for Him to astonish you and then expect Him to do that?

Jonathan and a Step of Faith

The Philistines were attacking Israel with thirty thousand chariots and six thousand horsemen (1 Samuel 13:4 NKJV).

There were only 600 Israelites with Saul. In addition, the only two people with sword or spear in the Israelite camp were Jonathan and Saul. And Saul is asleep under a Pomegranate tree.

Jonathan wakes up his armorbearer and the two take an incredible step of faith. Jonathan and his armorbearer slay 20 Philistines with his sword within only a few minutes. Then an earthquake hits. Finally, the commotion wakes up Saul. Jonathan took the first step of faith; then we see a miracle outside of that first step. The Philistines are routed. First, however, Jonathan had to take that initial first faith step.

Nehemiah and Faith

In Chapter 6 of this book you walked through that first prayer that Nehemiah prayed. It was a prayer from his heart to see Place again for his nation. He didn't ask God to build the wall; he asked for the opportunity for him to speak his vision to the king and for the king to have mercy.

Notice what happens. Nehemiah was a cupbearer to the King—a very high office. The King notices that Nehemiah is sad. Nehemiah has never been sad before the King before. Being sad before the king could cost him his life. It was a big risk. Nehemiah had the faith to step out of his cupbearer *personage* and be *person* to the king. Again, the healing begins as we become *person* (see Chapter 7). In Nehemiah 2:4 we see Nehemiah's request and his prayer of faith. And in Nehemiah 2:6-8 we see the King's response. We also see Nehemiah giving all the credit to God.

> *Then the king said to me (the queen also sitting beside him), "How long will your journey be? And when will you return?" So it pleased the king to send me; and I set him a time. Furthermore I said to the king, "If it pleases the king, let letters be given to me for the governors of the region beyond the River, that they must permit me to pass through till I come to Judah, and a letter to Asaph the keeper of the king's forest, that he must give me timber to make beams for the gates of the*

citadel which pertains to the temple, for the city wall, and for the house that I will occupy." And the king granted them to me according to the good hand of my God upon me.

Nehemiah 2:6-8

Some years ago I did a mission trip to India. Going over there with a stop in Singapore was certainly a first step of faith for me. Although I was with an experienced friend, for me the India trip would involve traveling in a very foreign culture. I remember on my last day in India I was working on a computer project and the computer suddenly stopped working. The power had gone out and was now back on; but the computer would not come up. I was trying to get the computer going again before I had to leave the next day. I didn't want to leave them with a broken computer, with me the last person to use it. When nothing seemed to work to heal the machine and my host asked me what I wanted to do, I said I wanted to make a trip to the silk store to get some silk for my wife to make a dress for herself. I knew the request seemed like a weird one with the problem I was having; but off we went to the silk store. In reality, I knew the silk store was a thirty minute drive away. That gave me an hour to pray for the computer, and that's what I did going to and from the store. After returning, a few minutes work on the computer brought it back up and working. That's real faith, as the resolution was external to anything I did.

When I got back and shared this story with a friend, he told of a doctor he knew who went to India and was doing surgery when the power went out. The light in the operating room went out and for a moment he was unable to complete the surgery. Then after a few seconds the light came on without the power coming back and he finished the operation. He was so impressed that when he got back to the States he wrote to the company that made the light and asked them about how that was done and queried them about the backup batteries that must have been in the light. They wrote back. There were no batteries in the light.

When I was hit with the GBS and prayed with others for

my healing, that was faith in a very real way in my own life. According to the doctors, I was never supposed to walk again. My neural system was destroyed. I had to take steps of real faith every day—action steps.

Faith Projection

One of the critical role of leaders is projecting their faith in the vision given to them by God into the larger picture and dimension of what God is doing and mobilizing the followers. As one pastor said, most of the goals of a modern church can be accomplished without God. All we need for those goals is people, money, and a shared objective. That isn't faith.

Nehemiah had this responsibility when he arrived at Jerusalem. He was the new kid on the block. Why would anyone in Jerusalem believe him? How is he going to mobilize the people to get them into the vision that he is carrying?

First, we see Nehemiah waited three days. Then God tells him to walk the walls of the city. He is to spiritually map the task. At that point he has not shared his vision with anyone. The Bible says no one knew his *heart*.

*Then I arose in the night, I and a few men with me; I told no one what my God had put in my **heart** to do at Jerusalem;…*

Nehemiah 2:12 (emphasis added)

As he walks the walls of the city alone, his burden and passion for the city grows. It is then Nehemiah stands and projects his vision to the leaders of the city. Notice how *he targets the needs of the people.* He also works top-down: starting with the priests, nobles, and the officials—the influential people or the "gatekeepers" of his culture.

And the officials did not know where I had gone or what I had done; I had not yet told the Jews, the priests, the nobles, the officials, or the others who did the work.

*Then I said to them, "You see the distress that we are in, how
Jerusalem lies waste, and its gates are burned with fire. Come
and let us build the wall of Jerusalem, that we may no longer
be a reproach." And I told them of the hand of my God which
had been good upon me, and also of the king's words that he
had spoken to me.*

*So they said, "Let us rise up and build." Then they set their
hands to this good work.*

Nehemiah 2:16-18

There was a time when the Lord told me to walk the perimeter,
or walls, of a particular neighborhood of my city. My first reaction
was that I needed to contact a leader who I knew in a specific
church in the neighborhood or the pastor of that church to walk
with me. God said no. I was to walk it alone in the [spiritual]
darkness like Nehemiah did Jerusalem. The perimeter was four
miles. If I walked one side at a time and back to the car, the entire
walk would be eight miles. It could be done in four days. Quite
a challenge for a kid who had been told by the doctors he would
never walk again. I struck out, but after half of a mile my feet
were in bad shape. God said it was urgent. I didn't know what that
meant, but I had a foot doctor do some repair and replaced the
shoes with new ones. I then started out again early one morning to
walk the first side (1 mile) of the neighborhood and then walked
back to the car (another mile).

I then went to a museum that had an exhibit of the spiritual
history of the Northwest. This was the last day for the exhibit, so
seeing the exhibit that day or never seeing it. I met two leading
city prayer warriors at the exhibit. I figured I walked a total of
over 6 miles that day. As I came out of the museum, I saw the
evening paper at a newspaper stand on the street. The headlines
shocked me. The previous night, a little over a block from where
I had walked that very morning, a church had burned to the

ground. Arson. I would have been the first person walking the area. I realized why God had said it was urgent.

On the next day, I walked over to the burned-out church. As I met with the people there carrying stuff out of what was left, I walked in on what was certainly sacred grounds. There, on the ashes that covered the baptistery window, I read the incredible words: "God is Love. No weapon fashioned against Him will stand." (See Isaiah 54:17.)

As I continued to complete my prayerwalk during the next few days, I passed lots of churches on the periphery of the neighborhood. In fact, all of the churches in the area with one exception were on the perimeter. By studying the history of the area, I realized why that was true. There was another reason as well, however. The churches, I realized, were planted by God as the gates to the neighborhood.

During the walk one day a leader in that neighborhood church called me on my cell phone. For some reason, she asked where I was—and I was honest and told her about what I was doing. She then asked more specifically—what was the address where I was? I was standing where the lady use to live.

Later this lady wanted to do the walk herself; but she felt burned out from all the work that she was involved in. I told her to wait. God would tell her when, with whom, and how to do her walk.

A few weeks later she called. Seems like a guy in a wheelchair in her church wanted to do the walk with her. She wanted to know if that was OK.

"Walk the neighborhood with him," I told her, "and the church will follow."

She did, they did, and some exciting things started as the church took hold of their vision.

What happened when Nehemiah walked?

Notice what Nehemiah does—he does a faith projection. He projects his faith into those who are to follow his vision. Notice also with whom he does this projection. He does the projection specifically to the leaders, or gatekeepers, of the city. This is a good general rule for any faith issue you are birthing.

Notice that Nehemiah had to have faith in the vision until he could project the same vision to others. Leaders project faith. Who projects faith to you; i.e., they have faith in the vision God has given to you? Who do you project faith to?

I was shocked, for example, when after losing my job a certain lady called me and she listened as I told her the news. Then she dropped a challenge that was incredible.

"Carl," she said, "you've got to run from your heart. Run from your heart. Why did you ever take that job you had in the first place? That's not your vision."

Faith projection.

The Steps to Faith

Since faith is the essential step for our journey to purpose and healing, let's take a moment to see some aspects of how to begin this journey.

Develop a passion and desperation for intimacy with God.

- Daniel experienced his visitation (Daniel 10) because he was desperate and humble.
- Abraham was desperately searching for a city whose builder and maker was God.
- Moses experienced forty years in the wilderness until he was desperate to lead a nation of over a million out of bondage.
- Nehemiah had the same information that his friends brought to him from Jerusalem; but it was only Nehemiah who had the desperation to spend four months fasting and praying for God's answer.
- And it was a desperate three wise men who traveled to see the tiny Christ-Child who was the expressed incarnation of

the Son of God. It was a desperate Zacchaeus who climbed a tree to see Jesus. It was a desperate woman who was washing the feet of Jesus with expensive perfume. It was a desperate Samaritan woman at the well. It was a desperate Nicodemus who came to Jesus in secret at night.

It is from this intimacy and desperation that we can begin to understand God's agenda, and then from this we can pray into it and expect it to be accomplished. It is already done in the heavenlies.

Submit to God

Those heroes of the faith—Abraham, Moses, Nehemiah, and more—shared something in common. They all submitted themselves to God so that God's hand could work through them in power. You must submit everything to God before you will see what I am talking about here. Can you do this?

Take the Word of God

As you read the narrative description of the soldier in Ephesians 6, you eventually reach verse 17. In this warfare picture, at this point the soldier is almost ready for battle but with all the other equipment he already has on; he needs help for the next two steps. The soldier cannot put the rest on by himself (or herself). It is the attendant who helps the warrior to put the helmet on and then gives the warrior his sword. In this analogy, these two are given to the soldier by an attendant—the Holy Spirit.

And take the helmet of salvation, and the sword of the Spirit, which is the word of God;

Ephesians 6:17

The "Word of God" is not used in the New Testament to refer to the Holy Scriptures. The New Testament did not exist at this time. The "Word" here translates as the *rhema* of God; that is, the spoken word (out loud) that has power in its speaking. Since the scriptures are given and inspired by God, speaking the right scripture at the right time does, indeed, become *rhema* (see Matthew 10:19). For effective faith ministry, we must understand God's agenda and then we can speak into it and expect it to be done, as it is already done in the heavenlies.

Understand the Warfare

God is waging warfare against the Enemy. God is coming to fight for your heart.

Rescuing the human heart is the hardest mission in the world.

John Eldridge, *Epic*

God should know—He's been doing it for centuries. Once we are desperate enough, God rips through the Enemy's bindings as if they were tissue paper. God is going to make a forced strike on the Enemy. I know. I've seen God do it and, believe me, it is awesome to watch. Miracle. Once it happens in your heart, it becomes testimony and this enables God to do more strikes on the Enemy both in your own heart and from the testimony to others to rescue their hearts from the Enemy. You will be astonished at what happens.

Recognize the Kairos Moments

If you start your day with that intimacy with Him, try to be desperate and bold enough to ask God to astonish you. Since God loves you very much and really wants to show you what He is doing, you should expect to be astonished. God will give you a *kairos* moment—maybe several of them— in the course of the day. We will look more at these windows of opportunity in Chapter 17. The problem is whether you can recognize them when they come. We are often so busy with our agenda that when God surprises us with joy and that moment comes, we don't even see it. We miss the joy. Take the joy.

Teach them to Your Kids

We are commanded (it is not an option) to share with our kids the commands God has given us and the stories that happened when we acted in faith.

Only take heed to yourself, and diligently keep yourself, lest you forget the things your eyes have seen, and lest they depart from your heart all the days of your life. And teach them to your children and your grandchildren,

Deuteronomy 4:9

Praise God

Going into the battle, you should praise God. While you are fighting, praise God. Once the battle is over (and before the next one) praise God for what He has done. Tell the story over and over again. The Enemy doesn't like praise music and stories and he will flee.

Taking a Leap of Faith

The life of Jesus tells us many stories about those He healed having to take the first leap of faith. The audacity of the faith Jesus asks for! One of my favorite stories is the healing of the ten lepers in Luke 17:11-19. The lepers would have been standing outside the city as Jesus was entering. It was illegal for the lepers to be in the city. Jesus did not speak the healing, but rather said for them to go show themselves to the priests. They were still lepers, and Jesus was asking them to enter the city (break the law) to go to the priests. The lepers had to take the first step of faith. The scripture says they were healed *as they went.* The priests would then have the responsibility of pronouncing them well. Only one of the lepers returned after the healing—a Samaritan. There are many stories like this in both the Old and New Testament. What step of faith is God asking you to take?

Dialog

1. When did you take a logical step based on known facts? For example, taking a new job based on an objective analysis of the company you planned to work for?

2. When did you take a step of faith in which you went into the decision blindly and saw a real miracle that cannot be explained by logical analysis? What was the role of prayer in this?

3. What are you doing that requires God's intervention? What do you think God wants you to do that requires His intervention?

4. Pray for God to astonish you today. Journal what happens.

Part IV: From Vision to Reality Leadership

In this final section we will look at some key elements of reality leadership: creating chaos, leading to Place, servanthood, compassion, and community. These are not the only components of reality leadership, but these are the ones most often lost to the leader today. For this reason, we will focus on these.

As in the previous section, we will focus on Nehemiah and see how he led from these same components.

Chapter 11: Leading to Reality: Upsetting the Equilibrium

Stay, thou are so fair.

Faust, speaking to the current moment and losing his soul in his decision.

Nothing changes until you upset what is, until you show people that where they are, the status quo, isn't working. People build a comfort zone, an illusion, so they don't have to change. They distort facts, lie, and ignore the facts—anything but change from where they are. The leader must upset the equilibrium; that is, create (and what appears to be) chaos. The new leader speaks and acts into the existing order, upsetting what is and creating chaos. This forces the "system" to reorder to a higher ordered system. This doesn't make sense from our older leadership models; yet there is a new and higher order that emerges from the disorder. The leader is not doing this just for the sake of creating chaos. Rather, the leader is drawing the followers to a new Place. People still trapped in the illusion see what the leader is doing as noise. There is a paradigm blindness on the part of those lost to the leader's vision.

When the Good News of the Gospel is alive in any person, whatever their kind of work may be, they become an inventive, searching, daring, self-expressive creature. He or she becomes interesting to other people. They disturb, upset, enlighten, and open ways for better understanding.

In the new paradigm, once the vision is put down (and continues to be put down), the leader then focuses energy not so much in planning, putting down programs, building structures, and evaluating; but rather the leader focuses on building relationships (networks, linkages, dynamic connectedness), and releases. There is no control. The result appears to the leader (and even the followers) as non-deterministic; but it really does have a pattern. Trying to control will distort the pattern.

Look what Nehemiah did. Families were given personal visions of building the wall near their house. The leader moves the vision down and involves followers in the shaping of the vision as they see it and their role in it. If you are building the wall near your house, of course you want that part of the wall as strong as possible. You are going to network with neighbors and others (building relationships) to find out how to do that. Community begins to happen.

Compare this concept with what Jesus did. The Church, when it was birthed, moved through the culture and upset everything; but we know almost nothing of the early church organizational structure and programs. And buildings? They met in homes.

I like the part in *The Shack*[1] where Sarayu (the Holy Spirit) takes Mack out to the Garden. The garden is very beautiful, but is described as "chaos in color". Some flower groups were blasting through random vegetables and herbs. Confusing, stunning, and beautiful. Sarayu tells Mack that, from above, the garden appears as a fractal; that is, there is really an order to what seems to him as chaos. As the day progresses, Sarayu tells Mack that the garden is really his own soul. We tend to see the beauty but lack, without the Holy Spirit, to see the real order in why God created us just the way He did and what purpose for which God created us. What the leader sees will look like chaos for those outside the vision.

The leader has to be a very secure person to lead from the new reality. What happens is very threatening not only to those he or she is trying to lead, but to the leader as well. What if they don't follow? What if God doesn't act? The leader has to believe that he or she is on God's vision and then trust in faith that God will make it happen. The leader sees things others don't see. Hears things others don't hear.

Margaret Wheatley, in her classic book *Leadership and the New Science*, shows how the old concept of leadership no longer works. Just as quantum physics gives us a non-deterministic world at the micro level, the larger world is also non-deterministic from a secular perspective. The leader has to lead from a different perspective. In fact, the leader has to create what seems to be chaos. He or she has to upset the equilibrium. **Change doesn't take place unless the leader can show that the present structure and status quo is not working.** This upsets those who follow, and then change can be initiated. The change will not take place until the people are desperate enough.

Jesus was a leader, but what He did was definitely upsetting to those around Him—even to the disciples and religious leaders. He upset the equilibrium. Look at His teachings:

- Losing is Finding
- Weakness is Strength
- Last is First
- Giving is Receiving
- Serving is Ruling
- Dying is Living
- Least is Greatest
- Poor is Rich
- Lose Your Life and You Will Find It

Definitely seems contradictory to "what is" or the status quo. Yet this is the *only* leadership model that will work today.

Now let's look at an example of a leader upsetting the equilibrium.

The Ski Story

A dear friend, Toni, asked me a few years after that Gullain-Barré Syndrome if I wanted to go skiing with her. She didn't ask if I could go, she asked if I *wanted* to go. Those are two *very* different questions. Notice that she was speaking to my heart. The leader must understand where the heart is of those being led and speak to that if anything is going to be changed. Toni was speaking faith into me where I had none. But I had to act on her faith or I wouldn't be able to see it. This is faith projection. She was sending an arrow strategically into my damaged heart. An arrow to heal it.

Before the GBS I used to ski every weekend during the winter and had even skied in the challenging mountains of Colorado. Back then I had managed the parallel turns on the intermediate slopes at Vail. Now, however, this was post-GBS and even walking was a miracle. Skiing?

"Sure, I'll go" I said. My ankles were still quite weak, and those ankles are very important for balance in walking. I still fell often. Toni mentioned that skiing should still work for me because the boots were tall and would make up for some ankle weakness. The quads were also weak. I had not skied in at least five years.

"Meet me Saturday at 8 a.m. at my place," she said.

"OK."

I tried an experiment at my house. I put on my old skis and boots. I took the poles. I then sat on the floor and tried to get up. I couldn't. My quads were too weak to lift me. So I'm going to go out there and if I fall I won't be able to get up. I then decided I would go and just rent some cross-country skis. Try the cross-country trails while Toni and her kids were skiing downhill. When I got tired, I'd rest in the lounge until they were ready to go home. I'd get some good exercise. I called my prayer warriors to let them know of my plans and asked them for prayers for my cross-country skiing. Their first response was, "Carl, are you nuts?" Then they prayed.

We drove up to the ski area early that Saturday and I stood in line at the ticket window with Toni. When it was my turn I asked for a map of the cross-country trails and where I could rent the equipment. The guy behind the window said there were no cross-country trails there and they had no equipment for that type of trails. I turned to Toni.

"What you gonna do?" she challenged."Sit in the lodge all day or downhill?"

"Downhill, of course." I replied. I bought my downhill ticket.

I soon had my boots and skis on and heading out the door of the rental building. After I went about 20 feet, I fell in the snow. Just like I predicted. I tried to get up. I couldn't. Just like I predicted. Toni tried to help me up, but she couldn't. I was helpless. I was getting to be a pretty good prophet; but that wasn't helping me now. Now what do I do? I made several attempts to get up and nothing worked.

I then remember looking into her eyes in desperation (there's that word again). Her eyes changed and there was a single command coming from her lips.

"Get up!"

The next think I knew, I was standing. My head was spinning. I was very astonished—more like shocked. I was trying to figure out what had just happened, because I probably would need it again in a few minutes. All I remember was a single command from her.

I stumbled over to the rope tow to start, trying to remember how I had skied before. I used to do parallel turns. Now it would be the rope tow and snowplows if I could even do that. The rope was moving, and I moved in place. I grasped the rope as it jerked me from my standing position to carry me up the hill. After about thirty feet I lost my balance and fell in the snow. I tried to roll away from the rope so the person coming behind me could get by. Then I heard a scream from my friend.

"Grab the rope, Carl! Grab the rope! He's holding them back 'til you get back on!"

The guy running the rope had not let anyone else on. I grabbed the rope again and it took me to the top.

At the top I started the horizontal run across the slope to pick up the energy for the parallel turn at the other edge. The turn did not work, however, as there was not enough muscle in the ankles and feet to lift me out of the snow for the turn. My body turned to face the direction for the return trip, but the feet could not clear the snow for the turn. I fell again, but picked myself up. I also realized I would have to resort to the snowplow for now. I made my way on down the slope zigzagging with something halfway between the snowplow and parallel turns (mostly snowplows) with Toni watching at the bottom. I would fall at each turn, pick myself up, and then would do the next leg of the zigzag down the hill. I was determined to do the parallel turn, but the feet would not cooperate. Then I hit the rope again and repeated the cycle. I think I set some type of Guinness records for the most falls going down the slope backwards and the number of falls in one run. But I was skiing again. Praise God! Toni watched me for awhile from the bottom of the slope; but she soon disappeared. I kept on trying, over and over again.

Toni returned at lunch time and we had lunch together; then we were all back to the slopes. She and her kids skied with me a while, then they went up the big slopes again. I was out there all day.

As I climbed in the car with her at the end of the day and we started back down the mountain, I was on a major adrenaline rush. I had skied. Primitive, but I had skied again— and all day. She was trying to tell me she was planning to stop for dinner with some friends before going home and asked if that was OK. She could have said we're going to go bungee jumping off the back side of Mt. Hood. Any challenge. Nothing was impossible.

The house where we stopped for dinner was the house of the parents of one of the kids with us that day. As we entered the house for dinner, I was gushing about what I had done that day. I was still on my adrenaline rush. Toni stopped me.

"No," she said. "Tell them the whole story."

Toni wanted me to share with the people who did not know the Lord what God had done in my life—starting with the healing of the GBS.

In this story you see a guy who had not skied in over five years just starting to walk again approximately four years after a paralysis where he was told he would never walk again. He had no vision of skiing again, but took the risk. You see someone else who was not forcing anything in her leadership, but was simply putting down a field that upset my equilibrium. Toni was creating Place and I bought into it. God honored my risk and it became testimony. Toni believed, then saw me skiing before I believed and saw myself skiing again. She led me from her belief. She held me accountable to the vision she believed and saw. She upset my equilibrium. She did *faith projection*.

Want more of the story? Remember, she disappeared after seeing me navigating the slopes that morning. At lunch that day she asked me if I wanted to know where she went after she disappeared.

"The kid who came with us?" Toni said. "He's a friend of my son. I took him up on the chair lift to the highest point on the mountain. It's icy up there and lots of moguls. I made a snowplow with my skis, put him in back of me between my skis, and carried him over the icy moguls up there at a very high speed."

"Do you know what you just did?" I asked.

"What?"

"Once you have taken that kid over those icy moguls up there at a very high speed, he will never be happy on the bunny slopes again."

"Yes." Toni continued, "We take a different kid with us almost every time and teach them to ski this way, with their arms around me. They get so excited that they often just take off skiing with the other kids in about 15 minutes. The kids want their friends to enjoy the fun and excitement with them.

"And I'll tell you something else." I said. "If we let him, Jesus will take us high up on the mountain and carry us over the icy moguls of life. Once He has done that with us, we will never be happy on the spiritual bunny slopes again."

This same kid came to the Lord at a Youth Conference with Toni and me at a nearby fairground not too many months later.

The leader is not so much creating a force as creating a field or Place and letting others choose to come into it. Remember the story of Amelia and George in Chapter 5, "The Illusion of the Lost Place"? Amelia's illusion left her with a bound heart with no doorknob on the outside. George created Place outside of that heart that upset the equilibrium, creating a field (Place), and she eventually opened her heart and let him in.

Remember also that the leader is not creating chaos for the sake of creating chaos. **The leader is putting down and living into a certain field or Place, a mission given from *Yahweh*— a very personal God.** It is that very field or Place that is disruptive to the current place *from which* those who follow must move. This leading also involves compassion and servanthood from the leader. If the leader tries to lead from his or her own agenda, they will fail. For this reason there must be a deep sense of intimacy between the leader and God. The leader must know the heart of God. The leader must also know the heart of those he or she is leading.

How Biblical Leaders Upset the Equilibrium

The Bible shows many examples of Biblical leaders upsetting the equilibrium and creating what appeared to be chaos to lead people to a higher order. It seemed to be a favorite game with God and those leaders.

Moses destroyed the entire Egyptian economic system and

led a nation to freedom. Even after leaving Egypt, the Israelites didn't want to change, griping constantly, and at times begged Moses to lead them back to Egypt. What Moses did with them in Egypt was not only disruptive to the Egyptians, but to where the Israelites were as well. When Pharaoh got angry with the persistence of Moses, Pharaoh made the Israelites work to build their bricks without straw. A very clever trick, as it turned the Israelites against Moses. Moses had to continually return to the Lord for directions, as getting the nation out of Egypt certainly did not look feasible. Moses worked to deepen his relationship with God, and at one point even asked to see a full view of *Yahweh's* Glory (Exodus 33:18). God honored his request. Twice Moses spent forty days alone with God.

Another leader upsetting the status quo was Nehemiah. He left a privileged position in the king's court to go back to Jerusalem and lead a nation with no vision, passion, purpose, or security. Nothing but depression at Jerusalem. He upset the status quo of the Israelites in Jerusalem, leading them back in 52 days to the chosen nation God had called them to be.

In the New Testament we see the Apostle Paul after his conversion leading the early Church in taking the Gospel to the Gentiles, upsetting a major Jewish illusion. Here was a guy who had been running around in very high places leading in the persecution and killing of the Christians. Now he has to convince the disciples and Jewish leaders that he has seen the risen Lord, the Lord had saved him, their mindset is wrong, and the Gospel is for everyone—including the Gentiles.

Later, in Acts 17, we see three specific areas Paul was visiting and what happened at each of these. Notice how Paul was upsetting the equilibrium. At Thessalonica, he met with them in the synagogue, and you see there was a mixture of Jews and Greeks. The Jews were probably well-schooled in their theology, and what Paul said about Jesus was very threatening to them. It upset their equilibrium. To the Greeks, however, this was fresh and they could accept it. The Jews set the city in an uproar and the Greeks had to help Paul get safely out of town. I like what the rabble-rousers there were chanting:

> *"Those who have turned the world upside down have come here too."*

Acts 17:6b

Paul goes on to Berea and found a better reception there in their synagogue. The Bible says those at Berea were more noble than those at Thessalonica. Soon, however, the rabble-rousers from Thessalonica came down to Berea and were stirring up the people there.

Paul goes on to Athens and notice the strategy at Athens. The Gospel, whenever presented, must be presented in terms of the needs of the people. Jesus always brought the Gospel in terms of the felt needs of the heart. While Paul is waiting in Athens for his friends, he does a lot of spiritual mapping. What are the needs of these Athenians? They had a lot of gods. They even had a statue to an "unknown god" in case they missed one. They were very spiritual, but had missed the reality—the real God. We don't see Paul in a synagogue. Paul stands in the public meeting place—the Areopagus. As he starts speaking, he first complements them on saying that he perceives in everything they are very religious. He references the statues of the gods, and then mentions their statue to the unknown god. Then he continues by saying "let me tell you about this unknown God". By the time Paul had finished, he had believers. Again, Paul was upsetting their equilibrium.

And then there was Jesus. He really upset things. His whole life and teaching echoed this. Look how He started His ministry with a bold vision statement.

> *The Spirit of the LORD is upon Me, because He has anointed Me*
> *To preach the gospel to the poor;*
> *He has sent Me to heal the brokenhearted,*
> *To proclaim liberty to the captives And recovery of sight to*

the blind,
To set at liberty those who are oppressed;
To proclaim the acceptable year of the LORD.

Luke 4:18-19

This is not the Messiah they were expecting.

After the coming of the Holy Spirit, the disciples and other followers began birthing the Church and there was a great upsetting of the Jewish religion. It was the Holy Spirit, working through Peter, who healed the lame man at the temple gate.

And he took him by the right hand and lifted him up, and immediately his feet and ankle bones received strength. So he, leaping up, stood and walked and entered the temple with them—walking, leaping, and praising God. And all the people saw him walking and praising God. Then they knew that it was he who sat begging alms at the Beautiful Gate of the temple; and they were filled with wonder and amazement at what had happened to him.

Acts 3:7-10

And that was only the beginning. God is still bringing the Kingdom today through His leaders. My ski friend did it with me. George did it with Amelia.

Conclusion

The leader is boldly taking those who follow into a Place they have not been. To do this, he or she must first show them that where they are is not the reality. He must disturb their status quo, upset "what is". This is very radical and involves risk on the part of both the leader and those who are following. The leader must be on God's agenda. To see and hear that agenda, there must be a very personal relationship of the leader with God.

And so I insist—and God backs me up on this—that there be no going along with the crowd, the empty-headed, mindless crowd. They've refused for so long to deal with God that they've lost touch not only with God but with reality itself. They can't think straight anymore.

Ephesians 4:17-19 *THE MESSAGE*

Notes:

1. Young, William. *The Shack*. (Newbury Park, CA: Windblown Media, 2007)

Dialog:

1. Who has upset your status quo recently? What did they ask you to change or risk? What did they do?

2. How did you feel about it?

3. Who have you challenged to change? What did they do?

4. How did you feel about it?

Chapter 12: Leading to Place and Vision

The Kingdom of Heaven is like…

Jesus

Most Christians repent enough to be forgiven,
but not enough to see the Kingdom.

Bill Johnson, *When Heaven Invades Earth*

The leader (and that is you) has to lead people (or a person) to a Place that the leader believes in and can already see as reality. Yet those being led can often neither believe in nor see the Place—yet. The Place is very real, but is only an illusion to those who have yet to believe or see it. How can the leader take those who follow to that Place?

Jesus faced the same challenge with those He was trying to lead and even today as He reaches in love to win your heart. One word of warning as we begin. You will never see what the leader sees unless you put your whole weight into the relationship. In Chapter 10 (*The Audacity of Faith*), we saw faith is based on a relationship. To see what the leader sees you must rest in the relationship. There is no other way. The risk is incredible. Whether it is a church you are thinking about joining as a member or a relationship with a lover, the principle is the same. Without the risk of putting your whole weight into the relationship you will never see what the leader sees.

Jesus never defined what this Kingdom of Heaven (Place) was and is. It was always "the Kingdom of Heaven is like..." . Jesus led by telling stories about what this Kingdom of Heaven (Place) was like. In doing this He put down a "field" that drew the followers into that Place. At times He referred to Heaven as the Place ("I go to prepare a Place for you...") . The stories Jesus told made it clear that this Kingdom of Heaven (Place) is not only past or future tense, but right here and now.

> *Another parable He put forth to them, saying: "The kingdom of heaven is like a mustard seed, which a man took and sowed in his field which indeed is the least of all the seeds; but when it is grown it is greater than the herbs and becomes a tree, so that the birds of the air come and nest in its branches."*

Matthew13:31-32

> *Another parable He spoke to them: "The kingdom of heaven is like leaven, which a woman took and hid in three measures of meal till it was all leavened."*

Matthew 13:33

> *Again, the kingdom of heaven is like treasure hidden in a field, which a man found and hid; and for joy over it he goes and sells all that he has and buys that field.*

Matthew 13:44

> *Again, the kingdom of heaven is like a merchant seeking beautiful pearls, who, when he had found one pearl of great price, went and sold all that he had and bought it.*

Matthew 13:45-46

At other times Jesus made very bold statements about this Place He was trying to lead you to.

From that time Jesus began to preach and to say, "Repent, for the kingdom of heaven is at hand."

Matthew 4:17

Blessed are the poor in spirit,
For theirs is the kingdom of heaven.

Matthew 5:3

Blessed are those who are persecuted for righteousness' sake,
For theirs is the kingdom of heaven.

Matthew 5:10

And as you go, preach, saying, "The kingdom of heaven is at hand." Heal the sick, cleanse the lepers, raise the dead, cast out demons. Freely you have received, freely give.

Matthew 10:7-8

And I will give you the keys of the kingdom of heaven, and whatever you bind on earth will be bound in heaven, and whatever you loose on earth will be loosed in heaven.

Matthew 16:19

Then Jesus called a little child to Him, set him in the midst of them, and said, "Assuredly, I say to you, unless you are converted and become as little children, you will by no means enter the kingdom of heaven."

Matthew 18:2-4

Wow! These were very bold statements. These refer to a Place that is here/now. They upset "what is". Unless those He was trying to lead could embrace and step into this Place with their *whole* heart, they could never see the reality of which Jesus spoke.

Notice there is no force on the part of the leader and the way Jesus led. He was living and speaking into this Kingdom, Place, or Field as if it was reality—and it was. Then He let the people choose. If Place was bold and strong enough, they may choose to believe and come into it. Then they could see the reality of what they could not see before. Crowds followed Him because they wanted to be where He was. He could only be at one place at a time. Wherever that was, something was happening. Wherever Jesus was became Place.

Once Jesus died and rose, He left to return to His Father. At the same time, He left the Holy Spirit to continue His work. He also left the Church, the Body of Christ, to do His work. The Holy Spirit is omnipotent. It can come anywhere people are desperate enough. The Kingdom work is no longer limited to a single location at a time. It can come into your own heart right now if you ask God for it.

Leading from Place

The leader's task is to seek the Kingdom, declare what is found, and then give it away! (Jack Taylor).

The leader leads by creating a field and leading from that Place at any cost. The leader embraces it and lives from it as reality. This creates what appears to be a force; but the force is only an illusion.[1] It cost Jesus His life. And John the Baptist. And most of the apostles. Then Jesus died on the cross. What is different in this story is that Jesus rose from the dead. That changed the direction of history. Then the Holy Spirit came at Pentecost and the Church was birthed. Then we see the healing of the lame man and the religious leaders are arresting Peter, a poor fisherman, for the healing of this lame man. The Kingdom of Heaven came and those present believed and experienced Place.

There is a wonderful objective equation that describes some of what the leader does and this is now known as a part of Gleicher's Change Theory.[2] It can be expressed as:

Dissatisfaction X *First Steps* X *Vision* > *Resistance to Change*

In looking at this equation, let me first be open in saying I don't like equations and even Einstein found no basis for a deterministic universe. The universe is deterministic, however, in one very real sense. It is not fate—there is an agenda at play. There is a war going on, and God will win. As Eric McManus says, whenever God is involved, the epilogue is not mysterious. God wins. His Kingdom will be established. God loves you and wants you part of this Kingdom Enterprise. Those are given facts. We really are in a deterministic universe. God determines it. God eventually wins. Keeping that in mind, let's return to this equation and see what we can learn from it.

First, those being led must have a desperateness (dissatisfaction) about their current place. The leader then must put down a bold vision or field or Place as a destination. Then the leader must begin to live into this at whatever cost (first steps). All of these must be under the authority and power of the Holy Spirit, with the leader responding from a calling and from his or her own spiritual gifts. In addition, nothing will happen unless these variables on the left are greater than the resistance of those being led. The bindings in those being led must be broken, and this takes the power of the Holy Spirit. Notice that the operators in the equation are multiplication signs, not plus signs. If any one of the three variables on the left is missing or close to zero, the change is unlikely to happen. All three must be there.

Now let's look for a minute at each of these. Before I start, however, look at one fact. Although it does not appear that way, the leader *does* have authority on what is on the right of the equation. If there are bindings there, the leader can pray for the Holy Spirit to reveal them to you and then you can break those by naming these specifically and claiming healing over them in the name of Jesus. Since God wants those bindings broken, you can expect with certainty that God will reveal where these are. I've seen this happen. It does take love, patience, and compassion, however. Sometimes a lot of it.

The leader's additional option is to make the variables on the left strong enough to burst through the resistance and make the change happen. On the left, let's look at what control the leader has with each of these.

Dissatisfaction

You might first think that this variable of dissatisfaction is outside of the leader's control. Quite the contrary. Church growth researchers today in America tell me it is rare to see in America's churches what those people following Jesus back then saw or what those apostles saw in the early church. For many people today, what people of the early church saw happening remains an illusion in their own church today and in the world about them. Yet in many places today the Holy Spirit is coming with far, far more power than I saw even when a volcano blew near my city. The problem is not that the Holy Spirit is not working today; it is our mindset and our own distortion of reality. We live in an illusion. The leader *has to lead the people out of that illusion. Once you have experienced what is really happening wherever* these fires are birthing, then you become dissatisfied with your old spiritual place and will risk anything to see the fires where you live.

It is not so much that we live in a post-Christian world; but rather we live in a post-secular world. People are experiencing the growing failure of our materialist and secular world that has gone bankrupt. Secular studies in my own city identify a primary need for meeting a strong spiritual hunger that is already there. I see this hunger even stronger in the younger generations who will need to be the coming leaders in this bankrupt world. At many conferences I attend, I see the spiritual hippies who go from fire to fire until the fire consumes them with the reality of what the Church is really all about.

How does a leader lead from this? Some years ago now I watched Tom Sine, a Christian futurist, leading workshops using a certain strategy and watched what happened as a result. He would begin the first evening with a keynote address with the primary purpose of shattering our vision of "what is". In a bold message he predicted *exactly* what we are seeing today—years after he led those early workshops I attended. Then Tom would break us into small groups based on various minivisions that we could choose from using a list he gave us.

Here are two examples from the list of two such possible minivison groups paraphrased from Tom Sine:

Urban Evangelism 2009

In view of the increasing secularization of the culture of the city, create an imaginative program of evangelism to reach the "hidden people" in your city. Use any of the new technologies and available resources that you can find.

Single Parent 2009

In view of the increasing number of single parent households in our culture, create a way in which your church family can:

- Include these households in the larger community of the church
- Provide support for both single parents and their children in all areas of their life and growth
- Involve the spiritual gifts of these families in the ministry of the church.

Once we chose our group, we had to start thinking what the vision for our group was really about and planning how to make the vision happen within a ten year period (the time line would be much shorter today). We had to start with no money (the economic system is bankrupt), a broken medical system, a humanistic educational system, failed political system—you get the idea. In the course of the weekend, we had to plan the whole process of getting each minivision operational. Tom worked with us, and each group posted their results on large butcher paper on the walls so you could see the synergy of everything that was happening as we went. At the end of the day we would walk out of the workshop; but if any of those little minivisions burned a real passion in the heart of any participant, the fire would be lit and something would happen. In some cases a participant might leave the conference with a personal minivision that wasn't on Tom's list. Now they had the dream to birth their own vision and had the confidence to start making it happen.

I watched Tom do this at a leading Christian college with students who were ready to change the world. I also watched him do it at a very conservative seminary. The initial setup was always the same—shatter the vision of what people saw as reality, then tease them with bold visions and let them dream visions to reality. What went up on the butcher paper with the two conferences was radically different. The people of which conference, do you think, were ready to make a difference? Ready to lead? Which group eventually created change in the world with viable leadership?

At the Prayer Mountain near Seoul, Korea in 1995, George Otis, Jr. shared stories of what he was seeing in his international travel. Otis did the same trick—he blasted our "what is" with stories of what God was doing today all over the world and you felt as if we were in that early Church some two thousand years ago. But it was all with here/now stories.

Later, in during December of 2006, Otis came through Portland and spoke. He said that we are at a very dark time in history; but we already knew that. A time when strange leaders have weapons of mass destruction with the intent to use them and other leaders seem powerless to stop them. When Otis did his *Transformations I* video back in 1999,[3] he had identified about 12 cities worldwide that were totally transformed by the power of God politically, socially, spiritually, and economically—any way you could measure it. Moreover, these were sustained transformations involving the entire city that continued there over time. This week he said the count is now over 250 cities and growing very rapidly. This is not just revival, but a supernatural outpouring of the Holy Spirit with stories you would not believe unless you knew the Holy Spirit. George spent the evening telling us some of the stories. Moreover, he had identified some over 500 places that you might call "salty places" where the fires have begun to burn and already have begun to explode. Like an appetizer for a meal, in these places there is already a deep hunger for the main course.

Moreover, Otis said taking our coffee into the Sunday Service and doing our chit-chat isn't going to do what needs to happen. It won't happen until there is a deep, deep, deep hunger for the coming of the Holy Spirit. In these cities where the fires broke people became desperate for spiritual awaking. Then the Holy Spirit came. Moreover, here is a stunning quote from Otis:

> *The greatest breakthrough today is where the Spirit of God comes down and attaches Himself to the broken and humble. It's where God goes when He wants pleasure.*

Vision

Soon after the completion of Disney World in Orlando someone said, "Isn't it too bad Walt Disney didn't live to see this!" Mike Vance, creative director of Disney Studios replied. "He did see it—that's why it's here."

Or think of Beethoven's Ninth Symphony and the beautiful "Ode to Joy" in it, written by a deaf Beethoven. But he *did* hear it. That's why we have it.

The leader has to put down a bold vision that strikes and draws passion in the very heart of those being led.

> *The power of transcendent vision is greater than the power of the scripting deep inside the human personality and it*

> *subordinates it [the scripting], submerges it, until the whole*
> *personality is reorganized in the accomplishment of that*
> *vision.*

Stephen Covey, *First Things First*

To quote Tom Sine, one of the reasons our personal faith has so little authority in changing the world about us is that we have never really fully connected with God's transcendent vision.

> *If you want to build a ship,*
> *don't summon people to buy wood, prepare tools,*
> *distribute jobs and organize the work;*
> *teach people the yearning for the wide, boundless ocean.*

Antoine de Saint-Exupery, *The Little Prince*

In other words, lead from Place.

The vision has to be clear—or those trying to follow will not see or hear it. How does one describe a sunset to a blind person who has never seen one? Jesus used stories.

Of course, the issue of leadership is much more than this simple equation. The leader also has to maintain communication within the culture ("place") of those he or she is trying to lead. Jesus used many agricultural analogies and other simple stories that the people of his time could relate to as well as using simple objects in the stories such as seeds and coins.

For the moment, however, let's look at some biblical examples of leaders who led from creating bold fields, or Place. We have already mentioned Christ and showed some of how He led from vision and fields, but what about other biblical leaders? How did they do this?

Moses is one classic example who we have already mentioned. He had to lead a rebellious nation through a desert to some kind of Promised Land. They had nothing to eat but manna for their journey and water was a scarce commodity. Over and over again they told Moses they wanted to return to the slavery they had left and even created an orgy to entertain themselves while Moses left them to receive the Ten Commandments. How did Moses lead them? The classic strategy is shown in Deuteronomy 11. In this incredible message he first tells them how God had honored them in the past with Place and His Presence. Then Moses told them how God was working with them in the present time. Finally, Moses gave them a vision about where they are going with God. And this was not a one-shot message. Moses constantly lived and breathed this message to them as they traveled through the desert.

What about Nehemiah? You see friends coming to him with a story about what they had seen in Jerusalem. The people of Jerusalem were depressed, without vision, purpose, security, passion, and certainly lost to any mission of themselves as a nation to which God had called them. Nehemiah had to go into that darkness and lead them out of that. He had to have a vision, strategy (first steps), funding base, support from King, and more. And the wall was built in 52 days.

Or Isaiah? Over and over again Isaiah described the coming Christ in great detail. Isaiah gives us the purist picture of the coming Christ, and it is bolder than even the Jews could accept. It is from Isaiah 61:1-2 that Jesus quotes in the synagogue early in His ministry. This was the vision statement that defined the life of Christ, and should be the vision statement for the Church, as the Body of Christ, today.

> *So He came to Nazareth, where He had been brought up. And as His custom was, He went into the synagogue on the Sabbath day, and stood up to read. And He was handed the book of the prophet Isaiah. And when He had opened the book, He found the place where it was written:*
>
> *"The Spirit of the LORD is upon Me,*
> *Because He has anointed Me*
> *To preach the gospel to the poor;*

> *He has sent Me to heal the brokenhearted,*
> *To proclaim liberty to the captives*
> *And recovery of sight to the blind,*
> *To set at liberty those who are oppressed;*
> *To proclaim the acceptable year of the LORD."*

> *Then He closed the book, and gave it back to the attendant*
> *and sat down. And the eyes of all who were in the synagogue*
> *were fixed on Him. And He began to say to them, "Today*
> *this Scripture is fulfilled in your hearing."*

Luke 4:14-21

Now look at your own life. What is the vision God is calling you to embrace? What burden do you have that drives this vision? What promises has God given you relative to this vision?

Core values are another factor important to the vision. Core values are the attitudes and beliefs that are held by an individual, organization, or nation. They are the foundation for behavior. *You should never sacrifice the core values for the sake of the vision.* Always hold on to the core values. Once the leader violates the core values of the group, organization or the nation, he or she has lost their leadership. And it is almost impossible to get it back.

The First Steps

The leader has to take the first steps. The initial risk is always on the part of the leader.

- Moses took the first step in rescuing the Israelites as he went back to Egypt and stood before Pharaoh.
- Nehemiah took his first steps as he negotiated with the King for financing and other resources before starting out through hostile territory to Jerusalem.
- Esther took her first steps as she asked the king to release her nation.

- The Apostle Paul took his first steps as he went to Jerusalem to share with the Jewish leaders about his conversion. Barnabas took his first steps when he supported Paul, who had been persecuting the Christians, in Paul's early faith.
- In I Samuel 14, King Saul and Jonathan were the only two of 600 Israelites with weapons as they faced a battle with the Philistines who possessed advanced metal technology. King Saul is sleeping under a Pomegranate tree. Jonathan wakes up in the night, wakes his armorbearer, and says he is going to take the Philistines on and "maybe God will help us". Jonathan takes the first step against impossible odds, and with his armorbearer slays 20 Philistines within a few minutes. An earthquake hits, and the noise then finally wakes up King Saul, and the Philistines are routed.

Other biblical leaders who took the first steps against all odds include Nicodemus, Zacchaeus, Ruth, and Rahab.

We have to take the first step as if there were no God. It is no use to wait for God to help us. He will not; but immediately if we arise we find He is there.

Oswald Chambers

Where are you taking the first step in your life? Maybe you aren't Jonathan facing the Philistines with impossible odds, but what about that lunch you had with a friend who wasn't a Christian? Did you share your story with your friend? Did you tell her about Jesus and what He has done for you? Did you tell her what it's like to have a personal relationship with God? Did you take that risk? Leadership involves being able to take that first step. Remember the ski story in that last chapter? Toni first challenged me to take that first step in skiing. Later that day as we had dinner with the family she encouraged me again to take a first step in sharing my faith with them.

When I was growing up in North Carolina, I loved the crape

myrtle tree. I could pull a bud off the tree that had yet to bloom, squeeze it in my fingers, and watch the bud pop open and "bloom".

"Hey, look!" I would scream with God-like authority, "I can make it bloom!"

Of course, I couldn't really make it bloom. And the "bloom" would fall to the ground and soon die, as the bud in my hand was no longer connected to the tree that could provide nutrients and life. The buds on the tree would soon burst into bloom on their own as soon as the pain of embracing the change and bursting forth was less than the pain of remaining trapped as the bud, and then you would see the beauty they were destined to show. And once the bud on the tree burst, that new bloom would stay on the tree, fed by nutrients and life.

And the day came when the risk to remain tight in a bud was more painful than the risk it took to blossom.

Anais Nin

When George Otis, Jr. began his research on what God is doing, he eventually released the now-famous Transformations videos.[4] The first video shows the total transformation of four cities from the power of the Holy Spirit. In reality, Otis was beginning to see these same fires breaking in city after city. He then began research on what each of the transformations shared in common. What were the common factors that led to each? He eventually published his results in a book.[5] Although he identified five factors that were the key factors, two of these appeared in every single story:

- Persevering Leadership
- Fervent, united prayer.

In almost every case, the change in the entire city was led from only one or two people who held the vision and were willing to take the first steps and risk to make the vision happen. In one story on the video there is a martyr. These leaders were willing to risk anything, even their life if necessary, to see the vision happen. And the vision did happen.

Nehemiah and Leading from Place

We see the dissatisfaction of the people from the report from Nehemiah's friends to him at the beginning of Nehemiah. We see him take the first steps in approaching the king and mobilizing resources and security. And once there he had a very specific vision (Place) and began to mobilize them by first working with the primary influencers, the gatekeepers of the people. Then he mobilized the larger nation through the influencers by striking at their hearts and felt needs.

> *Then I said to them, "You see the distress that we are in, how Jerusalem lies waste, and its gates are burned with fire. Come and let us build the wall of Jerusalem, that we may no longer be a reproach." And I told them of the hand of my God which had been good upon me, and also of the king's words that he had spoken to me.*
>
> *So they said, "Let us rise up and build." Then they set their hands to this good work.*

Nehemiah 2:17-18

The Authority of Leadership

There is another interesting factor about this equation when we look at the Church today. We often think we have very little influence in healing the wounds and hurts about us and creating the kind of Place that Christ talked about. *This is really an illusion on the part of the leader.* The leader is often trapped by an illusion, often as much or more than those he or she is trying to lead. By the death and resurrection of Christ, Christ's authority is again restored on the earth. The Holy Spirit acts today with each variable on both the left and the right sides of that equation to bring the Kingdom of Heaven right here on earth in the here/now. Paul spoke of this in Romans referring to the Israelites and their inability to see what God had done and was doing, quoting the prophet Isaiah.

> *Just as it is written:*
> *"God has given them a spirit of stupor,*
> *Eyes that should not see*
> *and ears that they should not hear,*
> *To this very day."*
>
> Romans 11:8

Many of us are just like those Israelites. In other words, if the leader is hearing from God and understands what God is doing—seeing it as reality—there is nothing stopping it from being accomplished if we believe. The Israelites could not see what God was doing as they stood on the edge of that Promised Land. There was too much resistance from them for God to use them. God's intention to take the land did not change. Moses interceded before God and the next generation went in. We must pray for God to send His Holy Spirit to discover our own personal bindings, then pray for the power of the Holy Spirit to release these so we can see and hear.

Notes:

1. Gravity is generally perceived as a force; but in reality Einstein showed gravity to be a field, a bending in space/time itself. In the same way, the leader is not using force; but in reality creating Place, a bending in space and time.
2. This formula is attributed to David Gleicher (cited in Beckhard, R. & Harris, R. (1987). Organizational Transitions. Reading, MA: Addison-Wesley).
3. For more information and recent reports, see: http://www.

sentinelgroup.org. Order the transformation DVDs if you haven't seen these.

4. *Ibid.*

5. Otis Jr., George. *Informed Intercession.* (Renew Books: Ventura, CA). 1999.

Dialog

1. Read Joshua 1. What is the vision God gave Joshua? What promises did God give Joshua? Any promise of prosperity? What risk could the Israelites expect with their vision?

2. What leaders in the Bible had visions who touched your heart?

3. What is the vision that God has given you? What is your burden? How does it relate to those leaders you mentioned in the second question?

4. Where is the opposition or resistance to your vision?

5. What biblical leaders were called to take first steps?

6. What contemporary leaders can you think of who took bold first steps?

7. What is a recent first step God asked you to take? Did you take it? Why or why not?

8. Can you think of a vision God is giving you? Another way to ask this is to try to identify what burden God has placed on your heart.

9. What are some first steps you can think of to make that happen?

10. What are some risks you have taken recently?

Chapter 13: Serving Leadership

If anyone desires to be first, he shall be last of all and servant of all.

Mark 9:35

But Jesus called them to Himself and said, "You know that the rulers of the Gentiles lord it over them, and those who are great exercise authority over them. Yet it shall not be so among you; but whoever desires to become great among you, let him be your servant. And whoever desires to be first among you, let him be your slave—just as the Son of Man did not come to be served, but to serve, and to give His life a ransom for many."

Matthew 20:25-28

The authentic leader leads from serving, a model that Jesus taught his disciples.

The only ones among you who will be truly happy are those who will have sought and found how to serve.

Albert Schweitzer

The Journey to Servanthood

When I was working with the local leaders for transformation in my own city, there were certain key people—bold visionaries—

that were dreaming, calling the city to prayer for the coming of the Holy Spirit throughout the entire city, and pulling the pastors together for prayer. These "John Knoxers" as we called them, were not pastors themselves. Instead, they felt called to serve the pastors; that is, to serve the city through the pastors. These "John Knoxers" have been identified in other cities and countries as defined by a quote by John Knox. Imprisoned during the late 1540's for supporting the Protestant Reformation in Scotland, Knox prayed daily, "Lord, give me Scotland, or I die". By the time he died in 1572, Scotland had been transformed and the Scottish Parliament had adopted the Reformation doctrines. Some of the first missionaries to America were from Scotland. Contemporary "John Knoxers" serve the pastors in their area, but their primary distinction and mission is that they are passionately praying and living for the coming of the Holy Spirit in their city or region.

Some of our own Portland city churches were strong and growing, some were dying. Some churches were lost to any real spiritual calling. To see the coming of the Holy Spirit, we would have to get all of these churches working together, with churches who were growing helping the struggling churches.

As I read the first chapters of Revelation and the letters to those early churches, I saw a collection of churches much like the churches of my city. Some were strong, others weak and dying. Some had lost their moorings and were following false prophets. One statement, however, was said by the angel to every single church.

> *He who has an ear, let him hear what the Spirit says to the churches.*

It didn't matter if the church was alive or dead spiritually; God was speaking to each. It was never an issue of whether or not God was speaking to that church. It was *always* a hearing problem. We realized, then, that God was speaking to each church in our city. It didn't matter where the church was spiritually. If the church was failing, it was *always* a hearing problem.

As I worked with these John Knoxers in my city, their organizational model was that of a servant leadership. These John Knoxers served the pastors. The pastors, in turn, were serving God. If the pastors did not hear and move, these John Knoxers waited and continued to pray for the coming Holy Spirit. As for myself, I was a servant to God and to these John Knoxers and I was soon taking ownership in Knox's vision myself. Nothing would happen unless the pastors heard and acted.

In one case an inner city pastor was paid by a major parachurch organization. As the larger parachurch organization fell on hard times and had to cut the inner city pastor's salary off, it was one of the megachurches in the city who picked up the salary of this pastor and enabled him to continue with his inner city pastoring. The transformation of the city is too much for one church to attempt. The churches must carry the vision together into the process, praying for the coming of the Holy Spirit to anoint all of them.

As the Holy Spirit began to move in our city, our city became a magnet that drew other pastors from across the world to see what we were doing. I remember one major conference where leading pastors and other spiritual leaders were coming to our city from all over the country. There were various sessions and workshops and it was really exciting to feel the energy as everything was going on with a vision we all shared. As one of these John Knoxers was leaving a session where he had spoken, I asked him a key question.

"These pastors who have come in—some of them are from megachurches. Some of them have big egos. Their objective is often to build up their own "kingdom". How did you explain to them what is going on here with our servant leadership model?"

"Well, Carl," he said, "I told them what I do is go around the city looking for small fires. Then I push the fires together and pour gasoline on them."

I couldn't have defined this servant leadership model any better than that.

What is a Servant?

In the Old Testament, the Hebrew word *sharat* was used of someone who performed menial tasks as part of accomplishing an overall goal. The word is used in Exodus 28:35-38 to describe Aaron's work as a minister and also in Exodus 24:18 to refer to Joshua as the assistant to Moses.

In the New Testament in the Mark 9:35 verse, the Greek word Christ used for servant was *diakonos*.

*And He sat down, called the twelve, and said to them, "If anyone desires to be first, he shall be last of all and **servant** of all."*

Mark 9:35 (emphasis added)

In the language of that time, this word referred to an attendant, a waiter, or someone who does menial tasks. With the birth of the Church, it was used to refer to a deacon, minister, or pastor.

Two Types of Leaders

Ken Blanchard and Phil Hodges in their wonderful book *The Servant Leader*, says there are basically two types of leaders: The self-serving leader and the servant leader. As we are each followers as well as leaders, you had better know which type of leaders you are following. How can you tell the servant leader from the self-serving leader?

Ken and Phil say that one test is how the leader handles feedback. Does the leader have structures to get feedback, does he or she listen to the feedback, and then how does the leader respond to this feedback. The self-serving leader is constantly trying to protect his or her agenda and authority and is really unsure inside, insecure. Anything that is negative is ignored or repudiated. There is an unbending attitude against change and those trying to upset the equilibrium. The servant leader is secure and open, building synergy in a dynamic environment, changing strategies as necessary to reach a common vision.

Another test is whether the leader serves or not. When a stranger came into our church and tried to usurp the existing leadership, I contacted a mentor to find a strategy for dealing with it. The mentor asked me a single question:

"How is he serving in the church?"

When I asked for clarification, he went on.

"Is he helping get the coffee going on Sunday? Does he help move chairs when setting up a room? Anything like that?"

"No," I said.

"Get him out of there."

A third test is how the leader trains for someone to follow him. A secure leader knows that eventually he must pass the torch, and he is constantly training others, the next generation, to pick up the torch to continue the race. The best manager I ever had at work was constantly training me to take over his job, and eventually I did take it over and became the manager myself. He moved on up in the organization; but I had high respect for him as leader. Jesus made it clear that those He was training would be able to do everything He was doing and even more. He trained them for that, and it wasn't an academic course. He took them into laboratory sessions.

The servant leader sees his or her position on loan. It is a gift. There is, however, a bit of self-serving leadership style in all of us. This is where we fail—it is the result of the Fall back with Adam and Eve. We each have to recognize that we have failed our mission at times and lead from what we have learned. The problem comes when the self-serving leader can't acknowledge to those who follow that he has failed. I know plenty of "self-called" leaders in that category. As a result of pride and fear, the leader loses his followers and never sees his or her vision. The leader must always lead from the heart and serve those who are following him or her as well as those that are a part of the larger vision.

Nehemiah knew he was on loan from the king. Even as he

began praying, you see him identifying himself to God as a servant of God.

> *And I said: "I pray, LORD God of heaven, O great and awesome God, You who keep Your covenant and mercy with those who love You and observe Your commandments, please let Your ear be attentive and Your eyes open, that You may hear the prayer of Your **servant** which I pray before You now, day and night, for the children of Israel Your **servants**, and confess the sins of the children of Israel which we have sinned against You. Both my father's house and I have sinned.*

Nehemiah 1:5-6 (emphasis added)

As he begins in Jerusalem, you can see how he leads as a servant in training the people, delegating and helping at times (Nehemiah 4:21-23). Notice that Nehemiah assumes the servant role here and, like the rest of the men, kept his clothes on and worked 24/7. Also you can see how Nehemiah ate with the Jews (Nehemiah 5:17); and it was from eating and working with them that he was able to learn of their oppression—the high interest rates charged to the poorer Jews by the wealthy Jews.

As mentioned in Chapter 11, the servant leader is putting down a vision and continues to put it down. Then the servant leader is not so much planning, putting down programs, building structures, and evaluation. Instead, the servant leader in the new paradigm is building relationships, networks, and linkages. Lots of faith projection and encouragement. Then the leader releases. There is really very little control.

Kings as Servants?

In 1 Kings 12 you see some interesting insights on servanthood. Solomon was considered by many contemporaries of his time to be the wisest king that Israel ever had. He asked God for wisdom, and God honored his request and gave him riches as well. Unfortunately, Solomon gained much of his wealth by taxing the Israelites very heavily and using slave labor. (Sounds like a lot of contemporary political "leaders" I know.) By the end of his life, Solomon was beginning to see the folly of his riches and his directions in life.

With Solomon's death, Rehoboam, his son, comes to the throne. In 1 Kings 12, you see the beginning of his reign. Rehoboam is not too good at following the Lord and had turned to idol worship. Another Israelite leader, Jeroboam, had experienced a falling out with Solomon and had escaped to Egypt. With Solomon dead, Jeroboam returns to Israel and comes with an assembly of the Israelites to request the new king to remove the heavy yoke of taxes and slavery Solomon had put on the Israelites. Rehoboam consults his elders and these elders spoke to him from their wisdom:

> *If you will be a servant to these people today, and serve them, and answer them, and speak good words to them, then they will be your servants forever.*

1 Kings 12:7b

In other words, Rehoboam must serve the people, not the other way around. Rehoboam doesn't like this advice and goes to his young friends who had grown up with him. These "yes men", of course, tell him to make the people work harder and he will be more famous than his father. Rehoboam follows the folly of his young men. Soon the ten tribes break with the two southern tribes, and Jeroboam becomes king of the northern tribes. Rehoboam has only the two southern tribes. There is great wisdom here for any new leader, including our own political leaders. They are elected to serve the people, to be a servant leader. If they forget this, they will fall in disgrace. That is very contemporary wisdom for politicians, busnesspeople, church officers, and pastors.

Jesus Teaches the Disciples About Servanthood

Jesus would be leaving His disciples soon and was eating His last meal with them in an upper room. It was Thursday, one day before His crucifixion. It would be their responsibility, with the help of the Holy Spirit, to start His church. Jesus still had a major lesson to teach them.

At this time in Palestine, the roads were very dusty. When a host had guests for supper, it was considered an act of hospitality for the servants of the host or his wife to wash the feet of the guests. The disciples had been fighting among themselves as to who would be the leaders in their perception of Christ's kingdom. Not one would stoop low enough to wash the feet of the others. The event happened during the meal. Judas was still there.[1]

At this point Jesus knew the final script had already started playing (John 13:1) and realized that He had only a short time to be with His disciples before leaving them and their distorted vision. Jesus rose from the table, laid aside His garments, and then picked up a towel. He poured water into a bowl and silently began to wash the feet of each of the disciples. No one said anything as they watched in a tense silence as Jesus moved to each of them in turn. Their hero, the guy who they expected to be their king, was now washing the feet of each of them.

As Jesus came to the impetuous Peter, Peter protests.

"Lord, are you washing my feet?"

Christ answered Peter emphasizing a key word:

*"What **I** am doing you do not know now."*

It is Peter who then relinquishes his agenda and we hear Peter telling Christ.

"Lord, not my feet only, but also my hands and my head!"

These followers would soon have the gift of the Holy Spirit. At that time they would understand what Christ was doing. Peter led later as he healed the lame man at the temple gate. The leader must lay aside the idea of being the hero and respond with his or her calling in true humility to the authority of Christ and the power of the Holy Spirit.

The Servant Leader and Transformation

George Otis, Jr. of the Sentinel Group tells how an unusual transformation in Singapore began in a prison from a man willing to risk servant leadership.

> "In Singapore my hosts arranged for me to have lunch with Jason Wang—a man who, until recently, was the deputy director of the nation's prison system. Inspired by the Transformation videos from the Sentinel Group, Jason told me that some months back he had began to pray that revival would flood the penitentiaries under his authority. Results came quickly.
>
> One night, at the prompting of the Holy Spirit, Jason donned civilian clothes and walked into a prison assembly. There, to the astonishment of the inmates, he took a basin of water and proceeded to wash their feet. Many were saved, and the presence of God filled the complex. Convicted of their sin, scores renounced their ties to underworld gangs.
>
> When television cameras broadcast Jason's actions throughout the nation, the impact was deeper than anyone could have imagined. One outcome was the high-profile "Yellow Ribbon" program that has seen schools, businesses, and churches unite in offering prisoners a "second chance" in society. A resounding success, the program has reduced Singapore's prison population by roughly 35 percent." [2]

For the leader to lead to the necessary transformation, the leader must lay aside his or her own ego (garments) and agenda, and then be willing to serve in the name of Christ.

The Servant and Vision

The leader starts with a vision, and then helps people, from a servant position, to take ownership on this vision. He or she is constantly listening to the needs of those they serve and communicating the vision to them in terms of their needs.

Sometimes the long-term goals are delayed or even sacrificed in terms of short-term goals of the servant heart. A member of the team may have a sudden illness, and the team will need to commit time, compassion, prayer, and financial resources for a period before they can continue forward with their vision. God has a divine inheritance for each of His kids, and only as servant can we receive it. (Matthew 25:14-30). In our submission as a servant leader, we learn the freedom of a servant leader.

Conclusion

The original title of this chapter was "The Leader as Servant". Then I realized I had it wrong. Serving is first, then leading. The title becomes "Serving Leadership". Now go another step. Suppose you drop the word "leadership", and the chapter title becomes "Serving". Suppose in reality I was tricking you to read the whole book about serving by using the word "leadership" in the book title?

Now here is the reality. The Apostle Paul begins many of his letters by referring to himself as a bondservant of Jesus Christ. So does James. So does Peter (2 Peter 1:1). So does Jude. The word used by these writers to refer to themselves is *doulos*. It refers to a servant, either voluntarily or involuntarily. In the New Testament, it generally refers to subjection without the idea of bondage. It is generally translated as bondsman.[3] Although these men were leaders; that was not how they saw themselves. They saw themselves as servants to Christ, even to the point of death.

Notes

1. There is some variation among the Gospels and translations as to the order of the events. The most accurate translation appears to indicate that the event happened during the meal. Jesus washed the feet of Judas. Judas left after the event. Judas made his final decision at the supper.

2. Excerpted from an information letter written by George Otis, Jr. on September 13, 2008. For more information on this and other transformation stories contact info@ sentinelgroup.org. Used with permission.

3. The bondsmen sold themselves into service for a price, for a period of time. Their word was their bond to stay.

Dialog

1. When have you seen this servant leadership model acting? Can you name names? What happened?

2. Where have you seen leaders who ignored the servant leadership model issue? Can you name names? What happened?

3. What servant leaders are influencing your life today? Why?

Chapter 14: Leading from Compassion

But when He saw the multitudes, He was moved with compassion for them, because they were weary and scattered, like sheep having no shepherd.

Matthew 9:36

Jesus wept

Mark 1:41

Jesus led with a deep sense of compassion. The Greek word translated as "compassion" is used 14 times in the Gospels, and means to have the bowels yearn, to feel with, a gut feeling, or to feel the pain of another. Many other times Jesus reached out from a deep, deep compassion and initiated the healing from His own pain at seeing what sin had done in the life of another or in the multitudes. The word isn't used at the healing of Lazarus; but Jesus wept as He stood before that tomb. The compassion was there with the Samaritan woman, the paralytic who was let down through the roof. In many of the parables of Jesus, He refers to a healing that took place through the showing of compassion, as with the stories of the prodigal son or the story of the Good Samaritan.

If you make a study of the healings of Jesus, you will find that this compassion is one of the common aspects of *every* healing. In its most prophetic form today, the healer takes on the suffering of the broken as if the brokenness and pain is his or her own and then prays into this for healing. This also can take the form of a spiritual mercy gift. This can be between two people as the pray-er takes on the pain of the person they are praying for. It can also, at times, involve praying for an entire people group and taking on the pain of that group. An example here is the ministry of John Dawson, Bob Beckett and others in their reconciliation work with the Native Americans.[1]

And when Jesus went out He saw a great multitude; and He was moved with compassion for them, and healed their sick.

Matthew 14:14

So Jesus had compassion and touched their eyes. And immediately their eyes received sight, and they followed Him.

Matthew 20:34

Then Jesus, moved with compassion , stretched out His hand and touched him, and said to him, "I am willing; be cleansed." As soon as He had spoken, immediately the leprosy left him, and he was cleansed.

Mark 1:41-42

When the Lord saw her, He had compassion on her and said to her, "Do not weep." Then He came and touched the open coffin, and those who carried him stood still. And He said, "Young man, I say to you, arise." So he who was dead sat up and began to speak. And He presented him to his mother.

Luke 7:13-15

And Jesus was certainly not the only compassionate leader in the Bible. Look at Moses, whose heart even as a young man yearned for his people held in the slavery of Egypt. Banished to the desert after a conflict situation, Moses finally stumbled on a group of young women at a watering hole who were being harassed by a group of thugs. He rescued the women from the thugs, then drew the water for the women, and also watered their flock. The story of his compassion had a wonderful ending. He got a dinner invitation, a wife, and a job. Later, after the rescued nation failed at the foot of Mt. Sinai, Moses interceded for them, even to the extent of giving up his place in heaven if God could not forgive their sin (Exodus 32:32). Later, even as the nation stood at the edge of the Promised Land and failed to take ownership on God's vision before them, Moses prayed and interceded again, saving the nation. Moses had a heart for God's people, a deep sense of compassion for them.

Nehemiah and Compassion

We see Nehemiah praying before God for the people (Nehemiah 1) and fasting for about four months as he interceded for the nation. Nehemiah had the same information that his friends did, but only Nehemiah saw the Lord's vision and had the compassion and burden for the hearts of the people. Even as they were building the wall, Nehemiah connected with the hearts of the people. Nehemiah ate with those who were of the lower class, heard their stories about high interest rates they were being charged, and stood with these to right the wrong of those charging high rates. Nehemiah led the construction, from when he first got the information until the wall was built, with his own deep compassion.

Compassion and the Mercy Gift

When my wife was sick and I prayed for her, I took on her pain and suffering as if it was my own. This compassion became an active force, or *dunamis*, in my own healing process. I reached out with a mercy gift, taking on her pain. In a real sense, I felt the pain more than she did. She was on morphine, I was not. I knew, from research that has been done on stress that with the loss of my wife there would be over a 90% probability of my body taking on a major disease in the next year with the particular type of stresses I was experiencing.[2] From this knowledge, I was able to put down strategies and prayers to deal with it. One component, for example, was the purchase of a very good keyboard for playing hours and hours of music. The only illness I faced during that time was shingles, and it was miraculously cured in a single afternoon after the praying of a group of prayer warriors. If the intimacy with God is there, this compassion is not a choice. It is just there.

The Dichotomy of Compassion

Organizations or organizational "leaders" often try an aggressive type of "slash-and-burn" type of leadership to accomplish their goals at any cost, such as aggressive tactics in Congress to raise money to build a little-used airport or road that will bear the congressperson's name. For long-term and any type of enduring difference, the compassion must be there—both at the personal and larger group level of those being led. A pastor, for example, is constantly trying to balance his or her time between ministering to the sick and broken in the church or mobilizing his people to bold visions and incredible adventures.

One of the most interesting examples of this was a session on *Dancing with the Stars* when professional dancer Julianne Hough was paired with the celebrity Olympic champion Apolo Anton. Julianne was a prodigy dancer, choreographer, teacher and singer and only 18 at the time. Apolo was an Olympic champion, having tied with one other person in the last Winter Olympics for the most gold metals. He was already training for the 2010 Olympics.

At their early dances, Apolo was very frustrated at not getting a 10 (the highest score) from each of the three judges. He was there to win and thought he was doing everything right. Both he and Julianne were highly competitive. Neither wanted anything less than the first place.

Eventually, the show gave us a camera view of the watershed rehearsal. Apolo was goofing off, making funny faces. Julianne was frustrated and disappointed in him for not seeing what she was trying to teach him.

"You want to win?" Julianne threw at him.

"Sure. I'm here to win."

"You are not going to win like that."

I saw what Julianne was telling him. In the Olympic race, the racer is focused on the goal. Nothing else is ever even seen but that goal. Everything is inward and anything not related to the goal at the end is shut out. The heart's passion is to reach that goal as quickly as possible. That is all the athlete can dream about, see, taste, or hear. Nothing else matters. No relationships, an invisible audience, no relaxing. The goal is everything. Too often a pastor or Christian leader does the same thing.

Julianne was trying to tell him that to win here everything was exactly the opposite—he had to see that the dance was outward. You are telling a story, and the dance is poetry in motion that communicates and expresses a story that involves the deepest part of the heart—a message that is beyond words.

At the next dance it was obvious that Apolo had learned it. After long hours of practice with her, he had learned something. The crowd went wild with a standing ovation. For the rest of the competition, you saw the two beating with one heart and Apolo taking risk after risk in his dances and he got continued standing ovations.[3] A few weeks later they stood together with his winning trophy. And Apolo was acknowledging that he was not the same person.

Neither was Julianne. She had created a field or place that not only led Apolo; but together they led the judges, audience, and television viewers into a story week after week. There was synergy, chemistry, and passion in their incredible dances.

This is what every leader today must do. He or she is not so much leading to a goal, but rather taking those led into a story that has romance and passion. And to do that, the leader must have a vision expressed as a Place, have a vulnerable heart, and show compassion. There is a profound relationship between the leader and those being led.

For a pastor, for example, this means it is not an academic or even a competitive goal of a larger attendance, bigger church budget, or a beautiful building that you are leading the congregation to embrace. The pastor is rather telling a story in action (and sometimes with words), the most incredible story ever told. The story is rich with romance, adventure, risk, and joy. If it is done right, people will choose to be a part of the journey and follow to join the story.

I was visiting Stan in the hospital. He was very sick with only a few months to live. With most people, I go to the hospital to cheer them up. In this case it was the reverse. Stan would take me to an awesome Place. Normally Stan would be on painkillers.

This day there were no painkillers and his mind was clear. He was depressed, however. His wife, Linda, was getting some badly needed rest and recuperation and was out of town for a few days. Unknown to any of us, Stan had only two more months before going home to Jesus.

As I stood there with him and talking with Stan, he looked at me and changed the subject.

"Linda is not the same woman I married four years ago," he said.

"I know," I replied.

"There was darkness there when I married her," he continued.

"I know," I replied again softly.

He looked away from me and out the window in the room. When he looked back tears were pouring down his face.

"There is no darkness there now," he choked through the tears.

"I know," I said again as now I choked up. "No darkness."

Then I waited. Waited to hear what he would dare to say next.

"Compassion," Stan said through his tears. "Compassion."

"I know, Stan. Compassion."

In claiming and naming this gifting, the one who received compassion experienced a healing and also received a blessing that goes out from the Holy Spirit. The one who showed compassion is also blessed and healed.

In another story, Donna was a nurse working in the emergency room of a hospital late one night. A young lady who had attempted suicide was brought in, screaming and swearing, saying she wanted to die, not be helped to live. This along with the fact that she was disheveled, dirty, appearing despondent, and wreaked a foul odor made it very difficult to want to be near her.

The doctor who was there that night ministered to her wounds, sewing up the deep cuts. As he did this, the doctor also wrestled with the fact that a deeper healing was needed considering that this same woman would probably return to the emergency room again later, perhaps more successful in her attempt the next time. With gentle words, he asked her questions to try to help him understand what was going on that brought her to her point of despondence. She calmed down some but still showed much evidence of her despair.

As the doctor finished and started to leave to help another patient, he asked Donna to hold the girl's wrists over the suture for ten minutes until the natural clotting could complete.

"What could I do, Carl, for those ten minutes?" she asked me. "I knew that she needed the Lord and I spent that time sharing about His wonderful love for her and, then asking her if she would like to give her life to Him who loved her so much and was so willing to help her." The whole time she listened intently, but it was hard to tell what her answer would be when I finally asked her if she would like to give control of her life to the Lord. Wonderfully she said, "yes" and she said she would pray with me as I prayed out loud for her. When I opened my eyes and looked at her, I could hardly believe my eyes. It was as if I was seeing her through God's eyes. She was smiling and beautiful!

After a few minutes another nurse came to take the young lady up to a room for the night. Then she came back down and spoke to Donna.

"What did you do?" she asked. "This isn't the same woman who we checked in."

"I know," Donna said. "It was really the Lord. I just asked him to work through my words and actions as I was with her."

A few hours later, this girl called Donna in the ER from her hospital room and asked her to come to see her before she left that night. Donna willingly did that and was amazed at the joy and radiance that flowed from this very recently despondent girl. She could see that God truly had been at work! The young lady wanted more help from Donna; but by hospital rules Donna could not give out her phone number or address. Donna was able, however, to do an incredible ministry there in that hospital room and point her to the next steps she needed to take. As Donna was leaving the hospital floor where this girl's room was, nurses shared their surprise and questions with Donna as they had a difficult time understanding how someone who was admitted for trying to commit suicide could be so bubbly and joyful acting. She wasn't like the others they had cared for who were admitted for similar reasons.

Again, in claiming and embracing this gifting, there is a blessing that goes out from the Holy Spirit to the one that showed compassion and something very special happens. That relationship and intimacy with God that was there in the Garden centuries ago becomes real again.

Notes

1. See Dawson, John. *Healing America's Wounds.* (Ventura, CA: Regal Books, 1994) and Beckett, Bob. And Rebecca Wagner. *Commitment to Conquer: Redeeming Your City by Strategic Intercession.* (Grand Rapids: Chosen, 1997)
2. Reported from studies by Thomas H. Holmes, M.D. and

Minoru Masuda, Ph. D. at the Department of Psychiatry at the University Of Washington School Of Medicine, Seattle, WA, dated December, 1972.

3. You can see their final Pasa Doble at http://www.youtube. com/watch?v=a3x5qScV4jU. You will also see the standing ovation they received. Julianne would have choreographed this and then taught Apolo how to do it.

Dialog

1. Can you think of other parables Jesus told that illustrated compassion principles in leadership?

2. Can you think of a time that you showed compassion? What happened to you in the experience?

3. The nurse in the last story has spiritual gifting in both leadership and mercy. How do these gifts relate? Are these gifts complementary or in tension with each other?

Chapter 15: The New Ekklesia

At the center of all this, Christ rules the church. The church, you see, is not peripheral to the world; the world is peripheral to the church. The church is Christ's body, by which he speaks and acts, by which he fills everything with His presence.

Ephesians 1:22 *THE MESSAGE*

The Church in the West today presents too easy a target for Satan. We do not believe we are at war. We do not know where the battleground is located, and, in spite of our weapons, they are neither loaded nor aimed at the right target. We are unaware of how vulnerable we are. We are better fitted for a parade than an amphibious landing.

Ed Silvoso, *That None Should Perish: How to Reach Entire Cites for Christ Through Prayer Evangelism*

The Church, as the Body of Christ, has the business of liberating the captives, recovering the sight of the blind, enabling the lame to walk, bringing the good news to the poor, and (yes) raising the dead.

(Paraphrase of a quote of Donald McGavran)

When we look at the issue of vision and leadership, this implies community. We can only discover who we are and why we are here in relationships—relationship to God, and in relationships with others. Being created in the image of God means that, like

God, we hunger for relationships. We cannot experience healing unless we are in relationships.

The visions that God gives us are so radical and transformational that, if we try them alone, the Enemy will certainly destroy us. No question about it. Christ came to establish His authority on earth and to restore the relationship of you to Himself. The Church, as the very Body of Christ, exists as the authority for the visions God gives us. Let me share a little of my own journey to find Church.

The Journey to Community

Although my conversion at a young age was very real, there came a point in my life after I left college that I had to find God on my own. I praise God for giving me parents of strong faith; but I didn't want a faith that had been handed down to me by my parents or by the institutional church as I knew it. After college I headed off to a nice job with IBM in the Washington, DC metro area. As a young squirt, I'm off to save the world. It's a shocker when you find out the world isn't exactly what you expected. Washington was imploding—high crime, March on Washington, Kennedy shot, and then Martin Luther King. I changed from a WASP (White Anglo-Saxon Protestant) church in the suburbs to an inner city church that met in a coffeehouse.

We could only seat about ninety at the worship service. When they opened the doors thirty minutes ahead of time for worship at the coffeehouse, there would be enough people waiting in line to fill those seats. The music one Sunday was Dave Brubeck and his jazz rendition of David dancing before the Lord. The speaker was always what the institutional church would call a layman (or laywoman). They could only speak for a few minutes, then he (or she) would open the service to dialog and the table microphones were opened. The communion was coffee and a sweet roll. Yes, there was an invitation. A lady heading to London one Sunday to do inner city mission work wanted to know if any of us would go with her.

I'd walk out of there feeling I had been to Church, but nothing I remembered of my old southern church was there. As least not in a physical form. Yet I felt like I had been to Church. In the classes at the church we wrestled with strange assignments that dropped me into an intensive community laboratory experience. One assignment was to find someone in the class I loved, someone I hated, and someone I felt indifferent about. I was to write in my journal about each. Then I was supposed to share a meal or coffee with each and write in my journal about how my opinions changed. So I had people who called me all week for coffee or dinner; but I never knew which category they had me in.

This church never had more than a hundred members. Even with this, the small church met as multiple smaller churches, with the coffeehouse church as one of these. The headquarters for the church was a house on Massachusetts Avenue. The primary service (where the pastor spoke) was at the headquarters each Sunday. It was at almost the same time as the coffeehouse service so that spiritual gluttons couldn't attend both services. From their viewpoint, they believed each of us were leaders and if the church got too large the community was no longer intentional and people sat around and watched instead of leading. Also, most people found the radical nature of their community and commitment was too much for them. It took two years to become a member of that church. It took that long, they said, before you could understand the radical nature of their community.

This church was a definite confluent event in my life. Yet it violated certain basic rules about the church that I had known from the past:

- I had been taught that growing my church would make a difference in my community. We weren't really committed to church growth; yet the community was transformed by this church.

- I had been taught that if you build the best church you can, people will come to it. In this case we took the church to the marketplace and met in a coffeehouse. We went to the people.
- I had been taught that if you train the church members you will have better evangelism. We weren't doing direct evangelism. God gifted us with an incarnational community and we took that community into the market. People saw what we had and chose to commit to Jesus and our community.

Later, I took a new job and needed to move from there to Illinois. I remember sitting and sharing with Gordon Cosby, the pastor of the Washington church. I told him how much the church meant to me and asked how, as I moved to another church, I could continue my spiritual journey. Gordon gave me advice I have never forgotten.

"Carl," he said, "God will give you a vision of what He wants you to do. It is a bold vision. Impossible by all human standards. You won't be able to accomplish it on your own, and probably not even in your lifetime. You must find a church who will support that vision and ministry and then live this vision with total commitment, even if it costs you your life. Nothing else has any meaning. If you can't find this church there, make it yourself. Bring in a group of committed Christians who can help you with the vision and let this become your church. But I'll give you one word of warning. If you take this vision into an existing traditional church, your vision will be so radical and challenging that the leaders of that church may come against you. You must stay with the vision. It is the only thing that matters."

If there is no community for you, young man, make it yourself.

Paul Goodman, speaking through a character in *Making Do*

I moved on to Illinois and soon found myself in a friendly church with little growth. With a few other young people, we met and talked about the problem. One of us, a very creative lady, was ready to pull out and leave the church. I grabbed a polystyrene cup, wrote "Church" on it, shredded it to a collection of small pieces, and then gave the pieces to her.

"Now," I said, "how would you put it back together?"

We watched in silence as this creative lady slowly crafted the pieces together into a beautiful new form.

With a few others, we formed a small radical group in the church who sang folk songs and mixed in some short dramatic skits with the folk music. I remember in Chicago a church asked us to help them with a weekend workshop. We talked with the congregation members as we prepared for the first evening. They told us their concern was of their young people leaving their church. That evening to start things I stuck a sign on a wastebasket that said "Church", stuck my foot in the wastebasket and staggered out to the stage and the microphone with the church-labeled wastebasket dragging me in a limp. That radical creative lady in our group met me on the stage.

"What's the problem?" she asked.

"Well, it looks like the church is holding me back."

That set the pace for the evening.

With our own church not growing, the church leaders decided what they needed to do was remodel the building to draw more people. So our little group formed a "ban the pew" committee. They could build, we told them, as long as they didn't use pews in the sanctuary. When people asked us why, our simple explanation became our motto: Screwed down pews meant screwed up people. Our group became incarnational with our city community, attending city meetings, working with community groups, marching with the anti-war protestors. Soon our little group had wonderful folk music, skits with dynamite messages, and other great stuff that led to performances in other churches and even a military base. Gordon Cosby was right. And we had a riot. Literally.

What is the Church?

The word used in the early Bible for the "church" was *ekklesia*. It was generally used at the time to refer to a political or any other type of assembly. The first mention of the *ekklesia* (as church) in the Bible is in Matthew 16:18. At this point Jesus is traveling in the vicinity of Caesarea Philippi, a center of godless worship at the time. Jesus turned to His disciples and asked them who other people were saying who He was.

> *He asked His disciples, saying, "Who do men say that I, the Son of Man, am?"*
>
> *So they said, "Some say John the Baptist, some Elijah, and others Jeremiah or one of the prophets."*
>
> *He said to them, "But who do you say that I am?"*
>
> *Simon Peter answered and said, "You are the Christ, the Son of the living God."*
>
> *Jesus answered and said to him, "Blessed are you, Simon Bar-Jonah, for flesh and blood has not revealed this to you, but My Father who is in heaven. And I also say to you that you are Peter, and on this rock I will build My church, and the gates of Hades shall not prevail against it. And I will give you the keys of the kingdom of heaven, and whatever you bind on earth will be bound in heaven, and whatever you loose on earth will be loosed in heaven."*

Matthew 16:13-19

What is going on here? Jesus would know what others were saying about who He was. That wasn't the issue. He knew who the disciples thought He was. That wasn't His intent here.

Remember that this book of Matthew in the Bible was like a membership manual in the early church. It was not "The Gospel According to Matthew". There was only one Gospel, and Matthew was not a book in the Bible. Matthew was written on a scroll probably no more than thirty feet long, so Matthew had to pick carefully what stories would go in it. Unlike Mark and the other Gospels, the stories in Matthew are told with passion and drama. It was the moral and ethic values for the early church (see the Beatitudes in Matthew). Miracles (*dunamis*) are described in detail, but the healing always took place instantly. Matthew is trying to say something very important to the Church in his "membership manual". This same Gospel where Jesus is talking about the Church is also the gospel (and the only one) that teaches what Jesus said about the Kingdom of Heaven (see Chapter 12).

Look at how Christ identifies himself and how they related to that. He wanted the disciples and soon the Church to speak and also to act in authority (*rhema*) as to who they thought He was. In asking the question, Christ refers to Himself as "the Son of Man." Peter replies that He is "the Son of God." So we see both the humanity and divinity of Jesus revealed in the discussion. Then Jesus says on this He will build his Church. Look at the Greek word for the Church Jesus used here—*ekklesia*. It translates as the "called out." Jesus is referring to the Church who will be birthed as the "called out" or the new "chosen people".

The next question, quite simply, would be from what are we called and to what are we called?

- We are called from the chaos, the brokenness, the Decapolis, the illusion of the Matrix (remember that movie?), the purposeless life.
- We are called to a purpose and an identity that are unique. We are called to love and be loved in a romance so intense that we are captured by this and want to stay there forever, and we will. We are called to peace, to place, to freedom, to hope, to duty, to sanctification, to grace.

Quite a statement for a Jewish mind in the early church to hear and understand against their current concept of the chosen people.

We don't know the size of the early churches or their organizational structure, but we know they had vision and passion. They were dying for it. The early leaders led from vision. They were more of a movement. You chose a personal relationship with Christ. Then you became part of a movement. Most denominations started as movements and then became institutionalized. Then they die. The Church doesn't die.

The Church Today

I see many Christians today who have left what is known as the traditional or institutional church. They see it has failed both them and the culture about them radically, and they are seeking something that speaks deeply to their spiritual needs. It's not that they are not spiritual or lack faith, it is just they can't find a church that speaks of a faith big enough for the story for which they are longing.

I like the story of Sherwood Baptist Church in Albany, Georgia who really wanted to make a difference in our culture. Stephen Kendrick and his brother Alex Kendrick, associate pastors at the church, did their research and discovered the three primary influences in our culture were television, movies, and the Internet. The Church wasn't even on the list. They took "movies" from this list and in 2008 released the movie *Fireproof*. They used local volunteer talent with the only exception being Kirk Cameron, a professional actor who is a committed Christian, who played the lead. And Kirk donated his salary to charity. Their budget was only $500,000. The movie became the highest grossing independent film of 2008 earning $33,456,317 domestically. The book that the Kendrick brothers wrote that is mentioned in the film (*The Love Dare*) is, as this is written, #41 in sales of all books on Amazon.com.

The DVD was released in January of 2009, and quickly had over 25 million in sales. Small groups exploring the issues in the film and the book have exploded in churches.

What does this say about the Church today? That Georgia church is only one type of church. There are many, many types of churches, but really one calling, a commission—The Great Commission. For the moment, let's get rid of the labels that are often used to describe the various church models you see today tags such as "emerging church", "cell-group", "seeker-sensitive church", "postmodern-sensitive" or "house church" or even "traditional" or "contemporary". These tags change to whatever the current flavor of the month is for the church growth specialists. Jesus didn't seem to care much about the model or denomination. When the early Church started, the issue was more about how to stay alive with the persecution they were facing. Christians were being tortured and martyred. I like how Paul and his friends were branded at Thessalonica:

> *But when they did not find them, they dragged Jason and some brethren to the rulers of the city, crying out, "These who have turned the world upside down have come here too."*

Acts 17:6

I don't see many churches or Christian leaders today turning the world upside down.

For starters, let's try to define a type of church that might act transformally today, whatever that would be. For one thing, this type of church would move away from an internal focus to emphasize redemptive participation in the community and the surrounding culture.

> *The church should stop mimicking the surrounding culture, and become an alternative community with a different set of beliefs, values, and behaviors. Ministers would no longer engage in marketing… The traditional ways of evaluating "successful churches—bigger buildings, more people, bigger budgets, larger*

*ministerial staff, new and more programs to serve members—
would be rejected. New yardsticks would be the norm: To
what extent is our church a "sent" community in which each
believer is reaching out to his community? To what extent is our
church impacting the community with a Christian message that
challenges the values of our secular society?*

David Horrox

I like the way Bob Waymire explained it to me. I was showing
him a three inch thick book I had done with my spiritual research
on the Portland area. Lots of demographics, maps, historical
research. Awesome book. Bob smiled at me, touched the book,
and then spoke:

"Carl, that's Light. Now you've got to be Salt."

Now let's look at some distinctives of this new Church as
Christ defined it.

- First, it is incarnational. As the body of Christ, it is the
  embodiment of the authority, power, love, peace, and
  grace of the risen Lord.
- It is a sent Church, going to the people. It is sent into the
  world; but it is not of the world. As I write this there is a
  sign near the front of my own church building that plays
  off a famous quote at the end of an Elvis Presley concert:

  The church has left the building.

  I love this quote. I like the worship experience at another
  church near me where the pastor says, at the end of the
  worship experience, "The service starts now".
- It is a servant Church, with the members serving each
  other first and then the world.
- There is no real distinction of laity and clergy. Each
  member is a servant leader in terms of their gifts and
  receiving in terms of the gifts of others. We will look
  more at this in the next chapter as we look at the issue

of spiritual gifts. There are distinctive functional leaders in the church in terms of their functional gifts (such as the pastor(s) or elders.) A pastor also may be part of the "laity", however, or vice versa.

- There is a deep, deep passion to see the Kingdom of God in the here and now.
- The community is more like an organism than organization.
- It is not a model, but a movement.

I don't like tags, but some of the new leaders today are referring to this type of church as a missional church. This implies it has a mission, is sent, and is intentional in terms of what Christ told it to do and that is expressed in the Great Commission:

And Jesus came and spoke to them, saying, "All authority has been given to Me in heaven and on earth. Go therefore and make disciples of all the nations, baptizing them in the name of the Father and of the Son and of the Holy Spirit, teaching them to observe all things that I have commanded you; and lo, I am with you always, even to the end of the age."

Matthew 28:18-20

Here's a quick comparison of this Missional Church with the current cultural church:

Current Cultural Church	Missional
Autocratic, hierarchical	Relational
Decisions	Disciples
Services	Service
Programs and Events	Processes
Demographics	Compassion
Organizations	Organisms

Uniformity	Diversity
Models	Missions
Seating	Sending
Models	Movements
Attractional	Incarnational
Professional	Passionate
Greek Determinate Thinking	Hebrew Holistic Thinking
Additive Growth	Exponential Growth
Ordered, Safe, Logical	Unpredictable, Creative

There is no specific model identified with this. The concept can be used with almost any model.

Now let's look at the issue of spiritual gifts and authority as it relates to the Church.

Dialog

Look back to the questions of the first chapter of this book. Now look forward.

1. Are you in a church today? Why or why not?

2. If you are in a church, what type of church are you in?

3. How would you like to see it different?

4. Suppose someone knocked on your door and said they were a pastor and this person said they were planting a new church in your area. This person asks what you would want in a church if they planted one. What would you say?

5. What is your reaction to the missional church as described here?

Chapter 16: The Church and Spiritual Gifts

Our greatest source of anxiety in our lives is our resistance and struggle against this destiny that is already written within our lives. We have great difficulty in accepting this gift, rejecting the very calling of God in our lives.

Elizabeth O'Connor

The Bible indicates that when God calls us, He gives us gifts for the vision to which we are called. Even in the Old Testament, we see references to gifting:

Then the LORD spoke to Moses, saying: "See, I have called by name Bezalel the son of Uri, the son of Hur, of the tribe of Judah. And I have filled him with the Spirit of God, in wisdom, in understanding, in knowledge, and in all manner of workmanship, to design artistic works, to work in gold, in silver, in bronze, in cutting jewels for setting, in carving wood, and to work in all manner of workmanship.

Exodus 31:1-5

After the Christ Event, the spiritual gifts were given to build up the Church in unity. We really don't see much in the Bible on this until after the birth of the Church. The most notable passage is probably the Apostle Paul's in-depth discussion in 1 Corinthians 12.

Now concerning spiritual [gifts], brethren, I do not want you to be ignorant:

1 Corinthians 12:1

The word "gifts" here is not in the original text of this first verse. The word "spiritual" here translates from *pneumatikos*, which more correctly translates as "spiritual things" or "spiritual gifts". That word, in turn, is built on the Greek word *pneuma* we met in Chapter 3. We get our word "pneumonia" from it. The shorter Greek word is used to refer to the Holy Spirit.

If you continue reading this passage, the word "gifts" is first used in the fourth verse.

*There are diversities of **gifts**, but the same Spirit. There are differences of ministries, but the same Lord. And there are diversities of activities, but it is the same God who works all in all. But the manifestation of the Spirit is given to each one for the profit of all: for to one is given the word of wisdom through the Spirit, to another the word of knowledge through the same Spirit, to another faith by the same Spirit, to another gifts of healings by the same Spirit, to another the working of miracles, to another prophecy, to another discerning of spirits, to another different kinds of tongues, to another the interpretation of tongues. But one and the same Spirit works all these things, distributing to each one individually as He wills.*

1 Corinthians 12:4-11 (emphasis added)

The Greek word used here for "gifts" in verse 4 is the Greek *charismata*, and translates as "a gift of grace or unmerited favor". This means spiritual gifts are something we receive from God that aren't earned or deserved. Gifts are given to us by God without restrictions or reservations. Peter Wagner defined gifts as *a special attribute given by the Holy Spirit to every member of the Body of Christ according to God's grace for use within the Body.* The purpose of the gifts is to build up the Body as well as for evangelism. Since building up the Body is a form of evangelism, the basic purpose of spiritual gifts is really evangelism. When Peter healed the lame man at the temple gate, the church grew. In Romans 6:23, Paul uses this same word to refer to God's gift in Jesus Christ, the greatest gift of all, and as the other gifts, is given with unmerited grace.

In verse 5, the word "ministries" is translated from *diakoneo*, which more directly translates as "service", or "servant ministries". The word "manifestation" in verse 7 is derived from the Greek *phanerosis* and means "to make clear or known".

Now let's read the same passage again referencing the Greek:

> *There are diversities of unmerited favors [grace], but the same Spirit. There are differences of servant ministries, but the same Lord. And there are diversities of activities, but it is the same God who works all in all. But the "making clear" [or bringing to reality] of the Spirit is given to each one for the profit of all.*

To understand the concept of spiritual gifts better, look at the Lord's Prayer[1] in John 17:

> *I do not pray for these alone, but also for those who will believe in Me through their word; that they all may be **one**, as You, Father, are in Me, and I in You; that they also may be **one** in Us, that the world may believe that You sent Me. And the glory which You gave Me I have given them, that they may be **one** just as We are one: I in them, and You in Me; that they may be made perfect in **one,** and that the world may know that You have sent Me, and have loved them as You have loved Me.*

John 17:20-23 (emphasis added)

Jesus is praying for the unity of the Church. The gifts are given to build up the Church, to witness to those who have yet to find Christ. There is no lone hero doing his or her thing when it comes to this gift business. In fact, whatever this vision that God gives us to accomplish will demand that others—the Church—come along side of us to accomplish the vision. Other gifts are needed that we don't have. This is God's way of keeping us humble. We are a leader in terms of the gifts we are given and a follower in terms of the gifts of others for the purpose of the common vision.

Now to each one the manifestation of the Spirit is given for the common good.

1 Corinthians 12:7-8 NIV

The body is a unit, though it is made up of many parts; and though all its parts are many, they form one body. So it is with Christ.

1 Corinthians 12:12 NIV

...to prepare God's people for works of service, so that the body of Christ may be built up until we all reach unity in the faith and in the knowledge of the Son of God and become mature, attaining to the whole measure of the fullness of Christ.

Ephesians 4:12-13 NIV

When the crippled man was healed at the temple gate (Acts 3), the church grew by 5,000 men in the one day. When the Gospel came to the Gentiles, that was a pretty major shift culturally and theologically for the Jewish leaders of the Church. This shift was validated by the gift of tongues.

For they heard them speaking in tongues and praising God.

Acts 10:45-46 NIV

Gifts are not like talents. Talents are something we are born with and develop through training and experience. Gifts, on the other hand, exist by God's grace and can change dynamically with time if necessary for specific needs. A musician may have both talent and gift, or perhaps only the talent.

Gifts are not given to the unsaved. The Holy Spirit acts in the unsaved to convert and then the spiritual gifts are given. The gifts are only given for the Body. The Holy Spirit, though, does work to quicken the heart of the unsaved and to draw him or her to an intimacy with God and salvation.

The Holy Spirit is first the Envisioner, then the Enabler. The Holy Spirit, as the *Envisioner,* gives us the vision of what God is doing and our personal vision and calling in response to His larger vision. Second, the Holy Spirit is the *Enabler,* completing the task in response to the call. The Holy Spirit enables us to respond to the call through our spiritual gifts. The process, then, is much like this:

God's larger vision -> our vision in response -> our call <- Gifts

The purpose of the process and call, in turn, is always evangelism—to bring people under the Lordship of Christ.

As each one has received a gift, minister it to one another, as good stewards of the manifold grace of God.

1 Peter 4:10

But the manifestation of the Spirit is given to each one for the profit of all:

1 Corinthians 12:7

We do not choose these gifts. They are already there and locked within our being (see Chapter 9). Our responsibility is to appropriate them in response to God's call on our life. We are not telling the Good News. We *are* the Good News. It is an incarnational thing.[2]

Functional Versus Motivational Gifts

There are several passages on spiritual gifts in the Bible. Let's take a quick look at some of these passages.

The first passage we just looked at is in 1 Corinthians 12. This letter was written by Paul to a pretty rowdy church. As far as morality and ethics went, they seemed to have none. They had turned the sacrament of the Lord's Supper into an orgy. There was incest. If you were the Apostle Paul, how would you write a letter to that kind of church? This letter is where you find some of the pinnacles of Paul's message to the Church.

Paul mentions the gifts of wisdom, word of knowledge, faith, healings (note the plural), miracles (*dunamis*), prophecy, discernment, tongues, and interpretation of tongues. Paul also places strong emphasis on the purpose of the gifts being that of building up of the Body. After the chapter on gifts, you see Paul's summary statement:

> *Though I speak with the tongues of men and of angels, but have not love, I have become sounding brass or a clanging cymbal.*

1 Corinthians 13:1-2

In Romans 12:3-8, Paul again mentions the spiritual gifts, their relationship to the unity of the Body.

> *For I say, through the grace given to me, to everyone who is among you, not to think of himself more highly than he ought to think, but to think soberly, as God has dealt to each one a measure of faith. For as we have many members in one body, but all the members do not have the same function, so we, being many, are one body in Christ, and individually members of one another. Having then gifts differing according to the grace that is given to us, let us use them: if prophecy, let us prophesy in proportion to our faith; or ministry, let us use it in our ministering; he who teaches,*

in teaching; he who exhorts, in exhortation; he who gives, with liberality; he who leads, with diligence; he who shows mercy, with cheerfulness.

Romans 12:3-8

In both of these passages (1 Corinthians 12, Romans 12) the word *charisma* is used to refer to these spiritual gifts. These gifts are given by God through grace—we do not deserve or choose them. They are given as part of the vision that God has called us to and to build up the Body. They are driven from our passion and burden, and as a result are often called motivational gifts.

Now turn to a third passage on gifts. You will find it in Ephesians 4. Again, Paul mentions the purpose of the gifts is to build up the unity of the Body.

*I, therefore, the prisoner of the Lord, beseech you to walk worthy of the calling with which you were called, with all lowliness and gentleness, with longsuffering, bearing with one another in love, endeavoring to keep the **unity** of the Spirit in the bond of peace. There is **one** body and **one** Spirit, just as you were called in **one** hope of your calling; **one** Lord, **one** faith, **on**e baptism; **one** God and Father of all, who is above all, and through all, and in you all.*

Ephesians 4:1-6 (emphasis added)

And then the gifts are mentioned:

But to each one of us grace was given according to the measure of Christ's gift. Therefore He says:

> *"When He ascended on high,*
> *He led captivity captive,*
> *And gave gifts to men."*

(Now this, "He ascended"—what does it mean but that He also first descended into the lower parts of the earth? He who

*descended is also the One who ascended far above all the
heavens, that He might fill all things.)*

*And He Himself gave some to be apostles, some prophets, some
evangelists, and some pastors and teachers, for the equipping
of the saints for the work of ministry, for the edifying of the
body of Christ, till we all come to the unity of the faith and
of the knowledge of the Son of God, to a perfect man, to
the measure of the stature of the fullness of Christ; that we
should no longer be children, tossed to and fro and carried
about with every wind of doctrine, by the trickery of men,
in the cunning craftiness of deceitful plotting, but, speaking
the truth in love, may grow up in all things into Him who is
the head—Christ—from whom the whole body, joined and
knit together by what every joint supplies, according to the
effective working by which every part does its share, causes
growth of the body for the edifying of itself in love.*

Ephesians 4:7-16

The word "grace" in that first verse is translated from the
Greek *charisma* again, but this gift list is different and refers to
functional gifts of the church. This time Paul is talking about the
people who are *functioning* under their gifts. The offices. This list
is sometimes called the five-fold gifts of the church and include
apostles, prophets, evangelists, pastors, and teachers. In other
words, a pastor is given certain operational gifts in the church by
virtue of his being pastor; i.e., he is called to function as pastor
in the church. Again, the purpose is to build up the unity of the
church, the members bonded in love, and an evangelistic outreach
from this to build the Kingdom.

In 1 Corinthians 12 we saw the motivational gifts. Later in
that same chapter on motivational gifts we see the functional
gifts.

*Now you are the body of Christ, and members individually.
And God has appointed these in the church: first apostles,*

second prophets, third teachers, after that miracles, then gifts of healings, helps, administrations, varieties of tongues. Are all apostles? Are all prophets? Are all teachers? Are all workers of miracles? Do all have gifts of healings? Do all speak with tongues? Do all interpret? But earnestly desire the best gifts. And yet I show you a more excellent way.

1 Corinthians 12:27-31

What is the difference between the motivational and functional gifts? I liked the way Dr. Joe Aldrich here in Portland explained it to me. His vision—and a very bold one—was to see a sustained movement of God in a city for the coming of the Holy Spirit and transformation, a coming of the Kingdom at the city or regional level. He told me the Greek language had two words for unity and oneness. One word referred to an organic unity. The second referred to a functional unity. Dr. Joe then led in the implementing of two structures in the city of Portland in preparation for the movement of God here. The first, the Northwest Renewal Ministries, worked with the prayer summits of our pastors at the coast and local prayer groups, praying for the coming of the Holy Spirit in our area to bring this organic unity to the churches. The second structure, Mission Portland, was a network of over thirty subnetworks (children, alcohol abuse, benevolent organizations, singles, etc.) that would work in tandem with the prayer network and churches to provide functional unity for the churches and parachurch organizations. In Chapter 19 you will see more of what happened to this.

These same concepts that Dr. Joe was using can be applied at the local church to see it empowered for Kingdom ministry.

The Apostolic Gift

Let's look at one of those functional gifts. This Ephesians passage mentions "apostles" as one of the five-fold functional gifts. What does this mean for the Church today? The word is translated from the Greek word *apostolos*, which translates literally as "one sent". In John 17:2, Jesus uses a variation of the word in referring to himself as sent by God. Some say it referred to those who had seen the risen Christ, with the Apostle Paul included. Paul saw the risen Christ on the Damascus road.

The word also had a wider meaning when used to refer to any missionaries sent out, such as in Acts 14:4 where Barnabus is sent out as a part of the group. In this passage Barnabus is referenced with the others as an apostle because he was "sent out".

Neither of these concepts do the meaning of *apostolos* functional gifting justice. If the *apostolos* word is used to describe those who had seen the risen Lord, that is not a functional definition and the Ephesians passage lists the apostolic gifting as a functional gift. If *apostolos* refers to one sent out, sent from what to what?

Think a minute. The spiritual culture of the time was almost identical to that today. The synagogues had gotten vary materialistic. Most of their Jewish tradition had now become ritualistic. None of that met the deep spiritual needs of the people. People were coming to Jesus and experienced healing and teaching. This upset the so-called religious leaders. The disciples and Paul became apostles all right. They were sent out (*apostolos*) to lead the Gospel through a cultural wormhole.[3] The Gospel was no longer in a nice, Jewish box. This was a radical new way to see what the Kingdom was all about. Now the Gospel was for everyone and was moving unhindered. Those early apostles had the challenge of being the transformal leaders to lead the Church through this wormhole.

In the same way today, we see failing church institutions and the need for that *apostolos* today that can help us carry the Gospel through the wormhole to people groups even in our own city that have not been touched by the message of Christ.

In your own life, who do you see with the functional gift of being an apostle to you? I can name several in my own life. They are always stretching me, creating chaos, visioning me to things that seem impossible. What they often tell me seems totally impractical. This forces me to move on faith.

Notes

1. The prayer earlier in the Gospels that begins "Our Father, which art in heaven..." (Matthew 6) is generally referred to as "The Model Prayer" and is the prayer Christ used in teaching the disciples how to pray. The prayer in John 17 is the prayer of Christ in the Garden, just days before his crucifixion. It is generally referred to as the "Lord's Prayer".

2. A great book for finding your spiritual gifts is Peter Wagner's *Your Spiritual Gifts Can Help Your Church Grow* (Ventura, CA: Regal, 1994)

3. In physics, a wormhole is theoretical structure in spacetime that forms a tube-like connection or tunnel for traveling between two separate regions of the universe. In the spiritual example, a cultural wormhole is connecting our past traditional cultural structures to a new and radically different world in which the Church must minister in.

Dialog

1. What do you see as your motivational gifts? Don't limit yourself to the standard list of 1 Corinthians 12.

2. Ask a close friend what they see as your motivational gifts. Are they the ones you thought they were?

3. How have you led from these?

4. Who is an apostle in your life? Why?

Chapter 17: The Church, Leadership and Authority

Sandy's death was real. My Gullain-Barré Syndrome was real. What was God telling me with my ride on that horse? I felt like I was on a stage, living in some kind of story of which I wanted no part. All God seemed to be saying was that I hadn't seen the last act yet, and what He had written He had written. What was reality and what was illusion?

If God has called me to lead—and He calls each us to lead— how did these experiences relate to that? What authority did I have now that I did not have before?

Exploring Authority and Power

The authority, like the gifting, is always in relationship to the Church as the Body of Christ.

- The call came to our church Elders that a teenage girl with parents in our church was dying in the hospital. Her fever continued to race higher and the doctors could not get the fever back down. If the fever could not be brought under control, there would be damage to her heart. It could even kill her. I joined with the rest of our elders and raced to the hospital, praying on the way. As we entered the room, we surrounded the bed and continued our prayers there at a more strategic level for her healing. In a few minutes we left the room. The fever abated 25 minutes after we left.
- Sometime later I was calling another lady and found her

weeping. The lady, a single mom with three kids, was being evicted from her apartment for leaving an empty gas can on her porch. She had thirty days (in winter) to move out with her kids. A few days later the elders prayed with her at church; but that seemed to change nothing. Two days later we traveled over to the apartment complex where we began a prayer march. Singing *Our God is an Awesome God* at the top of our lungs, we marched around and through the complex and then prayed and anointed each member of her family along with one other lady that wanted whatever it was we had. The eviction notice was canceled less than 24 hours later, and within a few months new managers ran the complex—including a Christian lady.

- In another story, a young man in our church just back from an international trip battled some type of virus for over a month with no relief. The elders traveled to his house one evening and began prayer with him. He was well and in church the next Sunday.

- Another time a request came to the leaders on the prayer chain that a lady in our church was in the hospital. She had double pneumonia with a low blood count, and we were told it would take the doctors a month to clear it up if she could survive at all. She was home in a few days and soon was back at church.

A common thread ripped through all of the healings. First, **the Apostle Paul tells us that the purpose of all these events was to build up the Church.** With the other elders and Christ, I had whatever authority and power was needed for that purpose. It had nothing to do with me and everything to do with the Church.

...and to make all see what is the fellowship of the mystery, which from the beginning of the ages has been hidden in God who created all things through Jesus Christ; to the

> *intent that now the manifold wisdom of God might be made
> known **by the church** to the principalities and powers in the
> heavenly places, according to the eternal purpose which He
> accomplished in Christ Jesus our Lord, in whom we have
> boldness and access with confidence through faith in Him.*

Ephesians 3:9-12 (emphasis added)

The Apostle Paul is talking about the mystery of the faith in that the illusion becomes reality; and reality as we perceive it is nothing more than an illusion.

> *When I was a child, I spoke as a child, I understood as a
> child, I thought as a child; but when I became a man, I put
> away childish things. For now we see in a mirror, dimly, but
> then face to face. Now I know in part, but then I shall know
> just as I also am known.*

1 Corinthians 13:11-12

You see the same message with the healing of the lame man in Acts 3. The purpose of the healing of the lame man was the same—to build up the Church.

Then how do we explain the death of my wife? Or the death of a dear friend that died a year ago with hundreds of people praying for him? Or the death of another friend that died of breast cancer a few months ago?

The Apostle Paul had such an incredible healing gift that people were healed from simply touching his handkerchief (Acts 19:12). Yet several times the Apostle tells us of praying for a healing that apparently was never answered (2 Timothy 4:20, 1 Timothy 5:23). And Paul himself had some type of "thorn in the flesh" from which he was apparently never healed.

Over and over again in his epistles Paul talks of the mystery of God's will. Unlike the English word, the Greek word for *mystery* in the New Testament means being outside the range of natural apprehension and can be known (perceived as reality) only by Divine revelation to those illuminated by His Spirit.

There were times when I have tried to step up and be the hero, the leader, and claim healing for someone. In those times I saw nothing until I could release my own ego and move to a place of humility and compassion. It was then, and only then, I could see the reality, healing, and authority. First you believe, and then you see. But what if the healing never happens?

Authority, Power, and Responsibility

There are three key words in the stories that are important here: *authority, power,* and *responsibility.*

- How was I healed from my GBS with the neural system completely destroyed? The doctors told me that they had no explanation. How did the illusion of the doctors become shattered? Where did I get the authority and power?
- I faced both guilt and anger in the loss of Sandy. Should I have had more authority and power there to rescue her? Where did I fail in her rescue? Was I in an illusion?

The Issue of Power

The Greek word used for "power" in the New Testament is *dunamis.* It is the same root word from which we get the English word dynamite. In the secular sense, the word refers to the ability to achieve certain ends. In the New Testament *dunamis* refers to a miraculous power, power outside of the laws of science and physics. Sometimes the word *dunamis* is translated as "miracles" in the modern New Testament, as in Acts 2:22 and Acts 13:8. The purpose of this power is to build up the Church, which is the Body of Christ.

> *Now to Him who is able to do exceedingly abundantly above all that we ask or think, according to the power* [dunamis]

*that works in us, to Him be glory in the **church** by Christ Jesus to all generations, forever and ever. Amen.*

Ephesians 3:20-21 (emphasis added)

This power comes from our relationship with God and the working of His Kingdom through us.

For the message of the cross is foolishness to those who are perishing, but to us who are being saved it is the power [dunamis] of God.

1 Corinthians 1:18-19

The Issue of Authority

In the secular world, authority and power often seem to refer to the same thing. However, they really have very different meanings. As already mentioned, "power" refers to the ability to achieve certain ends. "Authority", in contrast, refers to a claim of legitimacy, justification, and right to use this power.

Authority and power don't mean the same thing, but they always go together. I may have the power to race my car at over 100 mph on a city street; but I don't have the authority to do it. If I did do it, the consequences would not be good.

In our secular mindset, we really often define authority as meaning to use force to make others conform to what we want. In choosing such independence over relationships, the relationships become weaker or are destroyed. This is true at work, within our church, and within our marriage.

When the man and the woman were first created, they (both of them) were given authority over the earth. The relationships between the man and the woman and between both and God were not meant to be bound with authority and hierarchy, but more from a relationship of perfect unity and intimacy. It was the purest form of love. As the final Glory of God's creation, we were created in God's image and free to be in relationships with

Him and one another. Today, after the Fall, we are trained from birth to work within our systems with their related hierarchies and authority. The result is a binding on our relationships that never should be there. In heaven, that original relationship will be restored but we can choose to taste it here.

In God's original intent, "authority" had a deeper meaning than our concept we often think of now. The Greek word used for "authority" in the New Testament is *exousia*. We roughly translate it as "it is lawful".

The words "power" and "authority" are so closely related that Vine's *Expository Dictionary of New Testament Words* defines both when you look up "power". In Luke 9:2, Jesus sent the disciples out and gave them both power and authority.

Now travel back in time to when the world was first created and look at the issue of authority and power at creation. The humanistic scientists today have created a massive illusion that our world evolved from nothing.[1] This illusion is hammered into our brains as children until we think the illusion is reality. Our brain is then wired so that we can no longer even see the reality, much less act on it. We build a Tower of Babel called Technology, just like in the Bible story, trying to reach God on our own authority and power. That religion, taught in our public schools, is better known as Humanism. Humanism has nothing to do with reality. Look where it led those building that Tower of Babel. Look where it's led our political, economic, and other leaders.

God released authority to Adam on earth in the Garden. At the Fall, Adam released his authority on this earth to Satan there in the Garden. Satan had no authority on earth until Adam released it to him. Adam was there with Eve when Eve was tempted. Adam said and did nothing. Romans 5:12 says sin came into the world through one *man*. The relationship with God was broken. Adam had been given authority on earth by God, but with Eve failed to take this authority in the Garden with the serpent. There in the Garden Adam released his authority on this earth to Satan. Eve ate the apple in disobedience to God. Adam had been with Eve but had not said or done anything, breaking his relationship with Eve. They had stepped outside of the intimacy and relationship they had with God. They both had violated commands from God; and in addition, they had violated the relationship they had with each other.

Like Adam and Eve, we say we don't need God. I'm my own person. I'll build my own way to get what I want. My agenda is God's agenda and I'll get there on my own. God can help if He wants to; but basically I'm a good person and don't need God.

This, however, violates the very purpose for which we were made—to enter into a very intimate and personal relationship with our Creator. We have no purpose outside of that, and without that life becomes a wandering through a desert until we reach that understanding.

When Christ came and was tempted at the beginning of his ministry, Satan said all authority on this earth was his. That was a true statement. When Christ came, with His death and resurrection He took back that authority. With each version of the Great Commission, we see Jesus saying "ALL authority is mine." Once again, with the help of the Holy Spirit He left with us, we can reclaim that personal relationship with God and the intimacy that was lost in the Garden. We have His authority in His name. We have none in our own name. We have no authority in the name of our pastor, elders, deacons, or priest. Our only authority is in the name of Christ.

So what happens with authority? A good way to explain this is using as an illustration a conversation I once had with my wife. I told her I didn't understand about this feminism stuff. It made no sense to me. We didn't have any type of control or authority issues in our relationship with each other. If we disagreed on something, one of us—or maybe both of us—did not have the mind of God. We needed to pray through it and seek guidance until we heard the Lord speaking and shared a common mind. We would take no step until we reached that point. There was no hierarchy here. She agreed. This same story can be projected into your church. There should be a common vision, given to your church by God. This vision is accomplished in the church through relationships and intimacy with each other and God. (This leads to an interesting discussion question—see the Dialog for this chapter.)

Patrick Glynn, who started an interesting spiritual journey as an atheist at Harvard, explored the creation story with some leading scientists and came, with the scientists, to an amazing conclusion. It was impossible for all the variables necessary for our existence on this planet to come together for life as we know it unless something outside of the system was acting on the system. Moreover, with the other scientists they came to the conclusion that the idea of Man was there from the first nanosecond of creation. Patrick became a Christian and wrote a book[2] on his discoveries.

I believe the idea of *you* was there in the mind of God in that first nanosecond of creation. God created you for a purpose and relationship, and then gives you authority and responsibility in terms of that purpose and relationship. You are a leader in terms of this purpose. The authority and power you have as a leader is because of this relationship.

> *Blessed be the God and Father of our Lord Jesus Christ, who has blessed us with every spiritual blessing in the heavenly places in Christ, just as* **He chose us in Him** *before the foundation of the world, that we should be holy and without blame before Him in love, ...*

Ephesians 1:3-5 (emphasis added)

This verse is not about the Jews being chosen. This verse was written to an audience of mixed Gentiles and Jews (see Ephesians 1:12-13). What the Apostle is saying here would be an illusion to the Jews of that time, but was the reality of the coming Kingdom. In fact, the entire book of Acts shows the pattern of how the Holy Spirit led the Church out of this illusion. Acts was written by a

Gentile (Luke) to a Gentile (Theophilus), showing the breaking of the New Wineskins out of the Jewish illusion.

- The Gospel comes to the Jews—Acts 2-3
- The Gospel comes to the Half-Jews—Acts 8
- The Gospel comes to an Ethiopian—Acts 8
- Saul is called as missionary to the Gentiles—Acts 9
- The Gospel comes to God-Fearing Gentiles—Acts 10
- The Gospel comes to Hellenist Jews (Greek-speaking, often referring to the foreign-born Jews) —Acts 11
- The Gospel comes to the Gentiles—Acts 14

Soon the Holy Spirit has made it clear the Gospel is for everyone. The last verse of Acts refers to the Gospel now moving *unhindered* in the last years of Paul's life. No one and nothing could stop it. Today this is still true—nothing can stop it.

What happened at Calvary was not a power (*dunamis*) issue. The issue was one of authority (*exousia*). The death and resurrection of Christ removed Satan's authority on this earth and again reestablished Christ's authority on earth. Power does the work; but the power is under the authority of Christ and He controls the power. The power issue was won in heaven before the creation of man.[3]

Before leaving his followers, Jesus stood before his followers and gave them the Great Commission, beginning with *"All authority is mine…"*. We are commissioned to go in His authority. His authority was restored on Earth through what happened at Calvary. That is reality.

St Helens, a volcano near me, exploded in 1980. Thirty-four people were confirmed dead from the explosion and twenty-six others vanished and are presumed dead. The explosion had the power of 27,000 Hiroshima bombs. It created the largest landslide in recorded history, devastating 230 square miles and transforming what had been a lush green evergreen forest to a gray lifeless wasteland with no life. About 200 homes were damaged or destroyed. Many for hundreds of miles around were adversely affected by the ash in the air and ash traveled on winds over the ocean and around the world. Explosions don't create order. [4]

After some months, Sandy and I journeyed up through the debris and saw only chaos and destruction. Today Nature and Man have rebuilt the area; but the restoration of life in the area is coming from *outside* the site. Birds, animals, and humans brought seeds and life back into the area. In other words, whatever brought order at the creation of the universe came from *outside* the universe. Anything else violates certain basic laws of science. Authority and power at creation came from outside the system.

God still creates today. The authority and power for this is not our own, but from Him and for Him. That relationship and intimacy is there for our taking.

Responding to the Call

Another word that relates to authority and power is *responsibility*. When you are given authority and power to do something, you are held responsible for accomplishing it. Authority must always accompany responsibility. If God calls (*kalein*) us to do something, God holds us accountable for doing what He has called us to do.

God stands outside of time. He was there before creation, and will be there after this world is gone. There are moments when God calls us (*kalein*) to do something and gives us authority and power to do it. It is a moment in time where God is acting and the power and authority crosses with our calling to be a part of the Kingdom Enterprise. This is a window of opportunity in time, a God-Given moment, where we are called to act. God's giftings that we need for that moment are given to us to use. If we fail to act, the moment is gone forever. The Greek word for that moment and window is *kairos*.

Years ago the Israelites stood on the edge of their Promised Time. They were given both authority and power to take the land

and were called to take it. It was a *kairos* moment where God's agenda crossed their moment in time. They saw the reality of taking this land as an illusion. They did not believe and could not see, and the moment was then gone until the next generation. They spent the rest of their lives in the desert. How, like the Israelites, we often fail to move in faith under the authority and power of God and lose the *kairos* moment forever, remaining in our illusion and personal desert.

God spoke the *rhema* (words of authority and power) from Isaiah's mouth:

> *And He has made My mouth like a sharp sword;*
> *In the shadow of His hand He has hidden Me,*
> *And made Me a polished shaft;*
> *In His quiver He has hidden Me.*

Isaiah 49:2

This *rhema* is hidden so that it is protected. Only those who have chosen to be a part of this intimacy can hear it. The rest of the Isaiah chapter shows the purpose that God has in the coming Deliverer—to restore the intimacy that was lost in the Garden. A *kairos* moment was coming. The Deliverer did come. We live on a visited planet. All of history is focused on restoring the Sacred Romance, and God is chasing Man through time to complete the Kingdom Enterprise. God is ready to astonish you with your part in this story. It is now time for us to return to the Lordship of Christ in our life, seek God's agenda, and then speak the *rhema* into those *kairos* moments as they come today.

Remember that story of Elisha and the King? The dying Elisha told the King to shoot the arrow through the window. The window represented the *kairos* moment. The King only struck the ground with the arrows three times, however. He failed to take the authority and power for that *kairos* moment and eventually lost the moment.

This issue exists for each of us leading in the Church today.

There is an illusion that we are powerless with no authority. We see ourselves as geldings instead of the wild stallions God created us to be, and geldings can't bear fruit. We remain in our illusion. We don't see the *kairos* moments when they come every day. God calls us to participate in His Kingdom Enterprise. In Jesus teaching us the Model Prayer (Matthew 6). He was showing us how we can claim what is already done in the heavenlies to happen here with the *rhema* word. Once the Call is made, God has to wait until time catches up with what is already done in heaven.

Again and again the *kairos* window is lost.

How big is your God? God has created you for a vision He has for you. You are chosen. Are you willing, like Samuel as a child years ago, to tell God to speak and you will listen? Will you step through that *kairos* moment? Moments that appear on a daily basis?

As mentioned in the last chapter, authority and power are available to those who are followers of Christ through their spiritual gifts. Once we have heard our call and respond to it, God gives us the authority and power necessary to accomplish this call through our spiritual gifts. The motivational gifts are listed in 1 Corinthians 12 and include wisdom, word of knowledge, faith, healings, working of miracles, prophecy, discerning of spirits, speaking in tongues, and the interpretation of tongues. A real list would be much longer than this. These gifts are given to us for the Church, and the fact that they are distributed with different people having the authority and power in terms of their gifting should keep everyone humble. Paul emphasizes the unity that should be in the Church from these gifts working together. These gifts are often referred to as the motivational gifts, as they emerge from our calling to accomplish our ministry and are driven from our passion and vision.

Notes

1. The Second Law of Thermodynamics states that the entropy (disorder) of an isolated system that is not in equilibrium will tend to increase over time, approaching maximum value at equilibrium. (Rudolf Clausius) There are various expressions of this law, but basically it says a system runs down to disorder (chaos) unless acted on by some type of outside force that increases the order. You cannot create an ordered universe from within the system.

2. Glynn, Patrick. *God The Evidence: The Reconciliation of Faith and Reason in a Post Secular World.* (Rocklin, CA: Prima Publishing, 1997)

3. Sheets, Dutch. *Intercessory Prayer: How God Can Use Your Prayers to Move Heaven and Earth.* (Ventura, CA: Regal, 1996). This is the classic book on Intercessory Prayer.

4. A good DVD of the volcano story is *The Fire Below Us: Remembering Mount St. Helens.* This has been shown on National Geographic Television and at the Mt. Helens visitor centers. It has won multiple awards. Most showings, however, leave out the testimony of what really happened to Michael Lienau (the photographer) on the mountain and what the visitor centers and television are afraid to show you. If you want to see that, you need the extended special edition that has the additional story of the miraculous rescue of Michael Lienau and his crew and how it resulted in his coming to the Lord. Michael is a professional photographer who went into the blast zone with his crew *after* the volcano blew. While in the blast zone *he saw the volcano blow again* and barely escaped with his life. On his miraculous rescue and escaping, Michael gave his life to the Lord. The DVD is $29.95 from http://www.globalnetproductions.com/mshvideo.html.

Dialog

1. What does "being chosen" mean to you?

2. This chapter refers to churches and parachurch organizations that achieve such a level of intimacy as a community in which there is no single leader where "the buck stops" in the decision process. Do you believe this is possible? Do you know of any church or organization like this? (This author has seen it—it exists.)

Chapter 18: The Reality of Spiritual Warfare

*And the God of peace will crush Satan under **your** feet shortly.*

Romans 16:20a (emphasis added)

Finally, we must never forget that there is a spiritual war going on. With my own spiritual mapping, wise leaders told me not to worry so much about what the Enemy was doing. God would tell me what I needed for that. Focus on researching what God was doing and praise God for that. If I followed that rule, I would see the patterns of where the Kingdom was coming and could praise and lead from that.

Always remember that the battle is for the hearts of men and women—and for your heart. We will lose the battles at times because Satan is still roaming this earth. Eventually the King of Glory will win the war and we will be with Him forever. And we will reign with Him. The Evil One, Satan, will then be bound forever. We can praise God for what He has done, what He is doing, and what He will do through us. For the moment, however, there is the reality of the war. Even with this warfare, however, you can claim the reality that God can crush Satan under your feet.

The closer you get to the path God wants you on, the more danger you will face. It is not an "if" question. It's a "when" question.

In the Tolkein's *Lord of the Rings: The Two Towers*, you see the old King Theoden has experienced a miraculous healing and is now ready to relax and enjoy his new life. It is Aragorn that gives him a wakeup call:

Aragorn: *There is a war going on.*

King Theoden: *I will not risk open war.*

Aragorn: *Open war is upon you, whether you risk it or not.*

Whether to engage in war or not is not an option. If you are willing to stand in faith for what God wants you to do, there will be warfare directed at you. It's not an option.

Nehemiah and the External Warfare

Nehemiah faced warfare both internally and externally. On the external level, the most opposition came from Sanballat, the governor of Samaria. He had the most power of all the governors. Other governors in the area, including the previous governors of Jerusalem, tended to follow Sanballat.

> *But it so happened, when Sanballat heard that we were rebuilding the wall, that he was furious and very indignant, and mocked the Jews. And he spoke before his brethren and the army of Samaria, and said, "What are these feeble Jews doing? Will they fortify themselves? Will they offer sacrifices? Will they complete it in a day? Will they revive the stones from the heaps of rubbish—stones that are burned?"*
>
> *Now Tobiah the Ammonite was beside him, and he said, "Whatever they build, if even a fox goes up on it, he will break down their stone wall."*
>
> Nehemiah 4:1-3

Saballet does a good job of tearing the project up in an attempt to discourage the Israelites and to mobilize the opposition. Tobiah, the Ammonite, chimes in with his two bits.

What does Nehemiah do? His first response is prayer.

Hear, O our God, for we are despised; turn their reproach on their own heads, and give them as plunder to a land of captivity! Do not cover their iniquity, and do not let their sin be blotted out from before You; for they have provoked You to anger before the builders.

Nehemiah 4:4-5

Saballet's strategy fails. The Israelites continued to build the wall.

So we built the wall, and the entire wall was joined together up to half its height, for the people had a mind to work.

Nehemiah 4:6

Now Saballet is really ticked off. He starts to mobilize the Ammonites (Tobiah), the Arabs, and the Ashdodites. They plan a secret attack on the city from all sides. They plan to use force and create confusion. Nehemiah goes to prayer again.

Nevertheless we made our prayer to our God, and because of them we set a watch against them day and night.

Nehemiah 4:9-10

Two things happen now. First, the secret plan of Saballet got leaked to the Jews. As a result, the Israelites were able to arm and protect themselves. Second, as the Israelites began to lose heart Nehemiah began to encourage them. Although the scripture doesn't tell us, I think he encouraged them by telling them stories about what God had done for them in the past. Saballet's strategy failed again.

So often the visions that God gives us are so bold that we find ourselves getting discouraged just like those Israelites. The visions, when they do come, are as fragile as an avalanche lily I found growing by a mountain trail. Extremely beautiful, but so easy to crush in seconds with a misstep. In the same way, the visions God gives us are very often so bold that it is easy to lose heart. We must pray, remember what God has done in the past and now claiming the new vision in His authority. We must also encourage others with their visions in the same way; that is, sending faith messages into others so that they don't lose hope. Nehemiah held them to the vision.

Notice Nehemiah did not try to counter any of the criticisms of Saballet. Some of the criticisms were valid. The Israelites were not skilled and sometimes walked away from their jobs. There were gaps in the wall. Nehemiah kept them focused on their goal.

This second plan of Saballet failed as well.

And it happened, when our enemies heard that it was known to us, and that God had brought their plot to nothing, that all of us returned to the wall, everyone to his work.

Nehemiah 4:15

Now comes the third plan of Saballet. The wall is almost completed and Nehemiah gets a letter from Saballet. Saballet asks to meet with Nehemiah on the assumption of making peace. In reality, Saballet wanted to kill him. Nehemiah perceives this and doesn't go. The letter is sent four times. Each time Nehemiah says no. I love his answer.

So I sent messengers to them, saying, "I am doing a great work, so that I cannot come down. Why should the work cease while I leave it and go down to you?"

Nehemiah 6:3

Now Saballet sends a fifth letter in an attempt to bring Nehemiah down before the king in Babylon—and then sends this letter around as a rumor.

> *It is reported among the nations, and Geshem says, that you and the Jews plan to rebel; therefore, according to these rumors, you are rebuilding the wall, that you may be their king. And you have also appointed prophets to proclaim concerning you at Jerusalem, saying, "There is a king in Judah!" Now these matters will be reported to the king. So come, therefore, and let us consult together.*

Nehemiah 6:6-7

Nehemiah prays again.

> *Now therefore, O God, strengthen my hands.*

Nehemiah 6:9

Saballet tries again. Nehemiah meets with Delaiah who wants to give Nehemiah a prophecy. Nehemiah is to go to the temple and close the doors as a sanctuary against those who are trying to kill him. Nehemiah perceives, however, that Delaiah had really heard nothing from the Lord and, in reality, was paid by Saballet to lure him to the temple to kill him. Again, Nehemiah was able to perceive and protect his own life. They continued to work on the wall.

Nehemiah is Attacked from Within

The other attack on Nehemiah in this spiritual warfare is from within. Satan loves to attack from within. If the Enemy can create dissention and get the Christians fighting among themselves, he has won the battle. I love those early Star Trek episodes where Jim Kirk creates disunity in the enemy's camp. Once he's done that, he can watch the enemy self-destruct without having to fire a single shot.

As any leader steps out in vision with those who follow, there will always be those that try to control instead of serving. There will be those who try to manipulate people to their agenda instead of following the common agenda. They will try to destroy others to make themselves look good. You see all of that as Nehemiah tries to keep the people together as they build.

When Nehemiah first arrives in Jerusalem he was another governor in a long list of governors that had been sent to the area. Other governors had used their authority and position to place heavy taxes on the people. Governors had authority to tax as they wished. They also have a right to anything harvested by the farmers. Many of the Israelites had mortgaged their property or sold their kids or wives into slavery to pay their taxes. Nehemiah not only refused to live off the king's allowance, but also used some of his money to pay off the debts of some of the Jews there.

> *Moreover, from the time that I was appointed to be their governor in the land of Judah, from the twentieth year until the thirty-second year of King Artaxerxes, twelve years, neither I nor my brothers ate the governor's provisions. But the former governors who were before me laid burdens on the people, and took from them bread and wine, besides forty shekels of silver. Yes, even their servants bore rule over the people, but I did not do so, because of the fear of God.*

Nehemiah 5:14-16

He was not manipulating or controlling; but rather building relationships and a sense of unity with them. Moreover, he was working with the people (a servant leader) and eating with them (Nehemiah 5:16-17). He is praying again in Nehemiah 5:19.

> *Remember me, my God, for good, according to all that I have done for this people.*

Nehemiah 5:19

As a precious friend just told me, we should pray for more politicians like Nehemiah.

As Nehemiah worked with the people, he began to learn that the wealthier of the people were extracting money at high interest rates from those who are poor, with some of the poorer people again mortgaging their homes and selling family members into slavery. Nehemiah then calls the leaders of the city and nobles together and gives them a tongue lashing about their practices.

> *And I said to them, "According to our ability we have redeemed our Jewish brethren who were sold to the nations. Now indeed, will you even sell your brethren? Or should they be sold to us?"*

> *Then they were silenced and found nothing to say. Then I said, "What you are doing is not good. Should you not walk in the fear of our God because of the reproach of the nations, our enemies? I also, with my brethren and my servants, am lending them money and grain. Please, let us stop this usury! Restore now to them, even this day, their lands, their vineyards, their olive groves, and their houses, also a hundredth of the money and the grain, the new wine and the oil, that you have charged them."*

Nehemiah 5:8-11

Nehemiah had used his own money to ransom the Jews the nobles and city leaders had sold into slavery. Image how those nobles must have felt after what Nehemiah had done. They did as Nehemiah requested. Nehemiah could lead with the internal warfare because he maintained his moral and ethical authority.

Sounds pretty close to where we are in America today except we don't have a Nehemiah yet, do we? Time and time again I have written to the President and my Congressional leaders. The strategies they have led us on have consistently compromised their moral and ethical authority to accomplish specific ends. I voted in the last election to send one compromising leader in the Senate home. Others in my state followed me, and the senator was sent home. A leader should never compromise moral and ethical authority for the end goal. Never. Once you have compromised your core values, you no longer have any ownership from those who had been following you. It's all over. At that point you are no longer the leader and it is almost impossible to return as leader.

An Important Rule

When dealing with spiritual warfare, you are not so much coming against the Enemy as emboldening the vision. This is the strategy you see Nehemiah using. He is wise in the plans of the enemy, encourages the Israelites, and teaches them how to defend themselves while they kept working. Nehemiah consistently moves them to the final completion of the vision, encouraging them and cheering them on.

Key Principles of Spiritual Warfare

1. **Know that your authority is in Christ and only in Christ.**
   And Jesus came and spoke to them, saying, "All authority has been given to Me in heaven and on earth."
   Matthew 28:18-19

2. **Remember the reason Christ came was to destroy Satan's work on earth and rescue us from his power.**
   For this purpose the Son of God was manifested, that He might destroy the works of the devil.
   1 John 3:8-9

3. **Study the Scripture. Although Satan himself used the scripture at the temptation of Christ, knowing God's Plan and speaking the *rhema* leaves Satan powerless.**
   And take the helmet of salvation, and the sword of the Spirit, which is the word of God;
   Ephesians 6:17-18

4. **Spend much time in worship and praise.**
   Let the saints be joyful in glory;
   Let them sing aloud on their beds.
   Let the high praises of God be in their mouth,
   And a two-edged sword in their hand,

To execute vengeance on the nations,
And punishments on the peoples;
To bind their kings with chains,
And their nobles with fetters of iron;
To execute on them the written judgment —
This honor have all His saints.
Psalms 149:5-9

Worship has the power to neutralize the power of demonic attack upon the people of God, for wherever the spirit of praise resides, God is enthroned and neither flesh nor devil can successfully perpetuate their designs.
Jack Hayford, *Worship His Majesty*

5. **Repent and turn away from any unrepented sins.**
   Unrepented sins can block our access to God and his power.
6. **Humble yourself before God.**
   Look at what Michael, the archangel, told Daniel as to why Daniel as he came to rescue him.

   Then he said to me, "Do not fear, Daniel, for from the first day that you set your heart to understand, and to humble yourself before your God, your words were heard; and I have come because of your words.
   Daniel 10:12
7. **Pray for the coming of the Holy Spirit to your endeavor.**
8. **Remain in unity with other believers.**
9. **Put on the full armor of God (see Ephesians 6).**
10. **Step out in faith.**

Dialog

1. Where have you experienced spiritual warfare?

2. How did you deal with it?

3. What did you learn from that?

Chapter 19: The Awakening

The institutions, programs, organizations, and structures that we have built cannot contain what the Holy Spirit is trying to do. We must take the risk and open our hearts.

For fifty-two days the Israelites had been working on the wall and the project was finally completed. Many of the workers had been coming into Jerusalem from nearby towns and villages each day to work on the walls. They had been working around the clock on the project to complete the wall and keep the enemies at bay. It was a complete disruption of their normal life. Farmers had left their farms to work on the wall. Shops were closed. Now it was back to their farms and shops. Everything had stopped so that the wall could be completed as quickly as possible. Now they could return home.

What Next?

I remember what happened back in 1992 after the Billy Graham Crusade here. Some of us had been working for years to see it happen and it did happen. Awesome. Over 30,000 decisions for the Lord in a few days. Incredible success. Praise God! As we looked at the results, however, the Graham team told us of an astonishing revelation. Most of the leadership rose up locally—only a minimum from the Graham team. We had all the leadership, skills, talents, and gifts locally to keep what had happened going for a total city awakening. That awakening never happened. Some people were simply burned out. Many referrals were given to churches that did nothing, and the follow-up with those 30,000 decisions was never completed. Many people went back to their old life. Slowly the networks that had been created for the city work disappeared and the funding for the work dissolved. Proposals were written to carry things forward, but weren't financed. Several of the primary visionary leaders (John Knoxers) died. Spiritual warfare came in and we never saw the final awakening we wanted to see.

God is not asleep, however. Even as I write this, small fires are breaking out all over the city. It is another generation taking the lead. New leaders. Fresh ideas. New churches here are drawing the youth in massive numbers.

Now look at what happened back then after the Israelites built the wall. You see much of the same story of what happened in my own city back after the Crusade starting to happen with these people after the wall was built. They went home, overwhelmed, tired, and stressed out from the work—and they had more work waiting for them at home. But there was a difference here with this Jerusalem story. (I believe, unknown to us, this began here as well. Many seeds were sown.)

Back there in Jerusalem, what God had done through them slowly began to sink into their lives. Many emotions were sweeping through them. Two of these emotions were guilt and gratitude. They felt guilty because they had ignored God's law for so many years. Gratitude, because even though they had failed God, God had still shown mercy and blessed them. Without God acting, there would have been no wall. Also, I think they were missing the fellowship.

The wall was completed just six days before the beginning of the Jewish New Year. The holiday had long lost its religious significance. They had many Jewish traditions, but at this point they didn't even know how to do worship.

Something began to happen. Without any initiative from Nehemiah, both men and women left their houses and farms and began to drift to a square in Jerusalem. Nothing had been planned—it was just a spontaneous response. As the crowd continued to grow, someone made a decision that they need to hear from God. So they called Ezra.

Ezra was a priest and scribe that had returned with the second group of exiles. (Nehemiah led the third.) Ezra had been horrified to see the extent of the Jewish intermarriage of the Jews with nearby heathen women. With the congregation repenting, these marriages were dissolved as a part of this awakening. Now let's look at what happened after the wall was finished.

Now all the people gathered together as one man in the open square that was in front of the Water Gate; and they told Ezra the scribe to bring the Book of the Law of Moses, which the LORD had commanded Israel. So Ezra the priest brought the Law before the assembly of men and women and all who could hear with understanding on the first day of the seventh month. Then he read from it in the open square that was in front of the Water Gate from morning until midday, before the men and women and those who could understand; and the ears of all the people were attentive to the Book of the Law.

Nehemiah 8:1-3

They stood there and listened to Ezra read from the law for five or six hours. Now look at the response of the people.

And Ezra opened the book in the sight of all the people, for he was standing above all the people; and when he opened it, all the people stood up. And Ezra blessed the LORD, the great God.

Then all the people answered, "Amen, Amen!" while lifting up their hands. And they bowed their heads and worshiped the LORD with their faces to the ground.

Nehemiah 8:5-6

Notice there is no mention of the wall. The awakening is not called a celebration. What you see here is a spiritual renewal of their relationship with God.

After some five or six hours of the people standing as they listened to the law being read you would think they would be ready to get back to work. Instead, they decided the next day to celebrate the Feast of Booths that Ezra had read about to them. The Feast would last seven days, and during that time they would live in huts made from tree branches.

> *And they found written in the Law, which the LORD had commanded by Moses, that the children of Israel should dwell in booths during the feast of the seventh month, and that they should announce and proclaim in all their cities and in Jerusalem, saying, "Go out to the mountain, and bring olive branches, branches of oil trees, myrtle branches, palm branches, and branches of leafy trees, to make booths, as it is written."*
>
> *And there was very great gladness.*

Nehemiah 8:14-15,17b

As the story continues you see repentance, praise, joy, and a commitment of the Israelites to the vision God has given them in history and their new relationship with God.

The Rest of the Story

Nehemiah's vision was now completed. Nehemiah had led them to Place. The Temple was restored, there was obedience to the laws, and a real awakening of the hearts of God's people. (Nehemiah 10:28ff).

Nehemiah, before leaving Babylon for Jerusalem, had promised the king he would return to Babylon. He returns to Babylon in 433 B.C., twelve years after completing the wall. We don't know how long he stayed in Babylon, but he eventually returned to Jerusalem with the king's permission. What he saw on his return shocked him. Although the wall was there, the people had returned to their heathen ways. Tobiah, one of his previous enemies, now had his own room in the temple. Tobiah, an Ammonite, was not permitted by law to even enter the temple—it was illegal. Now he was living there! One of the priests had married Tobiah's daughter, another thing forbidden by law. The Levites were no longer supported and had returned to the farms, so the temple had been neglected—and with it the spiritual welfare of the people. There was commercial trading taking place on the Sabbath, another trampling of the law.

Nehemiah took charge, to a large extent violently. He led in restoring the city again and making sure the laws were restored and the people were obeying them. Then we see a final prayer as the story closes,

Remember me with favor, O my God.

Nehemiah 13:31 NIV

Contemporary Awakenings

There have been many awakenings in history. These follow a cyclic trend, but often they are related to each other or even build on each other. The invention of the Gutenberg Press in 1449 enabled the mass production of books. Martin Luther, born a few years later, was struck by the words of the Apostle Paul declaring that salvation was by faith and faith alone. On October 31, 1517 he nailed his famous Ninety-Five Theses to the door of Castle Church in Wittenberg, a common place for posting notes to open a discussion. The Theses were in Latin, which insured they would only be available to scholars. Someone, however, translated these to German and they were soon printed using the Gutenberg Press. Within two weeks they were available all over Germany and in a month all over Europe in a form that anyone could read. The Protestant Reformation had begun. Luther then began the translation of the Bible in the lay-person's language of German and completed it in 1534. Today the Bible has been published in over 2000 languages, including Klingon.

Early America

The founding of America was heavily influenced by the Protestant Reformation years earlier. The early settlements in America failed, for two major reasons:

- They lost their spiritual moorings. Columbus started with a mission to bring Christ to heathen lands, but soon got more interested in getting gold. Same thing with many of the next settlements. [1]
- The settlements could not build any level of community in a hostile land.

The Puritans, however, came over and landed in 1620. They were different. Although they weren't the first group to come over escaping religious persecution, they were the first to be able to make their settlement work. Their mission was an attempt to escape the persecution in England and Holland and to plant a New Israel in America. They were the cutting edge of the Protestant Reformation. They wanted to see a community committed to God. Their law book was the Bible. Unlike the stories of strict justice frequently told us about them, they really demonstrated a lot of compassion in their communities and they were ready to forgive if the sinner repented.

In a given area, the Puritans would first covenant together and build a church, and then the town would form around the church. There was a sense of intense community. The community was more like a large family. If one person sinned, it affected the entire community. Excommunication, when applied, was a serious judgment. You would be alone in a hostile environment.

Sin was taken very seriously. The family unit was very important. Children were disciplined in love. Failure of discipline was a failure of love. Since God is Love, the failure of proper parenting was considered idolatry.

The pastor was generally the most highly respected man in the community. He was generally a graduate of Oxford or Cambridge and had the highest formal education available. The early New England colleges such as Harvard and Yale were founded to be able to provide this formal education to the early pastors in America. The community relied on the pastors to keep them informed on what was happening in the world. Moreover, the community expected the pastors to have spiritual insights on the news as it was passed to their community.

The Lord prospered these early settlements for their faithfulness to Him. There were many miracles with those early pilgrims that enabled them to survive through the harsh times they experienced. More than anything else, however, their success was from their intense sense of unity and commitment to each other in Christ.

What happened to these pilgrims? Why did they essentially disappear from our American culture? As the pilgrim culture became blessed by God and survival was less of an issue, they became complacent and forgot the source of their blessings. Sure, they would go to church if the church was nearby; but as the sermon progressed they were more likely thinking of their farms and what they had to do when they got back home instead of focusing on what God was trying to tell them. Faith is not something that can be handed down from parents that loved the Lord or from participating in a church, baptism, or the Lord's Supper. Faith has to be hammered out in the fires of battle and adventure and nurtured in the soil of thanksgiving. Faith was lost as succeeding generations prospered.

The Lord warned the Israelites of this in Deuteronomy 8.

Beware that you do not forget the LORD your God by not keeping His commandments, His judgments, and His statutes which I command you today, lest—when you have eaten and are full, and have built beautiful houses and dwell in them; and when your herds and your flocks multiply, and your silver and your gold are multiplied, and all that you have is multiplied; when your heart is lifted up, and you forget the LORD your God who brought you out of the land of Egypt, from the house of bondage;...

Deuteronomy 8:11-14

The Lord also told them the consequences.

Behold, I set before you today a blessing and a curse: the blessing, if you obey the commandments of the LORD your God which I command you today; and the curse, if you do not obey the commandments of the LORD your God, but turn aside from the way which I command you today, to go after other gods which you have not known.

Deuteronomy 11:26-29

This judgment has already started in America today.

The First Great Awakening

The first Awakening in America was known as the Great Awakening and began about 1720, continuing until 1745. It happened before the American Revolution when the nation was still a British colony. It was part of a larger global movement known as Pietism on the European continent and Evangelicalism in England. John Wesley was perhaps the most prominent preacher of the movement in England. The movement was an evangelical reaction against the formalism and rationalism of the current religions and emphasized the fear of punishment in refusing to accept Salvation.

In America, the movement changed America after a Calvinist preacher named Jonathan Edwards preached his famous sermons on justification by faith alone. Jonathan Edwards was not what we would call a typical preacher. His most famous sermon, "Sinners in the Hands of an Angry God" was read word for word in a monotone voice. As he read, people would be caught up in their convictions of sin and swoon in the aisle. Yet Edwards was a humble theologian—no pulpit beating or brimstone-preaching evangelist.

George Whitefield was another famous preacher of the Awakening. It was said of Whitefield that he could move an audience to tears by merely saying the word "Mesopotamia".

The awakening was called "Great" because it was universal. It unified the Christians of different faiths to a common vision. There was some dissension with those who refused to change, but leaders such as Edwards and Whitefield had a unifying effect. Although we don't know the amount of church growth during this time, we do know it was dramatic. Mission outreach of the churches grew, particularly to the Native Americans. Several major universities were started, including Princeton and Brown. The laity began to have a stronger role in the church leadership. Denominationalism began to grow stronger.

There is a common teaching today that the American Revolution was birthed from objections to taxation without representation and primarily a political issue. This statement is not wrong, but it is incomplete. With the large evangelical base emerging from the awakening, people where tired of a king with a dying religious institution in England telling them what to believe and how to worship. Many men and women who converted during the awakening had defied various religious authorities to uphold their new convictions.

By the 1760s, Americans were getting more than angry with their relationship with England, with the Revolutionary War beginning in 1775. In 1776, it was Thomas Paine who used a press to print a series of articles called *Common Sense* that rallied the colonists of America to throw off their yoke of slavery and be free:

These are the times that try men's souls. The summer soldier and the sunshine patriot will, in this crisis, shrink from the service of their country; but he that stands by it now, deserves the love and thanks of man and woman. Tyranny, like hell, is not easily conquered; yet we have this consolation with us, that the harder the conflict, the more glorious the triumph. What we obtain too cheap, we esteem too lightly: it is dearness only that gives everything its value.

From *The Crisis*, by Thomas Paine

Just as Luther did more than two centuries earlier, Paine's publishing created a "swarm" that rallied the demoralized American colonists and led to a free nation.

Paine was not a Christian—in fact, he was against religion and Christianity. Yet he used an almost spiritual language in his writing that the evangelicals could relate to and was able to mobilize the colonies to a political awakening that many evangelicals saw as a holy war against a sinful and corrupt Britain. Unfortunately, this man who mobilized the nation lost his followers and friends due to his strong anti-religious views and eventually died in New York, lonely and abandoned.

The Second Great Awakening

The Second Great Awakening swept the nation from the late 1820's to the 1830's. At this point the colonies had won their independence and had begun shaping their own destiny. This awakening, in part, began out of the evangelical opposition of the deism associated with the French Revolution and grew in strength when Charles Finney, a charismatic lawyer who had turned preacher, led a revival in Utica, New York. Soon it hit Kentucky, Tennessee, and southern Ohio. Denominations instituted specific structures that enabled them to thrive and grow. The Methodists, for example, had a structure that depended on the circuit riding ministers that actively sought people on the frontier for conversions.

As the awakening movement grew, it created evangelical growth primarily in New England, mid-Atlantic, the Northwest, and the South. The Methodist and Baptist denominations grew faster than other denominations such as the Anglicans, Presbyterians, Reformed, and Congregationalists.

Another change with this Second Awakening was that of an Evangelical awakening to social causes: prison reform, temperance, women's rights, and abolitionism.

The Third Great Awakening

The Third Great Awakening was a period in American history from 1850 to 1900. This primarily affected the Protestant denominations and was marked with an increase in social activism. The Awakening was driven by the theology that the Second Coming of Christ would only come after Man has reformed the entire earth. Missionary movements became stronger worldwide.

This awakening was temporarily interrupted by the American Civil War. However, the war actually stimulated revivals in the South. Dwight L Moody, a leader in the revivalism of this period, founded the Moody Bible Institute. Ira Sankey, the great gospel hymn writer, worked with Moody on many of his revivals. In October 1871, Sankey and Moody were in the middle of a Chicago revival meeting when the Great Chicago Fire broke out. The two men barely escaped the fire with their lives. Sankey ended up watching the city burn from a rowboat far out on one of the Great Lakes. Sankey was also a friend of Fanny Crosby, another famous hymn writer of this period. Charles Spurgeon was also a leader during this time. Christian Science and the Salvation Army were founded during this period.

The Pentecostal Movement

The Welsh Revival of 1904-1905 in Wales soon came to America, and of particular note was the 1906 Azusa Street Revival in Los Angeles. The Azusa Street Revival is commonly regarded as the beginning of the modern-day Pentecostal Movement. The meeting place was nothing more than a dirt-floor barn with a capacity of 900, with meetings led by Brother Seymor, a black evangelist. The initial controversy here as the movement spread was not the issue of glossolalia (speaking in tongues), but rather a racial issue—many nationalities and ethnic groups (as many as 20 at one time) came together in all-night communion services,. A friend of Seymor believed it was against God's will for people from such assorted ethnic and racial groups to come together in communion and worship.[2] The attack from the enemy here, as in most cases, is seldom theological but more in the attempts to cause division and fractionalization. This strategy had its very roots in the early church (Acts 6) where the initial internal strife was not theological, but ethnic.

One catalyst for the start of the revival was the April 18, 1906 earthquake that hit San Francisco, adding a sense of urgency for repentance. The revival with its Pentecostal influence spread up the west coast and then to other countries—50 countries in two years. The revival in my own city of Portland eventually evolved to a third generation of "temple" churches: Bible Temple, Emmanuel Temple, and Portland Temple.

The Pentecostal movement that exploded at that time attracted primarily the blue-collar workers. Like earlier Protestant revivals, there was an emphasis on prayer, confession of sin, and repentance. It distinguished itself from the Protestant revivals by an emphasis on spiritual gifts, tongues, and healing. Typical services included spontaneous healings, prophecies, speaking in tongues, and other manifestations.

Peter Wagner writes[3] that most Christians were not prepared for this type of outpouring of the Holy Spirit. There was no Protestant theology to support this work of the Holy Spirit. The Protestants did the only thing they could and declared the Pentecostals heretics. In older books about false cults you will see Pentecostals listed along with Jehovah's Witnesses and Mormons. It took almost half a century for this movement to gain respect through the leadership of such men as David du Plessis and Thomas Zimmerman.

The years of revival forged new missions outreach across cultures and people groups around the world. World War I started a few years later, and with it this revival passed into history.

An Awakening Today?

Today, as a nation, we have strayed far, far from those commandments given by God long ago. Where and when will we return?

It is not a 1-2-3 program or process. It is not a matter of following some steps and if you follow those you will get there. That is the old deterministic Newtonian thinking. The old paradigm. We aren't there anymore. Returning is a *heart* issue—our heart's relationship to God and our heart for each other.

I remember a friend of mine going to Betty Mitchell at Good Samarian Ministries and meeting her for the first time. He was athletic, macho, with all the physical male image women love. Betty is a little elderly, gray-haired lady who doesn't look much like the apostolic leader she is. She's taught Bible in public schools. That gives you some idea of what she is like. And it's not the typical Bible teaching you get on Sunday morning. She doesn't compromise the message in any way.

This macho guy stood there showing her his muscles and very proud of them. This little gray haired lady spun around and hit him hard in the heart and watched him double over.

"Son," she said, "if the heart isn't right, nothing else makes any difference."

He got the message.

For finding your own heart, start by reading the prayers of Ezra (Ezra 9), Daniel (Daniel 9-10), and Nehemiah (Nehemiah 1). Realize they were praying for a nation that looked much like our own world as we stand here today. Look at these questions:

- What is common with their prayers?
- What was the burden that each had?
- What was their own heart condition?
- Who do they blame for the condition they are in?
- What are they asking God for?
- Did God answer their prayer?
- If so, why do you think God answered their prayer?

Can you pray like this? God isn't asleep. These fires of transformation are already starting to burn all over the world. Cities and even regions are being totally transformed. And what is remarkable is that in a given area it seems to always begin with one or two people praying for the coming of the Holy Spirit. And I don't mean a little chit-chat type prayer. These apostolic leaders today —are on their knees and praying 24/7 for this visitation. Weeping. Their hearts are torn and broken for this visitation and Place that is lost. And then the Awakening comes.

And there is another key issue. Perseverance. Transformation can take awhile. God has eternity and stands outside of time. He is waiting on us. Remember when the Israelites started returning and they began rebuilding the temple, they got discouraged and stopped for awhile. The Enemy will try anything to stop the awakening. We have to be ready and be willing to risk anything to see it happen.

Another factor is almost certainly to play a major part in the next awakening. Just as the Gutenberg Press had a major part in the Reformation in terms of making the Bible available to be read by anyone, The Internet is almost certain to play a major part in the next awakening. The growing influence of social networking and the energy and influence that can spread quickly through the culture provides for a true democracy if we are willing to understand and use the technology in the right way.

Spiritual mapping (seeing how God has worked and is working in an area, and understanding where the Enemy has bindings) is also a key part for those serious about seeing the awakening. Those friends of Nehemiah that came to him with their data had hard proof that Jerusalem was in ruins. Bob Becket, a pastor in Hemet, California, said he had prayer warriors praying for years for revival there and they stopped after they thought nothing was happening. But it was happening. If they had done their spiritual mapping, they would have known that.[4] The mapping would have shown them that their community *was* changing, transformation *was* starting to take place.

There was another problem Nehemiah faced and is very often there today. Once the visitation is there, how do you sustain and grow the Kingdom from that? And if you are holding on to that, the healthier challenge then becomes the question of how can this fire spread to other cities? How can what happened locally become regional and then, eventually, global?

Where are these fires of the Holy Spirit burning near you? Remember that church I mentioned in Chapter 1? Before that I was in a WASP church in the suburbs. One day I was riding with a mentor into the city. A guy who liked to shake up people with his questions. Yes, he walked with a limp. He turned to me and in a very quiet way ripped me apart with one single question.

"Where is God acting in your life?"

"Well, there is this strange church down in the heart of the city. It ministers out of a coffeehouse. I go there when I am depressed or lose heart. Every time I go there they sit with me and tell me stories about what God is doing there."

"Why don't you go join them?" he asked.

I did.

Today, as I write this, it is over 30 years later. I just recently changed churches. Same reason. I wanted to be where God was working.

Where is God working in your life?

Notes:

1. Marshall, Peter and David Manuel. *The Light and the Glory. 1492-1793: God's Plan for America.* (Old Tappan, NJ: Revell, 1977)
2. Dawson, John. *Healing America's Wounds.* (Ventura, CA: Regal Books, 1994) p. 218
3. Wagner, C. Peter. *The Third Wave of the Holy Spirit: Encountering the Power of Signs and Wonders Today.* (Ann Arbor: Vine Books, 1988) p. 16
4. Beckett, Bob with Rebecca Wagner Systema. *Commitment to Conquer: Redeeming Your City by Strategic Intercession.* (Grand Rapids: Chosen, 1997)

Dialog:

1. Is the story of these Israelites an academic excursion for you, or is God speaking to you through their story? What is God telling you in this?

2. Where are the fires of the Holy Spirit burning near you?

3. Why don't you go there?

4. Read the prayers of Daniel, Ezra, and Nehemiah. Work
    with those questions mentioned in this chapter:
- What is common with their prayers?

- What was the burden that each had?

- What was their own heart condition?

- Who do they blame for the condition they are in?

- What were they asking God for?

- Did God answer their prayer?

- If so, why do you think God answered their prayer?

Assignment: Can you pray for the coming of `the Holy Spirit
in your area?

Appendix A: Historical Perspectives and Nehemiah's Challenge

After Solomon, the Israel nation eventually split into two kingdoms: a Northern and Southern Kingdom. Neither honored the commands God had given them and each, in turn, was carried away in exile.

The Jews in the Northern Kingdom were carried away in exile first. Later, the Jews from the Southern Kingdom were carried off into exile by Nebuchadnezzar in 586 B.C. and Jerusalem destroyed. Isaiah spoke a startling prophecy during that difficult time about a king named Cyrus, speaking the words of the Lord:

Who says of Cyrus, 'He is My shepherd,
And he shall perform all My pleasure,
Saying to Jerusalem, "You shall be built,"
And to the temple, "Your foundation shall be laid."'
"Thus says the LORD to His anointed,
To Cyrus, whose right hand I have held—
To subdue nations before him
And loose the armor of kings,
To open before him the double doors,
So that the gates will not be shut:
'I will go before you
And make the crooked places straight;
I will break in pieces the gates of bronze

And cut the bars of iron.
I will give you the treasures of darkness
And hidden riches of secret places,
That you may know that I, the LORD,
Who call you by your name,
Am the God of Israel.
For Jacob My servant's sake,
And Israel My elect,
I have even called you by your name;
I have named you, though you have not known Me.
I am the LORD, and there is no other…'"
There is no God besides Me.
I will gird you, though you have not known Me,
That they may know from the rising of the sun to its setting
That there is none besides Me.
I am the LORD, and there is no other;

Isaiah 44:28 – Isaiah 45:6

Cyrus had not even been born at the time Isaiah spoke this.

Babylon was overthrown by Persia in 539 B.C., creating the large Medo-Persian Empire with Cyrus as King of Persia. Can you imagine his shock as probably one of his scribes (perhaps Daniel) read this prophecy to him? Soon Cyrus asks for a group of the Jews to return to Jerusalem to rebuild the temple. The book of 2 Chronicles ends with Cyrus asking for this group to return to Jerusalem for this very task.

There were actually three waves of the returning Jews. The first wave was led by Zerubbabel arriving in 537 B.C. with the task of rebuilding the temple. There were 42,360 pilgrims in this group. Haggai and Zechariah were prophets during that time. The temple work is eventually halted due to opposition. Darius I becomes king of Persia in 532 B.C. Daniel was in the King's court during this time and you can see Daniel's prayer and burden in Daniel 9-10. It gets real exciting if you compare Daniel's prayer with Nehemiah's prayer in Nehemiah 1. Nehemiah won't get to Jerusalem until 445 B.C.

Darius orders them to restart the building of the temple in 520 B.C. The temple is completed in 516 B.C.

The second wave of pilgrims arrived in Jerusalem in 458 B.C.; i.e., (a 58 year gap since completing the temple, and almost 80 years since the arrival of Zerubbabel). This group was led by Ezra, who was sent by King Artaxerxes I as an administrator for the area. There are about 2000 men and their families in this group. Like Daniel and later Nehemiah, Ezra carried an incredible burden for his people—a burden because he sees the intermarriage of the Jews with the nearby heathen. Like Daniel before him and Nehemiah later, he weeps and prays before God (Ezra 9), confessing his sin. A national revival begins.

You see all the rich characteristics of a leader here in Ezra—humility, servanthood, obedience, and compassion. Ezra was sent as an administrator; but he was also a scribe and priest. In all probability he wrote both Ezra, Nehemiah, and Chronicles. The book of Nehemiah is in first person, but was probably dictated to Ezra by Nehemiah. Originally, Ezra and Nehemiah were a single book.

In many ways, Nehemiah faced the same challenges as a leader in America today would face. The Israelite nation was at a confluent point in its history. Jerusalem was in ruins. As the Israelites began their return from Babylon, they found only rubble and desolation. The magnificent city lay in ruins with rubble all about. There was no temple, no walls, and no hope or vision. The Israelites left behind when Babylon carried them off were the poor, the despised, and the downtrodden. Rubble, just like the ruins of the wall. These had even intermarried with the nearby heathen women, adopted the heathen customs, and had compromised their spiritual heritage with the culture that was about them. Just like our prophets in our churches today are telling us.

The third wave of the returning Jews returned with Nehemiah. It was probably a small group. Nehemiah was chosen by King

Artaxerxes to lead this group. Nehemiah was sent as a governor, as others before him. It was a political appointment. Like Daniel, Nehemiah carried a burden to see the nation restored as Place, the channel through which the coming Christ would come. Nehemiah saw his task as a leader in rebuilding the wall. That would provide a visible security the nation needed. In addition, it would pull the nation together again.

These three leaders—Zerubbabel, Ezra, and Nehemiah, all played a prominent part in rebuilding the nation and preparing it for the coming of Christ. The Temple was back in a position of prominence; the priests were back in place with the law and the scribes. You also see the enmity developing between the Jews who had intermarried (Samaritans) and the Jews that did not.

Today, God again waits for leaders to lead from heart and compassion. He desires us to repent and return in faith to that intimacy with Him. To hear His agenda for our own personal life and to act on His call with whatever risks that involves.